CW00351514

MORE TALES FROM THE FORBIDDEN PLANET

MORE TALES FROM TH

EDITED BY ROZ KAVENEY

FORBIDDEN PLANET

TITAN BOOKS · LONDON 1990

MORE TALES FROM THE FORBIDDEN PLANET

Limited edition: 1 85286 330 7
Hardcover edition: 1 85286 331 5
Trade edition: 1 85286 332 3

Published by
Titan Books Ltd
58 St Giles High St
London WC2H 8LH

First edition: August 1990
10 9 8 7 6 5 4 3 2 1

Introduction © Roz Kaveney 1990

HOLLYWOOD CHICKENS © Terry Pratchett 1990. *Illustration* © Gilbert Shelton 1990.
THE WOMAN WHO DIDN'T COME BACK © Rachel Pollack 1990. *Illustration* Jamie
Reid 1990.
DINING OUT © John Sladek 1990. *Illustration* © Jamie Hewlett 1990.
BEST FRIENDS © Colin Greenland 1990. *Illustration* © Michael Kaluta 1990.
THE HEART BEATS © Ann Nocenti 1990. *Illustration* © Art Adams 1990.
THE HUMAN CHICKEN © Ian Watson 1990. *Illustration* © Oscar Zarate 1990.
FUN IN THE FINAL DAYS © Mick Farren 1990. *Illustration* © Savage Pencil 1990.
THE HORROR IN OUR LIVES © Jamie Delano 1990. *Illustration* © John Hicklenton 1990.
WASP SONGS © R M Lamming 1990. *Illustration* © Duncan Fegredo 1990.
WEBS © Neil Gaiman 1990. *Illustration* © Simon Bisley 1990.
DID YOU EVER SEE OYSTERS WALKING UP THE STAIRS? © Storm Constantine 1990.
Illustration © Steve Yeowell 1990.
THE PORTRAIT OF DARYANREE THE KING © Larry Niven 1990. *Illustration* © Don
Lawrence 1990.
ELLIPSES © David Langford 1990. *Illustration* © Rian Hughes 1990.
DEATH OF A SACRED MONSTER © John Clute 1990. *Illustration* © Dave McKean 1990.
BLACK MOTLEY © Mary Gentle 1990. *Illustration* © Charles Vess 1990.
Story title originally contained in Neil Gaiman's introduction to *Scholars and Soldiers* (by
Mary Gentle) and used here with permission.

Cover illustration © Moebius 1990
Design by Rian Hughes & Mark Cox

This book is sold subject to the condition that is shall not, by way of trade or otherwise,
be lent, re-sold, hired out or otherwise circulated without the publisher's prior consent in
any form of binding or cover other than that in which it is published and without a similar
condition including this condition, being imposed upon the subsequent purchaser.

Typeset by Spectrum Typesetting Ltd.
Printed and bound in England by Butler & Tanner Ltd, Frome, Somerset.

CONTENTS

INTRODUCTION

IT IS NOT always easier the second time; the first of this series had the advantage of being prepared against the tightest of deadlines, and having to be ready for a Worldcon. These of course seemed like disadvantages at the time, but time teaches wisdom ... In the introduction to the first volume, I was faintly satirical at the expense of *The Last Dangerous Visions*; forces, whether Nemesis, or more arcane Forces Beyond Our Control, have compelled me to be especially sincere in my apologies to Harlan Ellison, since an anthology that was supposed to appear in 1988 is appearing in 1990, and an anthology that was supposed to feature comics writers is a rather more general anthology of SF, fantasy and horror writing, drawing on the whole community of writers of those genres, comics and the spaces in between.

This is, in any case, no bad thing for an anthology that is appearing in the first year of a decade in which the easy division of publishing trade categories seems likely to vanish and the cross-over book, already prominent in the 80s, will grow ever more common. Further, now that we have all cottoned on to the reasons why people are drawn to genre fiction, the not especially obscure urges to feel affirmed through power fantasy or to console the fear of death through imaginary terrors, what better way to vary the formulae elegantly than by playing with mixed response? Many of these stories belong to more than one fantasy genre or to no specific one; if I can make one prediction about the 90s, it will be that this is how things will be from now on.

The 80s was a decade in which it was perfectly possible to find sword-and-sorcery country house murder mysteries or horror westerns – more importantly, it was a decade in which works answering those descriptions were not only published, but good. It was a decade in which the walls between the fantastic fiction genre ghettos crumbled definitively, so that a writer like Pat Cadigan is almost impossible to classify – is she a cyberpunk? or a splatterpunk? or just a writer who achieves emotional effects of a high order with whatever instruments the genres offer her?

It was also a decade in which comics may not have grown up or come of age, but have certainly moved forward from the stasis of the last few decades to a troubled and complex late adolescence; and in which the fantastic fiction genres, hitherto prone to disown comics as an embarrassing barrier to their own artistic respectability, were obliged to take seriously contributions from the comics. In any list of the most important, influential and acclaimed SF novels of the 80s, Alan Moore's *Watchmen* must be up there with Gene Wolfe's *Book of the New Sun* and Jonathan Carroll's dark fantasy sequence; other comics like *Love and Rockets* and *Cerebus* had a lot to teach the SF and fantasy fields about characterisation and how minimal yet effective it can be.

The progressive involvement of comics writers like Alan Moore and Neil Gaiman with prose fiction, the involvement of SF writers like Geoff Ryman with graphic fictions, indicates just how fruitful a closer relationship is likely to be.

Even among those writers who have not written for comics, it is a mistake to assume that comics have not had their effect; it is the stylization of comics as much as the simplicity of folk tales that had fed into Rachel Pollack's story in the present volume, and the rich stylish complication of the subcultures and underworlds of Mary Gentle's *Black Motley* owes as much to Jaime Hernandez as it does to Gene Wolfe.

This anthology then deals in cross-overs and interfaces; the point at which the ghost story becomes the alternate world story becomes the tale of hallucination and bad faith, or the point at which the sword-and-sorcery story can be read as myth or as space opera. One of the fruitful things about writing in a period where the audience is open to having one sort of story turn out to be another sort of story, or turn out to be a metaphor for something else entirely, is that options are open. Even when a formula appear most rigidly to being kept to, there is always the possibility of the trapdoor opening and the spider coming out; even when the formula is actually kept to, the possibility that remains up to the end of the story can be the spider in shadow. There is no innocence left in the tropes and traps of genre, no way of reading or of writing fantastic fiction that does not draw on a century of associations and ideas. We are all distorted echoes of another better story and our stories are no different.

The science fiction community, the fantastic community, the horror community and the comics community – these are fictions too, but fictions which reflect annual realities. We are all involved with the same ideas; we all read the same writers. There are writers here whom I am pleased to think of as friends, friends one rings most days or sees occasionally; others I have never met and know only through their work.

As was the case with the first anthology, this is an anthology of fiction by writers who have had signings at one or other of the *Forbidden Planet* shops. Accordingly, it is mostly an anthology of British writers or of writers resident in Britain, but their Britishness is less the issue than is the case with some other recent anthologies. This is an anthology less interested in the state of the nation than in the state of the genres, if not the state of the art.

The existence of specialist bookshops, and the economy of scale produced by the presence of all four kinds of fantasy under one roof, is one of the things that had made the crosses-over and cross-fertilisations of the 80s possible; it has meant that a significant part of the book trade is actually aware of the genres as something more than a warmed-through set of ideas from films, and that publishers have a chance to sell new ideas in the genres to a book trade that is informed about them and that cares. A close relationship between writers and the community that reads their work is partly dependent on the existence of bookshops and publishers that know and care about both, just as the trade depends on the artists and the consumers. There has to be partnership; there has to be trust.

Here then is a volume of fifteen stories and their illustrations; stories of barbarian swordswomen, and stories of ghosts, and stories of something else entirely. Enjoy them.

Roz Kaveney, *April 1990*

TERRY PRATCHETT

HOLLYWOOD CHICKENS

ILLUSTRATED BY GILBERT SHELTON

THE FACTS ARE these:

In 1973 a lorry overturned at a freeway interchange in Hollywood. It was one of the busiest in the United States and, therefore, the world.

It shed some of its load. It had been carrying chickens. A few crates broke.

Alongside the interchange, bordered on three sides by thundering traffic and on the fourth by a wall, was a quarter-mile of heavily-shrubbed verge.

No-one bothered too much about a few chickens.

. . .

Peck peck.
Scratch. Scratch.
Cluck?

. . .

It is a matter of record that, after a while, those who regularly drove this route noticed that the chickens had survived. There were, and indeed still are, sprinklers on the verge to keep the greenery alive and presumably the meagre population of bugs was supplemented by edible fallout from the constant stream of traffic.

The chickens seemed to be settling in. They were breeding.

. . .

Peck peck. Scratch. Peck . . .
Peck?
Scratch peck?
Peck?
Peck + peck = squawk
Cluck?

. . .

A rough census indicated that the population stabilised at around fifty birds. For the first few years young chickens would frequently be found laminated to the blacktop, but some sort of natural selection appeared to be operating, or, if we may put it another way, flat hens don't lay eggs.

Passing motorists did occasionally notice a few birds standing at the kerb, staring intently at the far verge.

GILBERT SHELTON - 1990

They looked like birds with a problem, they said.

. . .

SQUAWK PECK PECK CROW!
I Peck squawk peck
II Squawk crow peck
III Squawk *squawk* crow
IV Scratch crow peck waark
V (Neck stretch) peck crow
VI Peck peck peck (preen feathers)
VII (Peck foot) scratch crow
VIII Crow scratch
IX Peck (weird gurgling noise) peck
X Scratch peck *crow* waark (to keep it holy).

. . .

In fact, apart from the occasional chick or young bird, no
chicken was found dead on the freeway itself apart from the
incident in 1976, when ten chickens were seen to set out from
the kerb together during the rush hour peak. This must have
represented a sizeable proportion of the chicken population at
that time.

The driver of a gas tanker said that at the head of the little
group was an elderly cockerel, who stared at him with
supreme self-confidence, apparently waiting for something to
happen.

Examination of the tanker's front offside wing suggests that
the bird was a Rhode Island Red.

. . .

Cogito ergo cluck.

. . .

Periodically an itinerant, or the just plain desperate, would
dodge the traffic to the verge and liberate a sleeping chicken
for supper.

This originally caused some concern to the Department of
Health, who reasoned that the feral chickens, living as they
did so close to the traffic, would have built up dangerously
high levels of lead in their bodies, not to mention other noxious
substances.

In 1978 a couple of research officers were sent into the thickets to bring back a few birds for a sacrifice to Science.

The birds' bodies were found to be totally lead-free.

We do not know whether they checked any eggs.

This is important (see Document C).

They did remark incidentally, however, that the birds appeared to have been fighting amongst themselves. (See Document F: *Patterns of Aggression in Enclosed Environments, Helorksson and Frim*, 1981.) We must assume, in view of later developments, that this phase passed.

. . .

Four peck-(neck stretch) *and seven* cluck-scratch *ago, our* crow-(peck left foot)-squawk *brought forth upon this* cluck-cluck-squawk . . .

. . .

In the early hours of 10 March 1981, Police Officer James Stooker Stasheff, in pursuit of a suspect following a chase which resulted in a seven-car collision, a little way from the verge, saw a construction apparently made of long twigs, held together with cassette tape, extending several feet into the carriageway. Two chickens were on the end of it, with twigs in their beaks. "They looked as if they was nest building," he now recalls. "I went past again about 10 a.m., it was all smashed up in the gutter."

Officer Stasheff went on to say, "You always get tapes along the freeway. Any freeway. See, when they get snarled up in the Blaupunkt or whatever, people just rip 'em out and pitch them through the window."

According to Ruse and Sixbury (*Bulletin of the Arkham Ornithological Society*, vol. 17, pp. 124–132, 1968) birds may, under conditions of chronic stress, build nests of unusual size and complexity (Document D).

This is not necessarily advanced as an explanation.

. . .

Peck . . . peck . . . scratch.

Scratch scratch scratch scratch scratch scratch scratch scratch scratch scratch scratch.

5

. . .

The collapse of a small section of carriageway near the verge in the summer of 1983 is not considered germane to this study. The tunnel underneath it was put down to gophers. Or foxes. Or some other burrowing animal. What were irresponsibly described as shoring timbers must simply have been, for example, bits of timber that accidentally got carried into the tunnel by floodwater, as it were, and wedged. Undoubtedly the same thing happened with the feathers.

. . .

If Cluck *were meant to fly, they'd have bigger* (flap).

. . .

Testimony of Officer Stasheff again:

"This must have been around late August, 1984. This trucker told me, he was driving past, it would have been around mid-afternoon, when this thing comes flapping, he said *flapping,* out of the bushes and right across the freeway and he's watching it, and it doesn't lose height, and next thing he knows it bounces off his windshield and breaks up. He said he thought it was kids or something, so I went and had a look at the bushes, but no kids. Just a few of the chickens scratching about, and a load of junk, you know, you wouldn't believe the kind of junk that ends up by the side of roads. I found what was left of the thing that'd hit him. It was like a sort of cage with these kind of big wings on, and all full of pulleys and more bits of cassette tapes and levers and stuff. What? Oh, yeah. And these chickens. All smashed up. I mean, who'd do something like that? One minute flying chickens, next minute McNuggets. I recall there were three of them. All cockerels, and brown."

. . .

It's a (small scratch) for a *cluck,* a (giant flap) for *Cluck.*

. . .

Testimony of Officer Stasheff again (19 July 1986):

"Kids playing with fire. That's my opinion. They get over the wall and make hideouts in the bushes. Like I said, they just grab one of the chickens. I don't see why everyone's so excited. So some kids fill an old trashcan with junk and fireworks and stuff and push a damn *chicken* in it and blow it up in the air . . . It'd have caused a hell of a lot of damage if it hadn't hit one of the bridge supports on the far side. Bird inside got all smashed up. It'd got this cloth in there with strings all over. Maybe the kids thought the thing could use a parachute. . Okay, so there's a crater, what the hell, plant a bush in it. What? Sure it'd be hot, it's where they were playing spacemen. Not that kind of hot? What kind of hot?"

. . .

Peck (Neck Twist)-crow $= $ gurgle$/C^2$
Cluck?

. . .

We do know that at about 2 a.m. on the morning of 3 May 1989, a purple glow was noticed by several drivers in the bushes around the middle of the verge. Some say it was a blue glow. From a cross-checking of the statements, it appeared to last for at least ten minutes.

There was also a noise. We have a number of descriptions of this noise. It was "sort of weird", "kind of a whooping sound", and "rather like radio oscillation". The only one we have been able to check is the description from Curtis V J McDonald, who said, "You know in that *Star Trek* episode when they meet the fish men from an alternate Earth? Well, the fish men's matter transmitter made just the same noise."

We have viewed the episode in question. It is the one where Captain Kirk falls in love with the girl (tape A).

. . .

Cluck?
(Foot twist)$\sqrt{2}t\beta$ . . . $[\Sigma/\text{peck}]/\text{Scratch}^{2**\text{oon}}$ (Gurgle) (Left-shoulder-preen) $=$ (Right-shoulder-preen) . . .
HmmMMmmMMmmMMmmMMmmMMmm.
Cluck.

. . .

We also know that the person calling himself Elrond X, an itinerant, entered the area around 2 a.m. When located subsequently, he said: "Yeah, well, maybe sometimes I used to take a chicken but there's no law against it. Anyway, I stopped because it was getting very heavy, I mean, it was the way they were acting. The way they looked at you. Their beady eyes. But times are tough and I thought, okay, why not...

"There's no chickens there, man. Someone's been through it, there's no chickens!"

When asked about the Assemblage, he said: "There was only this pile of junk in the middle of the bushes. It was just twigs and wire and junk. And eggs, only you never touch the eggs, we know that, some of those eggs give you a shock, like electricity. 'Cos you never asked me before, that's why. Yeah, I kicked it over. Because there was this chicken inside it, okay, but when I went up close there was this flash and, like, a clap of thunder and it went all wavy and disappeared. I ain't taking that from no chicken."

Thus far we have been unable to reassemble the Assemblage (photos A thru G). There is considerable doubt as to its function, and we have dismissed Mr X's view that it was "a real *funky* microwave oven". It appeared simply to have been a collection of roadside debris and twigs, held together with cassette tape.* It may have had some religious significance. From drawings furnished by Mr X, there appeared to have been space inside for one chicken at a time.

Document C contains an analysis of the three eggs found in the debris. As you will see, one of them seems normal but infertile, the second has been powering a flashlight bulb for two days, and a report on the third is contingent on our finding either it or Dr Paperbuck, who was last seen trying to cut into it with a saw.

For the sake of completeness, please note document B, which is an offprint of Paperbuck and Macklin's *Western Science Journal* paper: *Exaggerated Evolutionary Pressures on Small Isolated Groups Under Stress.*

All that we can be certain of is that there are no chickens in the area where chickens have been for the last seventeen

---

* 'The Best of Queen'.

years.

However, there are now forty-seven chickens on the *opposite* verge.

Why they crossed is of course one of the fundamental riddles of popular philosophy.

That is not, however, the problem.

We don't know *how*.

But it's not such a great verge over there, and they're all clustered together and some of the hens are laying.

We're just going to have to wait and see how they get back.

. . .

Cluck?

Author's note: In 1973 a lorry overturned at a freeway interchange in Hollywood. It was one of the busiest in the United States and, therefore, the world. Some chickens escaped and bred. They survived – are surviving – very well, even in the hazardous atmosphere of the roadside. But this story is about another Hollywood. And other chickens.

RACHEL POLLACK

THE WOMAN WHO DIDN'T COME BACK

ILLUSTRATED BY JAMIE REID

IN THE OLD days, when a woman died, she returned to life after nine days.

On the first day after her death her friends laid her body on her bed. They tied ribbons round the hands and feet and placed a stone over the mouth. Then they would sit around the bed, as silent as their dead sister. Those who were bored, or sore, or hadn't liked the dead woman very much, told themselves they would need the same thing done for them some day. And they kept sitting.

On the second day they got up and cooked, their first hot food in twenty-four hours. When they were sitting round the bed again, they began to speak, telling what they knew about the woman. They told of favours she'd done them, fights they'd had with her. Someone might tell how the woman had nursed her when she had the 'flu, another how the woman had cheated her when they'd shared a house. They told whatever they could remember, the whole day long. The third day they buried her.

On the fourth, fifth, and sixth days they took care of their sister's business, paying her debts, writing letters for her, selling old clothes and useless junk, leaving only the things she would need for starting over. If the woman had enemies, some of the friends put on masks of her face and visited the people, doing what they could to satisfy the anger. When they got tired they reminded themselves of a woman named Carla, who had made so many enemies before her death it seemed like half the women in town were putting on masks and visiting the other half.

On the seventh and eighth days they prepared for the party. They hung banners in the woman's colours, they decorated the bar with her picture, they cooked or baked all her favourite foods. They cleaned and polished the bar, the furniture and even the silverware. They set out baskets of flowers up and down the street.

On the ninth day they paraded from the woman's house to the bar, setting out at sundown with drums and whistles, arriving just as the last sigh of daylight faded from the sky.

Then the party began. It went on for hours, everyone getting drunk or stoned, playing the woman's favourite records, until all of a sudden, when it seemed they'd forgotten about the woman herself, the door opened and there she stood.

The returned women always came in slightly wet, their hair damp and curly, the skin glistening. They walked inside and looked around, and everyone stopped, the only noise coming from a record player, or someone who'd tripped against a table or knocked over a glass.

After a moment someone would rush up with a drink, someone else with a roll baked in the shape of the Earth and covered with poppy seeds. As soon as the woman had taken a sip and a bite everyone started to talk again. But the nervousness would last, people spilling drinks or banging into each other. For there was something they had to do, even though no one knew why. Finally one of the younger women would go up to the returned woman and say to her, "What was it like?"

14

The woman would think a moment, maybe look away. "Sorry," she'd say, "I'm not allowed to tell you that." And then all the women would go back to dancing and getting drunk.

Sometime in the late evening, just as everyone was thinking it was time to go home, the woman who had come back would look around the room and see someone, maybe an ex-lover, maybe someone she'd never noticed before. She would ask her to dance. When the two of them had gone off together the party could end.

Sometimes the couple stayed together for months, even years, sometimes just for a night or a few days. But always, as the returned woman left the bar, holding on to her lover, something like a breeze would pass across her face, and she would stop a moment, squinting, or tilting her head, like someone trying to remember something. Then her friend would pull on her arm and they'd go home together. Later, if anyone asked her, "What was it like?" she'd shrug, or shake her head. "Don't know," she'd say, "I can't remember."

For a long time this went on. Then one day a woman named

Marjorie drowned when her boat smashed against a rock. Her friends built a stone circle at the water's edge and asked the sea to return her body. When it washed ashore they took to home and laid it on the bed.

Nine days later Marjorie returned, wearing yellow pants and a loose black shirt over her low breasts. A tall woman with thick shoulders and veined hands and long black hair, she stood in the doorway, wet and shining like the morning. It was strange to see her without glasses. No one had ever seen Marjorie without glasses before. The dead always returned with perfect vision, though it only lasted a few days before the world began to blur again.

Marjorie took a roll and a glass of bourbon. A few minutes later Betty, a neighbour of hers, asked her, "What was it like?" Marjorie threw up her hands and laughed. "Sorry," she said. "Secret."

All evening Marjorie danced about the room or sat trading stories with her former lovers. As it got late people started looking at each other, wondering when they could leave. Finally, Marjorie spotted someone, a young woman named Lenni. A newcomer, Lenni leaned against the pool table, drinking a bottle of beer. She was thin, with narrow hips and long fingers. She wore tight black pants and yellow boots and a blue silk shirt and silver chain with a black crescent around her neck. She tilted back her head to finish the beer, and when she brought down her eyes there was Marjorie.

"Want to dance?" the returned woman said.

Lenni had just broken up with a woman named Berenice. Berenice was so beautiful that some people said the Moon faded and then hid for three days a month because she couldn't compete with Berenice. And Marjorie had a slight scar on her left cheek below the ear, where a lover had cut her with a ring. So when Marjorie asked Lenni to dance, Lenni stared down at her empty bottle and shook her head.

No one in the room made a sound.

"Do you want to dance?" Marjorie asked again.

"I'm sorry," Lenni said, so low she could hardly hear her

own voice. "Maybe another time."

Marjorie stood up straight. She ran her fingers through her still damp hair. All her life Marjorie had hated it whenever anyone told her no. She'd gone sailing and smashed her boat because a woman named Kathleen had told Marjorie she couldn't see her any more. Now Marjorie stared at Lenni until the younger woman tried to walk away. Marjorie blocked her. "Why won't you dance with me?" she said.

Lenni shrugged. "I don't want to," she said. And then she smirked.

Jayne, who was running the bar that night, ran up to take Marjorie's arm. "Come on," she said, "let's dance."

Marjorie pulled loose her arm. "Shut up," she said. To Lenni she demanded, "Why don't you want to dance with me?"

Lenni crossed her arms. She looked Marjorie up and down and then she smiled.

Marjorie clenched her fists. She opened them and wiped her hands on her jeans. "Do you want to know what it was like?" she said. "Do you want me to tell you what it was like?" Lenni tried to slide away, but Marjorie grabbed her arm. When Jayne tried to separate them, Marjorie shoved her aside.

Marjorie told Lenni and all the others everything that had happened to her. She told them of a dark room, so large she couldn't see the walls, only a green floor and high above her a yellow ceiling. She told them of the sound of wings, and birds crying, of a cold wind shaking her body, cleaning off the smell of the sea. She told them of laughter and scuffling feet, and voices, as if the whole room was filled with people, but when she tried to see them she could only get a kind of afterimage in the dark – people lying together, or dancing in each other's arms. And then she was opening a red door and walking up stone steps with nothing on either side but a noise of grinding rocks. She became sluggish, afraid her unbalanced lump of a body would tilt backwards and roll down the stairs. And then something brushed her face, and she panicked, and began to run...

The story went on, while some of the women covered their

ears or banged on the tables. Lenni stood there, her arms folded, her chin down, her eyes tilted up. Only when Marjorie had finished, when all the other women fell silent again, only then did Lenni and Marjorie take a step back, staring like lovers who've goaded each other into some undesired act of violence. Marjorie turned around, saw all the frightened faces. "Shit," she said, "I wasn't supposed to do that."

"Marjorie?" Lenni said. She took a step towards her. Marjorie ran for the door, slipping once on a pool of beer. Just as she reached the street she heard Lenni shout something. She turned around.

In the bar the women heard a horn and a screech of brakes. When they rushed outside Marjorie lay dead.

For the next nine days the women followed all the customs. But on the first day they found it hard to keep silent, and on the second found it even harder to come up with something to say. After they'd buried her, no one could think of anything to do, anything they wanted to fix, any people they needed to see. Jayne thought of putting on a mask of Marjorie's face and visiting Lenni. But she kept postponing it, and postponing it, until the sixth day had passed and it was too late.

On the seventh day they did nothing. On the eighth they hung a few banners and bought some cake, but no one polished anything or put out any baskets of flowers. And on the ninth evening only a few women walked together to the bar, and when a couple tried to sing something the others didn't join in and they stopped after a single verse.

The party went on until dawn, but there wasn't much celebrating. The only woman who'd bought any new clothes was Lenni, dressed in red silk trousers and a long yellow shirt, with spangled green running shoes. But Lenni only stood in the back, leaning against the pool table with a bottle of beer in her hand. The women stayed until dawn. When they saw the sky brighten, and people walking to work, they knew that Marjorie would never walk through the door, would never stand before them, her skin glistening with water and light.

From that day no one who dies has ever returned.

JOHN SLADEK

DINING OUT

ILLUSTRATED BY JAMIE HEWLETT

AS THE TWO women came in, a small camera in the pale blue ceiling above the counter swivelled to catch their conversation.

"I don't know why this robot or whatever it is is such a big deal," said Brandi. "He could of called anyway."

"You know Cog. If you asked him, he'd just say, 'Nobody understands me.' That's supposed to make it all right," said Sherri, mysteriously.

"I mean, there are plenty of robots around already. And most humans are just so much servo junk, fastened together with a few tendons and stuff. Like Rod says — "

"Rod! You still going with *him*?"

"Yeah, hey listen, I had a little talk with Ginni. She goes, 'I don't know what you're talking about.' So I goes, 'No? You sure?' So she goes, 'No, rilly. Rod don't mean a thing to me.' So I goes — oh, hey, what are you getting?"

"Salad?"

They stood in line at a fast-food restaurant called Barry D. Lyte Salad Time Theater and Dessert Bowl. The camera followed them until they reached the pink-and-blue counter. The young man in pink looked at them with old eyes.

"Nielp you?"

"Two Tum-tum salads, please."

"Inny banebit sore nail gravy?"

"No."

"Innythin rink?"

"Two decafs."

"Kine?"

"One Irish almond mocha and one southern Moroccan orange half-roast."

"Kina dressing?" He asked, and by way of explanation:

"Onna sals?"

"One gorgonzola and one light epicure."

There remained only one question:

"Tea tier ort go?"

"Here," said Brandi, who had flawlessly followed the flow. After each answer, the boy had searched carefully over the

large array of squares depicted on a video screen, and pressed one. Each square displayed a tiny icon representing the item selected: Tum-tum salad, decaffeinated coffee, gorgonzola dressing, and a car for "To go."

The boy now stood mute while the total bill was displayed on a larger screen behind him: *$34.80*. To make sure they understood it, a mechanical voice read the number aloud:

"Thirty-four dollars and eighty cents, please."

"Are you sure you don't want me to catch this?" asked Sherri. "I could eyeball it."

Hearing her, the young man started reaching for the Accuret customer retinal reader.

"Wouldn't think of it." Brandi opened her thief-proof wallet and extracted a $50 bill. A man at a table near the window took a close interest in the transaction. The boy accepted the bill, turned and fed it into a machine. Change rattled down a chute in front of Brandi. Seconds later, two trays laden with fast food shot down another chute.

"Joy your meal!" called the boy, as they turned and looked for a table.

"Thank you," Sherri said automatically, though the boy had already turned to say to the next customer, "Nielp you?"

The next customer was a man wearing a skimmer and striped blazer. He stepped closer to the counter and mumbled something about pizza.

"Kine?"

"Anchovy and okra. What do I care?"

"Innythin rink?"

"Decaf, crème de cinnamon delite," replied the man, naming a popular flavour.

"Tea tier ort go?"

"To go . . . I guess. We're all going, right?"

The man looked round the restaurant. Two cameras watched him. "Lots of people here. People just like me. My name is Lube Cordwall, by the way. Pleased to meet you. Likewise. It sure is a small world. Though not quite small enough. I eat at Barry D. Lyte Salad Time Theaters never, seldom, sometimes, a lot, all the time."

The boy ignored him. Only the pale blue cameras watched.

"Hey, I'm wearing the colours, see?" He snapped a finger against the stripes of his blazer, pale blue and pink. "Barry's colours."

Ignoring him, the boy pressed a picture of a car. He then waited, mute, while the total bill was displayed on the big screen behind him: *$29.40.* A mechanical voice read the number aloud: *"Twenty-nine dollars and forty cents, please."* The man ignored it. Ignoring was going on. There was plenty of ignoring here at Barry D.'s, the man observed.

He tried again. "Lube Cordwall is the name," he announced to the restaurant at large. No one looked at him. They were all busy. Well, by thunder, they would know the name of Lube Cordwall tomorrow!

Two thin people over in the tiny smoking section – a glass cubicle in the corner – were hurrying through their meals, as though anxious to put food aside and resume smoking. A woman in a playsuit was trying to hurry her three children. But like other children, hers concentrated on wearing special paper party hats. They dawdled over their barryburgers and cheesyface pizzas, while taking every opportunity to pull at their sweet drinks. In spite of all that could be done to harry and upset them, they continued to joy their meals.

"Joy your meal!" the boy behind the counter was all set to say, but never got the chance. Mr Lube Cordwall fumbled in a shopping bag and came up, not with money, but with a bundle of sticks wrapped with tape, trailing coiled wires. He set it on the counter.

"This is a bomb," he said pleasantly. The boy stared at it, mute, while the mechanical voice read the number again, louder: *"Twenty-nine dollars and forty cents, please."*

"This is a bomb, and I will set it off unless everyone does exactly as I ask. First of all, I want all the customers in here to stay where they are, continue eating, and just ignore me."

This wish was easily granted, since no one had noticed Lube.

23

"I also want to see Barry."

The mechanical voice now said, rather stridently: "*Your order is twenty-nine dollars and forty cents, please. PLEASE PAY NOW.*"

"I said I want to see Barry."

"Barry?"

"Yes, you know – Barry." Mr Cordwall made awkward dancing motions, and the boy nodded.

Everybody knew Barry D. Lyte, the huge dancing teddy bear in the TV commercials. He turned up now and then at Barry D. Lyte restaurants to pass out balloons and paper hats. His ears were hamburgers, his eyes were blueberries, and his muzzle was a 'regular size' (10-oz) plastic drinking cup.

"I want to see him pronto."

"*Your order has been cancelled,*" the mechanical voice said, its tone subdued, regretful. "*Please re-order, or stand aside so the next person can be served.*"

"I want to see Barry, pronto."

"Uh – ullgetta manger." The boy ducked out of sight, and in a moment was replaced by the manager, a plump young man whose badge identified him as Junior Cheever.

"Problem, sir? What can I do for you?"

"I have a bomb here, Junior. I was just telling the kid, I want to see Barry. The bear."

"You want to see Barry?"

"I want to see him here. Dancing. Or I blow the shit out of this place."

Junior focussed mismatched eyes on him. "How about a free salad instead? And we'll throw in a free regular-size diet soda? How would that be, sir?"

"Nope. I said, I want to see Barry."

"Well." Junior grinned at the hideous device. Sweat sprang up on his forehead. "Well, I'm not sure. Barry isn't scheduled to be in our part of the country this week. I don't know just where he is."

"Oh, that's too darned bad. It means I'll have to set this thing off." Lube reached for something that looked like a switch.

The coils of wire trembled.

"Wait, wait. Listen, let me make a few phone calls, maybe I can get Barry for you."

"Okay. Meanwhile, lock the doors. Nobody goes in or out of this place."

Junior said, "Couldn't you let the kids go?"

"No, not until they see Barry dance."

The order was passed along, and employees glided out to lock all of the doors.

Junior went to the wall phone behind him and dialled 911.

"There's a man with a bomb here, at Barry D. Lyte, on Oliver North Boulevard. That's right. He made us lock the doors . . . Yes, this is the manager, my name is Junior Cheever."

Lube Cordwall shouted. "If you're calling the cops, tell them I want to see Barry the dancing bear." He picked up his bomb and vaulted over the counter. "In fact, let me talk to them."

Junior handed over the receiver, which was about to drop from his shaking, sweat-slippery hand.

"Hello? Who am I speaking to? Hello, sergeant, this is Lube Cordwall speaking, I'm the guy with the bomb. L-U-B-E, Lube, C-O-R-D-W-A-L-L, Cordwall. Never mind my address, sarge, let's cut the gab and get down to business. Let me talk to the hostage crisis squad, will you? I do have hostages here, yep, about forty people. Hello? Yes, I will hold, but not for very damn long."

Lube assumed a waiting posture, leaning against the wall, feet crossed, drumming his fingers on the explosive device. Junior wilted.

People were trying to leave. A man and woman herded their three tiny blonde children to the door, where all five of them began to bang and shout. An employee hurried out to speak to them. All five sat down, and only the man continued to shout. The children were absorbed in watching a police car with flashing lights arrive outside.

An elderly couple got up from their table and made their way towards an exit. The man carried a tray of debris from their meal – crumpled paper napkins, styrofoam boxes, plastic drinking cups. The woman preceded him to a large green plastic frog. This frog's huge mouth was covered by a flap marked THANK YOU. The woman pushed at his flap, while the man tipped in the contents of their tray. Above the frog was a large orange toadstool, holding up a stack of trays. The man added the empty tray to the stack. Immediately, a deep, froggy voice said:

"Thank you kindly, folks. Come back and see us real soon, now."

The old couple chuckled and turned to the exit. They rattled at the locked door for a moment. The woman then said something sharp to the man, who shrugged. They went back to their table and sat down.

"Hello, is this the hostage crisis officer? Listen, officer – OK, listen, Joe. I have about forty people, at least a dozen children. I'm about to set off a bomb unless you meet my demands . . . Okay, my first demand is, I want to see Barry D. Lyte, the dancing bear. I want to see him right here. I want Barry to come here and dance – you got that?" He hung up.

Outside, two more police cars entered the parking lot, then two more. Their flashing lights kept the confined children entertained, for the moment.

A man in a business suit got up from his table and rattled a door. Then he rattled another door. When he had tried all exits, he came to the counter. With a folded newspaper, he tapped Junior Cheever on the shoulder.

"You're the manager?"

Junior nodded.

"Why have you locked the doors?"

"You're breaking the fire laws, for a start. This could even be abduction."

Lube Cordwall said, "It *is* abduction. You are all my prisoners."

"Says who?"

"Says me and this bomb."

The businessman looked thoughtful. "I see." He tapped his nose with the folded paper for a moment. "What is it you want?"

"He wants to see Barry, the dancing bear," said Junior, his voice breaking. He was very young, and his management training course ("Five keys to a Happy Customer") had not prepared him for anything like this.

The businessman evaluated this news. "How about some money instead. If we took up a collection—"

"Nope," said Lube Cordwall. "Maybe later I'll ask for stuff like that. Money, safe conduct, a plane to Baffin Island. But just now, I want to see Barry."

The businessman hated to give up. "What if *I* danced? I could put a couple of hamburgers on my head, and a plastic cup over my nose—okay?"

"Just sit down."

Outside, more police arrived, with more flashing lights. They had cleared the street and parking lot of people, and their cars were drawn up in a solid barricade, circling the restaurant. Their small remote cameras rolled in close, while the TV news cameras shot from high behind the barricade.

The police did not seem to have a unified purpose, so far: some officers stood leaning against their cars in plain sight, chewing gum and talking over a coming softball game against the employees of Dirkton's Taproom. The precinct's starting pitcher had been wounded on the hand by a parrot while serving a summons on its owner.

Behind the police lines, a truckload of paramilitary police arrived. Holding rifles at port arms, they ran in place for a moment, then rested.

Simultaneously, a child began to scream and the phone warbled. Lube answered. "Yes? Hi again, Joe. Yes, I am still just fine. Plenty to eat here. Great companions, you can hear one of them screaming now. I sure appreciate your concern.

"What do I need? What do I need? I've been telling you, I need a dancing teddy bear. Yeah? *So where is Barry?* No don't give me all these stories about how you're really trying. If I don't see that damn bear in five minutes, *I will blow up this place and everyone in it!* You got that?"

The child stopped screaming as he put down the phone. It was suddenly so quiet they could hear the faint creaking sounds of the tiny mansard roof and the sound of grating carrots from the kitchen. Outside, a camera focussed on two police officers:

"You think this bozo could really boom the place?"

"Nah, we get a lot of these, one a month. I don't worry."

"You know what worries me?"

"What?"

"What worries me is a starting pitcher. You think we got any chance with Greenspan starting?"

"Jeez I don't know, first base looks pretty bad too, Ron Ronson got traded to the twelfth precinct, what does that leave us with?"

The manager seemed slowly to come back to life. "Well," he said cheerfully. "If we're all gonna die, we might as well have a good last meal."

"*Die?*" said a woman customer, her voice rising with every word. "Last *meal?*"

"No, wait. I mean, since we're all gonna be here awhile we might as well have a good meal. I'll get my boys and girls busy."

The restaurant employees moved like zombies, dishing up hamburgers, french fries, pizzas, salads, all the rich provender of the earth. They loaded it on fibreglass trays and carried it to every table. The house cameras followed one, then another, as though confused by all the unorthodox movement.

"On the house," the employees were instructed to say. "With Barry's compliments. And we're real sorry about this problem, folks." Junior served some of the food himself, smiling ("Give 'em a happy face. Doesn't cost you a dime," said the training manual). There was no happiness, however in his mismatched eyes.

The problem continued to lean against the wall near the phone. He continued to clutch the coils of wire while he scanned the parking lot for a sign of the dancing bear.

Barry was nowhere to be seen. Instead, a short, smiling middle-aged man came from the parking lot and knocked at one of the glass doors. He was wearing a sloppy Hawaiian shirt, Bermuda shorts, sandals, and a baseball cap. Only the badge clipped to his pocket identified him as a policeman. He put his lips to the crack between the glass doors and called through.

"Hello, Lube. I'm Joe Howell. We talked on the phone. How are you?"

"Impatient," Lube Cordwall called back.

The man chuckled sympathetically. "I can understand that, all right. Well, Barry is definitely on his way. Should be here any minute. Uh, meanwhile, anything else we can do for you?"

"No."

"If you want to talk, we've got a direct line to the phone there. Just pick it up, and I'll be on the other end."

"I see."

"Well, gotta go. So long, Lube. Take it easy."

The cop waved, as if to an old friend, and wandered off.

Outside the sun was trying to set. The streetlights were glowing red outside, trying to blaze up to their normal yellow. The police had turned on their car headlights, and set up a few bright lamps, trying to turn the parking lot into daylight for the cameras. Overhead, a helicopter trained its light and camera on the glass doors.

The elderly woman got up and marched over to Lube. "I've had about enough of this," she said. "My husband is a sick man. He has asthma. You'd better let us go."

"Why?"

"*I just told you why.* Clean out your ears, mister. If you'd listened years ago, you wouldn't be in this fix. Don't you feel ridiculous, standing around in a Barry D. Lyte restaurant with a bomb in your hand? Nothing better to do, I expect. You're a mess, mister."

"Who asked you?" he said shrilly. "Go sit down." His hands tightened on the coiled wires.

"No I won't sit down. My husband is sick, I want to take him home. Besides that, I have a million things to do today. I can't sit around here all day. You'd better let us go. You'd better let everybody go."

"No!"

"Selfish!" The woman had completely lost her composure.

"Go sit down, Goddamn it, or I'll blow you up!"

"Blow yourself up, why don't you? And don't you threaten me, Mister Selfish. Why don't you try thinking about others for a change?"

Junior took the woman by the arm and started moving her away. "Ma'am, I think you'd better sit down. This guy is dangerous."

"Fiddlesticks. Let him blow himself up somewhere else."

"*Goddamnit,*" screamed Lube Cordwall, "*I am going to do it now. We're all going. We're all going.*" His fingers flexed on something – a switch among the coiled wires – and instinctively everyone flinched.

30   But there was no explosion. Barry had arrived in the nick of time.

All ready to push the button, Lube had taken one last look outside and spotted the huge head bobbing up behind a police car. The hamburger ears seemed to glow in the strange light.

"Barry," he shouted. "You got here just in time. Hey, Junior, let him in. Hurry up, let him in."

Junior scurried to unlock a glass door, as the great familiar, happy bear face approached the restaurant. Barry was larger than anyone imagined – at least eight feet tall. Even so, his enormous bow tie, pink and pale blue, seemed too big for him. It wobbled as he walked with his characteristic rolling gait, swaying from side to side, cocking his head to one side and then the other. Like an overgrown puppy tied up with a ribbon. Kids all over the restaurant were cheering, all of them almost as gleeful as the mad bomber.

The dancing teddy bear stopped in the space before the counter. He was facing Lube, as though he sensed Lube was the man in charge here. The bear did not speak – Barry D. Lyte never speaks – but when Lube Cordwall spoke, the hamburger ears turned to catch every word.

"I knew you'd come," Lube said in a childish voice. "I knew you would come and dance." His face had gone slack, and spittle drooled down his chin. "All I had to do was wait."

Barry nodded. Then he began to nod, one, two, three. The drinking-cup nose moved as though conducting an invisible band, two, three. The blueberry eyes rolled with an unheard rhythm, a-one, a-two, a-three. The great white-gloved hands spread their three fingers, clapped without sound, two, three. Finally, a foot – the size of a small stool – lifted and came down softly on the tiled floor – three and one and two and. Barry began to dance.

It was an odd dance, without sound. The restaurant was not silent of course. Kids were laughing and shouting, some of them clapping and banging on tables. Barry himself made not a sound, however. The giant feet in spectator shoes rose and fell delicately, silently.

The door remained open, unnoticed by Cordwall, and a few frightened souls slipped out and made their way across the parking lot to safety. Others were too exhausted to move, or afraid, or simply unable to tug their children away from the entertainment. For many years, they would regret not making the move.

Everything was fine while the dance lasted. Then at length, Barry brought his heels together, flung out his hands, and bowed his head.

"That was very nice," said Lube Cordwall, not applauding.

"More. Dance more."

Barry danced for another minute. When he stopped, he was a little closer to Lube Cordwall. Lube said, "More again."

The eyebrows, which were large french fries, shot up in humorous surprise. But Barry D. Lyte obeyed. He finally stopped again, closer still.

Lube said, "More! More dance!"

Barry did not deliver more dance. Instead, he held up a

white-gloved finger for attention. His grin grew wider, and somehow it did not seem so friendly. Lube had a moment to look into the blueberry eyes and reflect that this bear was very large and very close.

The grin suddenly split open. Barry's head broke apart, and a large reptile snout poked forth. Glittering reptile eyes came behind it – they were fixed on Lube Cordwall. In a second, reptile claws tore through Barry's papier-mâché head and shoulders so the large reptilian creature inside could begin slithering out, reaching for Lube.

Some mistakenly claimed later that it looked like a crocodile, others that it was a miniature Tyrannosaurus Rex (but the tapes would have shown otherwise). The younger children were never able to talk about it at all. But it would be waiting in their nightmares, like endless repeats of old shows. The cheers turned to screams.

The cameras would have recorded a snakelike creature, though equipped with efficient clawed hands that held the man still, while the enormous jaws began to cover him with saliva.

A mouse caught by a cat suddenly stops moving. It gives up and relaxes. This is the 'still reaction,' a numbing recognition that life is up. The great explorer of Africa, Dr Livingstone had the experience himself, when attacked by a lion. He found himself relaxing – he felt no pain, though the animal was tearing his shoulder.

Lube Cordwall stood rigid with fear for a moment, before he let go of his bomb device and went limp. The stink of reptile saliva rose through the restaurant.

Numbness crept over the restaurant. People stopped eating, stopped screaming, stopped trying to claw their way through the glass walls. They simply sat and watched. Children sat in puddles of their own urine and watched.

The creature began to swallow Lube Cordwall, head first. The straw skimmer crunched into the great gagging mouth, then Lube's head and shoulders, in pink and blue stripes, then the rest of him. The legs made a last convulsive kick as they disappeared.

After a few moments, the police went to work. A bomb squad man carried away the dynamite, past the cameras, which now began to work again. Other officers came in to remove the rest of the patrons. Children were rushed off to see police paediatricians. Their parents were wrapped in foil blankets and fed sedatives, then wheeled away on low carts. The cameras followed them, carefully avoiding the reptile.

Finally the police reptile handler came to get his animal. It had now stopped thrashing about and lay still, eyes opaque, no movement except a faint pulsing of its distended belly. Covered in a blanket, it could be wheeled away without attracting attention.

Inside and outside, the cameras rolled about, watching and listening.

"I told you this bozo wouldn't boom the place."

"Hey, you think we should start Borden instead of Greenspan?"

"Borden's bad news. Anyway, what about first base? Jeez, with Ron traded, what does that leave us with?"

The disgusted policeman watched a pink camera roll through the door, where it turned and veered past the booth where two women picked at their salads.

"Okay, tell me how come you're still going with Rod."

"Yeah, well listen, last week I was supposed to have a date with Cog, you know? Only Rod calls up and asks me to go to the lake. So I goes, 'You think you can call me up just like that and ask me to go to the lake?' And he goes – "

COLIN GREENLAND

BEST FRIENDS

ILLUSTRATED BY MICHAEL KALUTA

SHE CALLED ME. She called me by name.

I was sitting alone in a crowded restaurant. Camilla had excused herself and gone off to powder her nose while I drank my coffee. When we went out for a meal, I liked to drink a cup of coffee afterwards, for I never have the opportunity at home. Camilla believes coffee after noon is bad for the complexion; but she never sought to dissuade me from this luxury of mine.

I suppose I was not being very good company, in any case. There were problems at work that took much of my attention. It was easy to believe that the fair-haired young woman two tables away was smiling at someone behind me; or else she had mistaken me for another man.

It was then that I heard her speak my name.

"Ralph. Ralph!"

She had materialised, without my seeing quite how, at our table. She stood with her hands on the back of Camilla's vacant chair. She did seem to be young indeed, almost young enough to be one of Penelope's school chums, I thought, and I thought that was probably it.

"I'm sorry," I said, or began to say.

"You remember me, Ralph," she said with perfect equanimity. "Of course you do. I'm Susan."

Her voice was light, and not at all suggestive; and yet, yes, suggestive of a certain assumed intimacy, so I tried to conceal it as I cudgelled my memory.

I will not say I was not taken with her at once. I was. But I held back. Susan: the name meant nothing to me.

"Susan," I said.

"It's been ages. Ages!" She sounded happy. It would have been churlish not to encourage her.

"Yes," I said. "A long time. My goodness." I sounded foolish, even to myself.

"Fancy meeting you here," I temporised; which only sounded worse.

"Fancy," said Susan.

The inanity of this verbal ping-pong was becoming embarrassing. If she had nothing more than this to say to me, I

remember thinking, why had she approached me in this forthright fashion? Yet her smile was the smile of one with good news to deliver; or perhaps her smile was the good news. I hoped for a clue.

"I saw you come in," she said, not very helpfully.

"We often come here at the weekend," I replied, "Camilla and I."

Which was no more than to speak the truth.

It did not daunt her.

"It's nice here," she said. She was looking around – at the ceiling, I remember especially – as if she had never seen the inside of a restaurant before.

"Yes, it lets Camilla out of the kitchen one night a week, at least," I went on. Now I thought I must sound a hopeless case, cheerfully mired in domesticity.

"Camilla?" she echoed. "That's a nice name. Is she nice?"

So that was one slight fear allayed, that she was some friend of Camilla's, that Camilla would come back from the powder room any minute and disentangle us. I felt rather ashamed of that fear as I let it go. I did not like to let my wife cover for a failing of my own. I believed it indicated a moral weakness in the relationship. It all came to the same in the end though, I suppose.

"Yes, she's very nice," I said; while I thought: pre-Camilla, then. For even if in the purlieus of the City attractive young women had not been as rare as unicorns, I could scarcely have forgotten one so fresh, so unmarked; one who would thereafter address me in public by my Christian name. Pre-Camilla. Of course, one had had one's flings, if you could call them that; one's youthful pashes, one's disappointments, during the war, and up at Aberystwyth. But never so numerous that I could not, even now, recite the names of my queens and the dates of their brief reigns in my heart. She was not one of them. Pre-Camilla: she must be older than she looked.

All this categorical speculation I went through in a moment in my head while I smiled and silently cursed and invisibly trembled; for what was I to do with her? How could I introduce her? I could not even account for her presence.

Yet one must be gallant, especially while approaching forty, beyond which opportunities for gallantry become increasingly few, and all those avuncular.

"Won't you join us?" I asked, plunging into the abyss.

"Oh no," said Susan, withdrawing a little, visibly shrinking, in fact. "Not yet," she said. "I just wanted to let you know I'm here."

Which I thought was an odd way to put it; especially when the next thing she said was: "I've got to go now." And she waved to me, there in the middle of a crowded restaurant: her extraordinary, awkward, silly little wave, made by holding her hand up and opening and closing her fingers. I found it hugely distracting.

Then my visitor had turned and gone, back to her own table I supposed, and Camilla was coming at last. I felt considerable relief. A ghastly *faux pas* had been averted. The abyss had graciously declined my sacrifice, and returned me to the land of the living.

But I had to say something. Camilla was sure to have noticed her, and it would be suspect, I thought, not to say something.

"The damnedest thing," I said.

"Well, I hope it's not so bad you need to swear, darling," said Camilla, sitting down and reaching across the table for my hand to show she forgave me. She smiled pleasantly. She had seen nothing.

"Susan? We don't know any Susans. What surname?"

"I haven't the slightest idea."

"Well, didn't you ask?"

"I could hardly do that, my dear."

"Where is she?" Camilla turned in her seat to look; but since Susan's departure a large bald man with a great number of chins had been seated in her place. There were people coming and going all the time. Susan was nowhere to be seen.

"Fair hair?" Camilla mused. "Suzanne, probably."

"Who?" I asked.

"Darling," said Camilla reproachfully. "Suzanne Pearce. Frank Pearce's wife. They live at number thirty-seven," she said, as if addressing a rather stupid little boy.

"Must have been," I said.

It occurred to me that I had not even looked to see if she was wearing a ring.

"If you've finished, darling, perhaps we could pay," said Camilla. "I'm sure they need the table."

Susan. Someone I'd met at the university? One of those miscellaneous women, impossibly fragrant and self-assured, that held impeccable dinner parties and were continually rumoured to be sleeping with the president of the Students' Guild. They always had terrifyingly acute memories.

I, on the other hand, have not. If you had asked me, any time in the next couple of weeks, I would honestly have said I'd forgotten all about her. I had other things on my plate. In fact, when the telephone rang unexpectedly one particular dull and rainy Saturday afternoon, I was up to my eyes in papers I'd had to bring home. Nevertheless, I sprang from my seat to answer it.

"It's me," she said, a habit neither grammatical nor informative, which I normally detested in people. I knew, however, who it was. I felt a strange hollowness, almost a breathlessness, as if a cavity had opened up in the region of my sternum.

"Susan," I said.

Camilla was in the next room, helping Penelope make a frock. It would be all right if I kept my voice down a bit.

There were peculiar noises in the background, atmospherics on the line, I supposed: a sort of buffeting, windy sound, and something that sounded exactly like chains hanging idly, clinking together.

"Where are you?" I asked.

"Silly," she said. "I'm here. I told you."

I thought then, and I was rather surprised I hadn't thought it before, that it might after all be a practical joke. The women at the office. They had never liked me. Some of the chaps had a way with them; not me.

But a man is master in his own home, I told myself; and wherever Susan was, she was on the other end of the phone, where she could do me no harm. Besides, she had charmed me.

The chaps at work: what would they have said to Susan? I knew the sort of thing.

"What a pity you're not here," I said gamely.

"But I am," she insisted. "Here I am." Then, before I could even begin to tire of her childish nonsense: "Where's Camilla?" she asked.

I lied to her. I do not excuse myself for it.

"She's out," I said quickly. "She's gone to see her mother." I held the telephone closer to my mouth. "There's just us."

"Ralph and Susan," she said.

At that mere utterance a warm glow suffused me, rising up through the cold and tremulous place in my breast.

"What can I do for you?" I asked.

"Why don't you come out to the park?" she said.

I looked at the front door. Rain was blowing against the glass.

"It's a filthy day," I said, as calmly as I could.

"But we always used to go to the park," she persisted. "You used to like the park."

"Did I?"

"Ralph. You know you did."

I hadn't the first idea of what she was talking about.

"Are you sure it was me?" I asked, quite playfully.

"There wasn't anybody else," she said. "There never was. Come to the park, Ralph, do. I've been waiting for you, you know. I've been waiting ever so long."

There was no sound of the receiver being replaced at the other end, but the blustery noise changed slightly, and when I said, "Hello? Hello? Susan?" there was no reply.

I laid the handset gently back in its cradle. The wind blew another gust of rain at the door. I felt a powerful urge to seize my mackintosh and rush out to the park, to see if she was

41

there, just to see, and damn the consequences.

Of course I could not do any such thing. I knew that. That was the way it was. That was what I had chosen.

I went back into the lounge and closed the door.

Penelope came through from the dining room.

"Who were you talking to, daddy?" she asked.

"Hm?"

"On the phone," she said.

I looked at her standing there, picking ends of cotton off her fluffy cardigan.

"Nobody," I said.

"No it wasn't," she said. "It couldn't have been nobody because you talked to them."

Her hair was in pigtails, but when she let it down in the evening after her bath, it would flow soft and shining over the shoulders of her dressing gown. She worried about spots. She was almost a woman herself.

"I tell you, darling, I really don't know who it was," I said quietly, hoping her mother wouldn't hear.

Penelope wrinkled her nose.

"She wouldn't tell me," I said.

"You said 'Susan'," she objected.

"Did I, darling?" I said. "We don't know anyone called Susan."

"There's Susan Chapman in the lower sixth," said Penelope.

"Darling, I'm sure it wasn't any of your friends," I said truthfully.

"Susan Chapman's not my friend," said Penelope at once. "She's a pig. She sticks chewing gum under the seats. She borrowed my hanky and wiped her pen on it!"

"How's the sewing coming along?" I asked her.

She held my hand and took me to see.

That night I dreamed I was sitting in front of one of those mirrors actors have in their dressing rooms, with light bulbs all the way around the frame. I could see my face in the mirror, which is something I can't recall being able to do, usually, in a dream. My face was caked with thick white make-up, like a clown's. A door opened behind me, and I saw someone come in. This person, whether a man or woman I couldn't say, made a remark, I don't remember what, only that it was rather sad. Then suddenly I saw something I hadn't known was there, lying on the dressing-table, something grey and shabby and folded that frightened me. I had to put it out of sight at once, so I picked it up, but the thing was rotten and came to pieces in my fingers.

I woke abruptly. It was very dark. The afternoon's squalls had at a quarter to nine in the evening turned to steady and sullen rain. I could hear it still, thudding on the roof and splashing in the street. The alarm clock had stopped some minutes before twelve. I suppose I had omitted to wind it up.

The dream was lingering, hanging on me, like a bad taste in the mouth. With some idea of finding out the time I got out of bed, put on my dressing gown and slippers, and went out of the bedroom, closing the door softly so as not to wake Camilla.

I looked in on Penelope, who lay as she always did, on her right side, frowning in her sleep as if concentrating furiously on something.

I don't think I looked at her clock. Perhaps I had already forgotten what I was supposed to be doing. At any rate, I left her room and went downstairs.

Through the glass of the front door the street light was sparkling. There was a faint white shimmer on the bottom few stairs and on the newel-post. It made it look as if the pattern of the carpet was moving around beneath my feet, wriggling about.

I went into the lounge and, in the dark, almost walked into the piano stool. The shadows of the trees outside ran up the curtain into the corner of the ceiling. I pulled the curtain aside and looked out into the rain.

The street seemed bleak and unreal in some way, like theatre scenery, although the rain was real enough. I would need my mackintosh.

What was I thinking of? It was the middle of the night, or at least some awful small hour of it. It wasn't time to go anywhere but back to bed.

I remember, as a boy, I never used to understand it when people spoke of the 'small hours'. To me, on sleepless nights, when I was unwell, those were the longest hours of all.

In the wet light of the window I looked down at my feet and saw that I was not, as I'd thought, wearing my slippers. What I had put on in the darkness of the bedroom were my outdoor shoes. I had even, without realising, tied the laces.

I took my mackintosh from the peg and my keys from the hallstand and went out into the rainy night.

They lock our local park at night. No one is supposed to get in or out. I stood under the heavy trees that reach out over the fence and looked across the lawns towards the playground. I could see the silhouettes of the swings standing up above the hedge. It was too far, and too dark, to see if anyone was in there.

Duncombe Park is not like the park I used to go to as a child, St Margaret's Park. St Margaret's Park had a playground twice the size, and an ornamental pond where goldfish swam in brown water under thick, glossy weed and the wet black leaves fallen from the willows. It had a bandstand I could get up on, out of season, and pretend it was a ship, or a tent, or the greenwood hideout of Robin Hood and Maid Marian. Duncombe Park has only the putting green, and the smaller playground.

I stood outside Duncombe Park that night in the rain, thinking: There could be anyone in there. Anyone could get in, I realised, if he were truly determined. I thought there might be somebody in there that minute, in the bushes, watching me.

It was like the time I played hide and seek. I played hide and seek, as a child, once at my uncle and aunt's in Northumberland. I rarely went out to play with other children, because of my complaint. We were playing in the little scrubby wood at the bottom of their garden, while the grown-ups were having tea. I was "it".

I remember feeling then that someone was looking at me out of every bush, though actually the other boys had abandoned the game already, without telling me. The air smelt sour and slimy. My cousins came trooping into the clearing where I stood hesitating. My cousin Norman had an old paint tin clutched to his chest. He had found it somewhere. It was full of dirty water. He dumped all the water on the ground at my feet. It splashed my sandals and socks, and up my legs. I realised, that night outside Duncombe Park in the rain, that he would have thrown it all over me, if he'd dared. They called me "bog brush", because of the way my father always made the barber cut my hair so short, so that it would last me.

I was not a vindictive child. I didn't tell on my cousins, even when my parents made me come indoors. My mother told me to stop running around. "You'll have an attack," she said, scrubbing at my shins with a handkerchief. My father looked at me contemptuously from where he sat on the edge of the settee, because I did not know how to behave, because I would get "in a state", as he put it.

"I wasn't running," I told them. In fact I felt perfectly well.

There was no way to convince them of that. In any case, I could never tell how long it would last. My attacks could come on very suddenly.

The rain was falling all about me through the overhanging trees. My parents live in Canada now. They emigrated there when my father retired. What would they have said to see me that wild night, out in the rain in my pyjamas, clutching the railings of the park like a mad ape?

The weather worsened that season, as it so often does. In town I seemed to be always fighting for my umbrella with the wind that had turned it inside out. The streets were full of muck and rubbish. Along by the allotments the short cut to the station was infested with browsing slugs. Work was difficult. I was, I suppose, becoming absent-minded, always thinking of other things. Camilla, I now think, cushioned me. At any rate she behaved with great forbearance. How complicated life can become, if we let it.

I was sitting at home one morning going over some figures. I had been off-colour, I believe, for a few days, with something of a recurrence of my old problem. I paused for a moment, staring out of the window at something other, no doubt, than the wet and dreary day. In reality, I suppose, I had drifted off.

What recalled me to myself was a noise upstairs, a faint intimation that I was not in fact, as I knew myself to be, alone in the house. Camilla had accompanied Penelope to school and gone on into town to shop. She could not have come in without me hearing her, distracted though I was. She could never come into the house without singing out "Hello!" Lately, in my indisposition, she had become almost solicitous.

The noise made itself heard again. It was not a furtive noise, more a sort of soft, blind, fluttering noise. I wondered at first if a bird could have got in upstairs. Yet Camilla would not have gone out and left a window open, whether I was working at home or not. She thought such things her responsibility, and quite rightly too.

At another time, perhaps, I might have dismissed it altogether and continued with my work. On such slight evidence it was more than likely there was nothing there at all, and I should waste my time and trouble investigating.

Yet I got up from the table and went swiftly and silently upstairs.

She was in the bedroom, sitting, if you please, on our bed.

"Goodness, you startled me!" she said, as if I were the intruder there. She pressed her hand to her breast in a way I should have thought coquettish in another. She was wearing a mauve jumper and a blue tartan skirt and looked more than ever like one of the girls who came home with Penelope now and then. I doubted everything again. I decided she must be somebody obvious, somebody with a perfect right, under an arrangement I had been told about but had forgotten, to be sitting there in our bedroom in broad daylight.

"I didn't know you were here," I said. "Did Camilla let you in?"

"No, Ralph," she said. "You let me in."

I supposed I had left the back door unlocked again. Camilla was always chiding me for it.

"Well, don't sit up here on your own, come down," I said, like the cheerful host. "May I offer you a cup of coffee?"

She shook her head.

I looked at my watch, without, however, registering what time it said. "A sherry, then."

"Sherry," she said. "No, I don't think sherry's what I want."

She got up then with a lovely lithe movement and took my hands. Her hands were cold, as if she'd just come in from outside.

"Come and play, Ralph," she said.

I did not resist her pull. I indulged her, letting her draw me towards her. I felt like a man in a dream, who behaves as if everything were perfectly normal and logical when his waking self would cry aloud that on the contrary nothing makes any sense.

Susan drew me, not, as for one alarming moment I thought, further into the bedroom, but out to the landing and the top of the stairs.

"Susan, I can't play with you now," I said.

"Soon, then," she insisted.

"Another day," I said.

"You've got to," she told me.

"Have I? Have I got to do everything you say?" I asked, teasing her.

"We could play that, if you like," she said.

She smiled at me with a heart-warming candour, and then again I doubted her intentions. She seemed so innocent. And so maddeningly familiar, but from some other circumstances, surely, not from here at all. I knew I had made a mistake, pretending to know her, and sinking into this absurd relation with her, this bare-faced masquerade.

"Susan," I said.

"Ralph," she said.

"You shouldn't be here, you know," I said. "It's out of the

question."

"No, Ralph," she said.

How wonderfully vexing I found it, her way of answering no to everything I said!

"There isn't anywhere else," she said. "I'm yours."

I had always longed for a woman to say those words to me. I imagine every man has. I knew I should look into her eyes.

She held on tightly to my hands.

Below, the front door opened and Camilla came in, vigorously wiping her wellington boots.

"Hello, darling!" she called.

I came to leaning over the banister, peering uncertainly down at her.

Camilla was standing on one leg on the doormat, lifting up her other leg to pull off her boot. "What are you doing?" she asked.

I looked around the landing.

"I thought there was a bird up here," I said. "I thought I heard something."

"A bird?"

I went into our room and looked around. There was no sign of anything untoward, but the counterpane was crumpled, as if someone had been lying on it negligently. I straightened it and went downstairs to my wife, who was standing in the hall in her stockinged feet, surrounded by groceries. She offered her cheek to be kissed.

"Nothing there now," I said.

Camilla looked at me critically and felt my forehead. "You haven't been overdoing it, have you, darling?"

I said I thought I had nodded off for a minute or two.

"Why don't you go back to bed?" she asked. "I'm sure you'd feel better for a proper rest."

Nothing was wrong, I told her.

"I'll bring you up some soup," she offered. She picked up one of her shopping bags and padded off into the kitchen.

"It's a filthy day out there," she said.

"I had a most odd dream," I said. I had decided to put it like that. "It was about a woman."

I carried the rest of the shopping through to the kitchen and set it on the dresser. Camilla was at the sink, running water into a saucepan. I can see her now, as clearly as if it were yesterday. She had rolled up her sleeves, but had not yet put on her houseshoes, though I had often warned her against walking barefoot. There could be things left lying on the floor, I used to say, dressmaking pins for instance, that she might step on and injure herself.

"Do you remember that woman," I began, "what was her name, Susan, was it? Susan something, what was it now . . . "

Camilla put the pan down sharply in the sink.

"It's her," she said. "Her. That woman in the restaurant."

I thought her reaction a little abrupt, and covered myself. "Oh, I don't know, did we meet her in a restaurant? Let me see . . ."

"I knew it," she said. "I knew it. I'm not a complete fool, Ralph, you know. I knew there was something. It's her." She turned on me accusingly. "You needn't try to deny it."

I was amazed, astounded, to see tears in her eyes.

"I didn't say anything. I pretended I didn't know," she said. "I tried to keep you away from her. I — "

She broke off, and pulled herself together.

"No more, Ralph," she said. "I made myself a promise, when all this started. I made myself a promise," she said briskly, "and I'm going to keep it."

She pushed past me into the hall.

"Camilla!" I cried. "What's wrong? Where are you going?"

She was wrestling her boots on again, and tying her headscarf.

"I don't know who she is, Ralph," she declared, "but I've got a jolly good idea what she is." Her face seemed to clench in anger. She shouted at me. "Aren't you ashamed?"

I felt myself move jerkily along the hall towards her, my hands reaching out for her, like a badly operated marionette.

"Camilla! Calm down! What is it? What do you mean?"

This seemed only to infuriate her further.

49

"Do you think I don't know?" she demanded. She was almost shrieking.

"Dearest, please!" I remonstrated. "The neighbours – "

Camilla threw the door open wide and rushed out into the rain.

Naturally I followed her. I caught up with her and took her in my arms, or attempted to. But there is a limit to how far one is prepared to carry on one's domestic altercations in the open, in the pelting rain, especially in a peaceful, respectable neighbourhood like Addison Close. Camilla was incoherent and heedless. She exhausted me. I had to let her go and return indoors.

The first thing I did was to turn off the kitchen tap, which Camilla had left running. The water had filled the saucepan in the sink and was overflowing needlessly down the drain. I sat down at the table again, where in something of a daze I noticed that I had left the cap off my fountain pen, and I put it back on. Yet while I remained thus outwardly calm, I think I was beginning to panic.

What was I to do? What if Camilla did not return before nightfall? Should I tell the police? What if she stayed away for several days? Who would look after Penelope? Who would prepare our meals? What would they think at the office if I were to arrive looking unkempt and uncared-for, in yesterday's collar and cuffs?

What, above all, had I done to deserve this treatment, this melodrama of slammed doors and tussling in the street?

I did not, however, have long to wait.

I was still sitting there staring blankly at the confused and cancelled figures that covered the papers in front of me, and trying to marshal my thoughts, when the doorbell rang.

"Camilla!" I cried, starting up from the table. She had gone out in such a temper she had forgotten her front door key.

But it was not Camilla.

It was Susan standing there, in a white cardigan and a summer frock the colour of dandelions. It was still pouring with rain, but Susan had been careful and hadn't even got her feet wet.

"Come out and play, Ralph," she said.

I could see she didn't look so young now, now I remembered her.

She took my hands. Her hands were cold. "Come and play," she said, and I followed her out into the rain.

Duncombe Park isn't as good as St Margaret's Park. There isn't a fishpond, or a bandstand. But there are swings, and when you swing up high, you feel as if you're going to fly away, up into the sky.

We like the swings best, Susan and I.

ANN NOCENTI

THE HEART BEATS

ILLUSTRATED BY ART ADAMS

FLAT TYRES, IMMOVABLE mounds of them. Stacks of blind televisions, tubes blown out, gouged black eyes staring. The exploded coils of sprung bedsprings, beds that now mock the idea of sleep. A twisted, blackened trumpet, the occasional wind playing its one sour note. Reels of unravelling celluloid, someone's home movies. A landscape shaped by jutting ironies, heaps of satire, rusted humour. Metal scrap, dead rubber shreds, silicone bones, flaccid plastic, a screaming clash of waste, all defying Mother Nature's hunger, arrogantly proclaiming her teeth not sharp enough to break them down, drag them back whence they came. Dust to rust to dust. They were wrong. In the end, she claimed us all. She needed us, eventually, to push up her daisies.

Lately, I'd taken to hanging out in junkyards. I was so angry, at mankind, at all kinds of men, for the world he had built, that it gave me great pleasure to see his wondrous achievements piled in rotting heaps. The Great American Junkyard. Where all the accomplishments of technology ended up. Magnificent stinking monuments of twisted metal, gape-toothed pianos, slack-jawed refrigerators, Cadillacs on their backs like flipped turtles, flat tyres pawing helplessly at the sky, billboards sporting pretty girls with stained faces, broken hope chests, frayed love nests . . . all the dreams and ideals confused and twisted into material objects and finally discarded. I wasn't alone in my love for junkyards. That's where I met Skunk.

I was relaxing in a beautifully cracked antique tub, the kind that squats on clawed lion paws, thinking about what it must have been like before the big bang, the one where the universe as we know it was first created, when man was a mere gleam in God's eye. The dizzy speeding particles, the void and vacuum. All that great nothingness, which still smiles behind all man tries to do to fill it. You're probably thinking I'm some kind of nihilistic dropout anarchist. I'm not – I have a job, a VCR, a wife, a house, a TV, a car, a pet and all that, but some-times on my way to work my car takes over and drives me, like it or not, to the junkyard. My car drives faster than I do, and one day I envision it speeding head on into a garbage heap,

making both of us, as last, permanent parts of the techno-graveyard.

Anyway, I was lying in the dry tub, a naked headless Barbie doll propped up on my chest, thinking about losing things in black holes, of the moment before a white dwarf explodes, of particles spinning crazily through space . . . when I heard a low whistle.

She was the most beautiful Road Kill I'd ever seen.

Animal-black hair with a white streak down the centre. Face obscured by vibrant purple and fuchsia bruises, a smashed headlight strapped over one breast, a glass shard necklace that cut her as she moved, tyre tracks streaked down her front, splatters of blood on her back, pieces of skunk skin hung from her hips and other edges. I'd heard of the Road Kills, seen them on news television, occasionally glimpsed them running in packs at the edge of town. They're the latest manifestation of costumed disaffected youth. As with greasers, hippies, and punks before them, they had a manifesto of sorts. They're dropout kids who considered themselves to be damaged goods, but still up and walking. The products of smashed families, of a society crushed under its own social pile-ups. The walking wounded. Sensual car wrecks. They live in that moment when man and his blinding headlights traps animal on the highway. Animals transfixed by the beam, the brilliant white light that promises transcendence. Man was always making promises like that, with his sleek products. But it always ends in another road kill. So they dressed as road kills, accidents waiting to happen, in honour of that conceptual moment.

"When a man gives up on live girls and takes up bathin' with baby dolls, what's his shrink possibly got left to say to him?" She'd snuck up on me, and having done so, couldn't look me straight in the eye.

"My shrink is my wife, and she won't know about this one."

"Lovely. Well come on, gimme a hand, will you? I'm looking for my mate, I just wanna make sure he ain't buried in this heap somewhere." She reached in to pull me out of my bath, her necklace tinkling, a jagged glass edge etching a thin crimson crack on her lovely porcelain neck. She smiled once, quickly, an unforgettable smile. If I live to two hundred, I will still be haunted by that brief smile.

"What does he look like?" I let her drag me out of the tub, gave up my naked doll for her to toss away with a smirk.

"I don't know. You see I have this recurring vision of a big mother red Mac truck, circling out there on the lonely highways, and somewhere on its grille, somewhere right between the headlights, is my name. That big old truck's got my name on it, and it's lookin' to run me down. 'Specially when life's goin' pretty good, like when I actually feel happy sometimes. Then I know it must be movin' close, comin' right around the next bend."

"Your mate is a truck?"

"Yeah, you know, the one of my dreams. Why not? My idea of a good marriage. One meeting. One powerful embrace. One unforgettable kiss. Intense, over fast, no disappointments. Got my name on him and everything. We're wed for life, like swans."

"Swans. They mate for life?"

"Yeah. Only better marriage is that of the queen bee. Hundreds of males chase her, only the strongest gets to mate, and even he dies trying. She's the queen. The whole hive takes on her personality, she's so powerful."

"Uh-huh. So what are we looking for now?"

"Just gotta check out the front ends of all these car wrecks, make sure mine ain't here."

"But wouldn't it be good if you found the truck? It would mean it was already wrecked, and could never hit you."

"So what's the fun in that?"

We picked our way to the top of the heap. On the way up, she prised an ornament off the accordion hood of a rusted sports car. With a twist of wire, she fashioned a barbed halo, and fastened the tortured thing around my head, so that the ornament, a woman with outstretched arms and flowing silk in cast silver, now headed the prow of my forehead.

"I feel as a Christ crucified."

"That's the ticket," she said.

"Listen, this was fun, but I've got to get home, kick the dog, kiss the wife, you know."

"Will she be mad, that you're late?"

"Yes."

"Never beg mercy from the enemy."

"My wife is not my enemy, she's my shrink."

"You know the Ten Commandments?"

"I used to."

"Well, I found a copy of 'em, an' read them, and they're all wrong, you know? So I'm writin' new ones." She dug into the amazing folds of what alluded to a skirt but was made of bits of car metal and upholstery woven together like chain mail. She pulled out a scrap of paper and began reading.

"Thou shalt never beg mercy from the enemy. That's number one. Thou shalt never be bored. Thou shalt have no regrets. Thou shalt always have a way out. You know, a back door. So whatta you think?"

"What was wrong with, 'Thou shalt not kill or steal or . . .'"

"Had to be re-written. Times change. It's a whole new game show."

"I'm tired of rules."

"Oh, these aren't rules as you know them, these I change every day."

"I gotta get home to my shrink."

"All right, be a good boy. But you're foolin' nobody." She reached around me and felt my back. "Not even a bump. You ain't sproutin' wings. You're no angel." She rubbed my head. "Ah! But here you got some bumps. You got horns comin'." Her mouth slipped into that smile of hers. The smile behind the universe.

I listened to her laughter all the way down the hill, as I rubbed my head and glanced at car grilles for my name.

"Hi Heather."

"Yeah? Where've you been? What's your excuse tonight?"

"Never beg mercy from the enemy." I felt Saxophone, our dog, nuzzling my fingertips. I ignored him.

"I'm not your enemy, I'm your wife. Come, I want to show you something. And why can't you be nice to Saxy? Don't you like your own dog anymore?"

"I'm jealous of him. I don't understand why I'm the man and he's the dog, yet he's allowed to go out at night and prowl, and I'm not."

"I really shouldn't have to explain to you the difference between a man and a dog." As we walked down the hall, Heather talked about vital organs. Mostly the heart. She said she had a dream about her heart. That in the dream it still beat for me, but it had grown unwieldy, loud, lumpish, was telling inappropriate jokes, and, like a drunk at an otherwise well-mannered party, had to be asked to leave. This lout of a heart had forgotten how to behave. Instead of pumping steadily, calmly, at an even, reliable tempo, like a bass drum line that holds an ethereal melody aloft, this ornery heart picked up a knife and fork and began to beat a clanking, embarrassing drumroll on the kitchen table, scarring its fine-grained surface. It had no idea what a fool it was, had no idea it should have left, gracefully, many many hours ago. She said she finally reached down her own throat and ripped out her own heart, severing all arteries, ties and communications, and threw the cad of a heart across the room where she could no longer hear its migraine beat.

I listened, politely, and wondered what she was trying to tell me. My wife often speaks in slippery pagan parables. Heather led me into the bedroom, over to the window. A pigeon had built a nest on the ledge. Not out of string or sticks, but out of wire and bottle caps and razor blades and other metal bits. "I feel like that pigeon," said my lovely wife. "I feel like I live in a harsh world, and I've feathered my nest with dangerous objects." She turned to me and stared into my eyes significantly, pinning me in her knowing beam. I felt like a road kill.

59

I stayed home for a solid week, to try and save my marriage. The house was a mess, there were a lot of obsolete emotions, rotten feelings, broken spirits lying around, like another kind of junkyard. Maybe if I explain the context of our world, this new age, you'll understand how things had gotten so bad.

They were bankrupt times. The youth all had their own corporations, they wore huge gold or silver pendants of their company logos around their necks. To them, the Holy Madonna was an ageing rock star and J. Edgar Hoover invented a vacuum cleaner. They weren't sure what the cleaner was for. Jesus Christ was just a swear word, nothing more, and not a particularly potent one at that. Romance was now defined mostly by real estate. A woman chose a man if he lived near a convenient subway to work, or had a big enough apartment. If he had high ceilings and good light . . . well, love could be negotiated, and if the apartment had a balcony, marriage was in the progress charts. The elections were put off, due to lack of nominations. Out of 250 million people, there weren't any good men around. Do you begin to understand? Bankruptcy, everywhere. All paper, no gold. Nothing new was ever created, it was a society living off old images. The magazines still offered glossy pictures, but the people written about weren't even as deep as the paper they were printed on. But even in the thinnest of times, man is still seducible. There were still things . . . of interest.

I had lived in seclusion with my wife for as long as I was able. But I began to notice the fringe groups. There's always the fringe. Like the Road Kills. They seemed to be a kind of roving Heartbreak Club. Still, they were authentic, they had charm. Especially when they tripped and stumbled. Now that I'd finally met one, I couldn't get her out of my mind. I managed to slip out at midnight once when I heard her howling outside, and we ran through the bleak acid rain night, breaking and making rules. I thought things would work out, until one night my wife caught her prowling around outside, bothering the garbage cans.

The heart beats on doors it should never open.

That night she suggested the therapy. My wife's a psychiatrist, so she didn't come right out and say it. She talked circuitously for seven hours first. She spoke of labyrinths and imagination, of unlocking the secrets of the grape and the olive. Of snail shells and circular staircases. Of wine and olive oil and who first seduced them out of hiding. Of the unlocked closets of the mind. Rooms one wasn't allowed to enter in childhood, so were never gotten around to as adults. Doors never opened. The heart beats . . .

She thought I was drifting, she wanted the nest cleaned up. She wanted the eternal vows renewed. She said I should open her up and crawl inside and shove my heart up next to hers and pump . . . She said I should love and trust and never let her down. Or I should do it with the Skunk. Or someone, anyone. Just do it, for real for once. But this halfway stuff is the stuff of cowards, and you know what they say, cowards die a hundred deaths, heroes die once. Take your everloving pick.

61

I'm a physicist. I told her I'd lost something in a black hole, and could never retrieve it. She told me to shut up and take the therapy or she'd leave me. I love my wife. I love her with all my heartbeats.

The therapy was brand new. It was experimental, dangerous, illegal, untested, unreliable, unethical, irreversible, immoral, murderous. When I protested, my wife said that love required sacrifice.

Several days later I found myself in a room like the inside of a refrigerator, strapped to a bed with a burst of colourful wires rising like a fountain out of my chest. The wires ran from my heart to various computers. From my heart to theirs. The top of my head had disappeared into a huge smooth machine, where more wires were plugged into my scalp. They now had access to my every impulse. Printouts monitored the imagery running across the backdrop of my mind, which, now that everyone was looking, I had trouble keeping clean. The psych-techs all gave me dirty looks. This little hook-up, this new-age version of the 'couch' was supposed to allow me to take a stroll through my own mind. A journey, an odyssey to bang on and open all the closed doors. I was supposed to wander the labyrinth of memory and emotion, chase skirt tails, follow balloons, trace the flight of my past. Track down those original moments, original sins, those first strikes, the events that bombed my childhood and made me into this bizarre conflicted baroque Gordian knot complex that can't love his wife the way she wants him to. Her smiling face, body rigid in a straight-back chair, shoved up close to my chest where she could keep one eye on my heart – that was the last thing I saw before . . .

The landscape of the mind. A minefield. A junkyard. But this time my junk, my dynamite. I began to suspect that to take a walk through your own mind is a good way to discover you hate yourself.

I couldn't see much, it was dark, smokey, there were walls and alleyways and what looked like a giant snail shell. A monstrous ant with a string tied around his waist turned a corner, his leash held by an unseen hand. There were piles of mundane objects, like this stack of clocks. Faces, hands, ticks, chimes. I headed that way,wondering. Lately I'd had a thing about clocks, I'd catch myself staring at the second hand of my watch as it beat its relentless reliable way around the face – even, democratic, unequivocal, never-ending. Tickticktick-tickticktickticktick. I'd stare in horror at its sure-footed tick, pushing me someplace I didn't want to go, bringing me a step closer with each tock. There was no stopping it – like the blind armies and tanks of war – ever-moving, determined to march its merciless way right over you, its prisoner. Run you down before you've had a chance to figure out just what you're doing in the road of your unfolding life.

"Heather?" I knew somehow the wires to my head were phone lines that transmitted my thoughts to her and the doctors. So perhaps she could hear me. "You there, honey?

You see what I see? Clocks. Time. Something I'm afraid of. Okay? Does that help? Are we getting anywhere? Am I cured yet?"

I tried to walk on, but my feet were heavy. I took a few dragging steps, but the weight was too much. I looked down. There were two children there, a boy and a girl, one wrapped around each leg.

"Who are you?"

"Daddy!" said the boy.

"Daddy? I have no children."

"We know, you wouldn't have us!"

Oh Christ. I hated this. "Heather! You see this? Kids! So I'm afraid of time and kids! What's next? Jobs and houses and wives and vacuums and TV dinners? We knew all this! I feel trapped and boxed in and caged and I want to escape! To form a tribe and run in a pack and run into walls and slam dance and bleed! We knew this! We know this! So what? Get me out of here!"

I began to run, the children melted away. The landscape became increasingly dark, violent, jutting. I was hit by a bright light, and blinded, I spun, confused. I ran hard, and crashed straight into the arms of my Road Kill. Head on collision. Before I could recover my senses and feel my head for the crack I knew was splitting open up there, she enveloped me, crushed me in a hard metal embrace, her arms locking me to her, lips smashing into mine. Everything in me crumpled and buckled and I felt a shower of glass sweat. We kissed to the taste of blood, and when I pulled away I saw that her mouth was bleeding, her teeth jagged and cracked like the edge of a busted-out windshield, her jaw dented, her lips twisted, two crumpled fenders. I jerk back and see that she is a wreck, a huge hole right through her chest like a window – I could see right through her. And her skin was rusting.

"What happened to you, Skunk?"

She grinned this crazy grin and pointed to the hole in her front end. "This is from when my dog died." She raised an impossibly twisted arm. "This is from that time I figured out

63

how to wiggle out of a straitjacket." She pointed to the back of her head, which I luckily couldn't see. "This is from. . . Oh, hell. Who cares. I don't feel like pullin' out the purple heart file right now, baby. Let's just say I've had a hard life, I got a lot of wounds, okay? Leave it at that?" She fingered a necklace that was made of tiny purple hearts. They seemed to still be moving.

"Frogs," she said.

"Huh?"

"Frogs' hearts. I can take 'em out, still beating."

"Yeah. Handy skill to have. . ." I said softly. "Heather!" I screamed at the top of my voice, or so the phrase goes, but it felt more like the very bottom depths of my voice.

Skunk reached out and grabbed my hair, yanking my head back, either to kiss me or slit my throat. I never found out which, because I was back in the hospital, and Heather was yanking the wires out of my scalp, along with a painful lot of hair. I could see the technicians rushing in, see lights flashing and ticker tape tickering and computers sputtering in anger and madness. Heather belted me in the eye, and as I sank back down, the last thing I saw before I passed out was my jealous little wildcat wife hauling off and belting two psych-techs at once . . .

The next thing I saw was a cracked headlight, peering down at me.

"You awake yet?"

The headlight was strapped to my Heather's forehead. I let my eyes wander over the damage she'd done to her chassis, and I knew I was at the scene of an accident. She'd done herself up like a Road Kill. She looked great, my thumper picked up its tempo to double time. She held up her arm, which had a side view mirror strapped to it. It was pretty cracked, but I could see she'd done me up as a Road Kill too. I wondered where she got the animal skin that flapped off my head, admired the shiner her punch had given me, laughed at the sexist way she'd strapped the gear shift to me. She led me by the hand to our car, which she must have had a good time driving into a few walls to get it undressed. It was zebra streaked in spray paint – black and white with spatters of red. Heather was quiet, content with simple gestures and smiles.

"Where are we going?" I asked, beginning to grin one of those stupid grins that won't wipe off for hours. Heather shrugged and started the car. "Wait a minute!" I yelled, seeing the spray cans on the floor. I got out and began spraying the front grille. My wife came around just in time to see me cross the 't' in "Heather".

She smiled, asking why with her eyes. I kissed her, smearing her black lipstick all over her face, and mumbled, "Now we're wed for life, like swans."

We got into the car.

IAN WATSON

THE HUMAN CHICKEN

ILLUSTRATED BY OSCAR ZARATE

MOLLY AND JOE lived on the narrow-boat *Meadowsweet*, chugging along the English canals, mooring wherever they chose for as long as they chose. They rejoiced in the good, free life. They'd been together for the seven years since they left art school, at which time Molly's parents were killed in a plane crash in Saudi. This was bitter news. However, Molly's share of inheritance and insurance bought her and Joe the *Meadowsweet*. Molly's roots were cut – she wasn't too close to her older brothers, one of whom was an accountant, the other a junior solicitor. Why shouldn't she and Joe cast off their moorings entirely from the mundane world? They felt special and different, as the boat-folk of old had felt with the melodeons and Measham teapots and ribbon-ware plates, their rose-and-castle decorations painted on doors and walls and utensils, their private rituals and traditions as to how to dress or how to knot the rope buffer for the fender of a butty boat; those were a breed apart.

Actually, the water-gypsy life had been forced upon those boat-folk of old by the arrival of the railways. During the great Canal Age preceding, narrow-boat men usually left their families ashore dwelling in proper houses. Compelled to cut costs, the canal carriers incorporated home and boat, family and crew; whereas Molly and Joe gained the freedom of the waters thanks to a little legacy. Nevertheless, Joe and Molly – who were both into naïve art – felt that they were carrying on a folk tradition alien to the modern world. Now they earned their modest living expenses by painting roses and castles upon water-cans and pots and pans for the tourist shops at boatyards, as well as from sale of their own naïve-art canalscapes; not that they ever hoped to be "discovered" by an art dealer. Nor by any form of authority.

Molly and Joe hadn't bothered with any wedding ritual, but after six years afloat they trusted their life and the future well enough for Molly to become pregnant one midsummer. Come the drizzly windswept start of March of the following year *Meadowsweet* was moored in open countryside a few miles north of Oxford when Molly's waters broke a fortnight early.

Though they hadn't consulted any doctors or gynaecologists, no more than the boat-folk would have done, they had both studied a book about pregnancy and childbirth. *Meadowsweet* was only a quick taxi or ambulance hop from Oxford's John Radcliffe Hospital with its maternity wards. Yet labour occurred so suddenly and proceeded so rapidly that Joe didn't dare leave Molly to dash ashore to a phone. Within less than an hour – with the ease of a Third World delivery in the fields, or a wild creature's accouchement, *molto allegro* so as not to be pounced on and eaten – birth took place on board *Meadowsweet*.

Maybe it was fortunate that no third party was present to witness the event. Maybe it was *un*fortunate, since how now would anyone but Molly and Joe credit this? *They* were both very disconcerted, for Molly had given birth from between her legs, as most women do, not to a baby girl or a baby boy – but to a chicken.

This was a fully grown chicken, same size as a lusty newborn human baby, an eight-or nine-pounder with feathers of buff gold, still slicked and matted from birth. Already it was fluffing these out to dry, flapping the crooked arms which were its wings as it perched at the bottom of the bed. Their offspring's body was roomy, its head broad though refined. Its beady eyes shone bright and prominent as it gazed at its human parents.

Molly squealed a little but this set the chicken to squawking in reply.

"My God, what'll we *do*?" asked Joe. "It isn't as if it's a freak or a monster! It looks perfectly normal. It just isn't human, that's all. It's a blithering chicken. You just gave birth to it. We both made it together, didn't we? Of course we did. You didn't sneak ashore last summer and have an affair in a barnyard with a rooster."

"In that case it's a *human* chicken," gasped Molly. "It's our child. We're special, aren't we? We're different. This is the most special, different thing that ever happened to us!" She began to sob, then dried her eyes on the sheet.

Should they try to register the birth? *Could* they? Hardly! Who had known that Molly was pregnant in any case? Only casual acquaintances along the waterways. No one was likely to think it odd that there was, or wasn't, a baby.

Molly recalled the book on childbirth they had read. "Do you think it might have jaundice?" New born babies often developed a mild touch of jaundice during the first few days.

"Bit hard to tell, with feathers that colour!" said Joe. "I mean, it's sort of yellow anyway. But its hair. . . can't call it *that* . . . the stuff on its head, and the flap under its beak – "

"The comb," she told him, "and the wattles." Molly had included poultry in her paintings (though she didn't make a thing of it) so she had found out the names of the parts, and what went where.

"Those look a bit blue, don't they? As if there isn't enough oxygen in the blood. Maybe it isn't breathing properly."

Indeed the chicken's wattles and comb were bluish, shrunken, and scurfy; they looked cold not warm.

"I think," said Molly, "those only turn red and smooth, and swell up when birds are laying. I think they ought to look like that."

"You think," repeated Joe, "our baby ought to look like that: feathers and claws and a beak?"

"Why not?" cried Molly, defending her offspring now that she was more used to the idea.

Their child began to squawk again. Head bobbing, it pecked at the blanket.

"It's hungry. We should feed it." She patted her breasts but these did not feel damp or full or sore, and already she suspected that milk had no intention of coming. "Run to that farm over the field and ask them what you give chickens to eat. They can sell you some food. Or we might already have the right stuff on board! Don't worry about me; I'm not tired. I'm not even hurting. While you're away I'll start getting to know it."

"Er, Molly, should I ask how to feed a baby chicken – or a full-grown one?"

They both stared at their feathered child.

"Well, it's newly born," allowed Molly, "though on the other hand—"

"It's full-size already, isn't it?"

She shook her head. "I don't think so, not if it's a *human* chicken. It's still only a baby. Might need a grown-up chicken diet, though."

"Yeah, let's offer it everything the farmer says. It'll know what it needs."

She smiled. "*It* needs a name. You'd better ask the farmer how to tell a chicken's sex."

"Yeah. Then we'd best shift the boat before he gets nosey."

Their chicken proved to be female so they called her Arabella, only reflecting later how this hinted at the word "crops", thereby suggesting both farmyards and the first organ of their feathered daughter's digestive system. Thus does the subconscious refuse to forget whatever disconcerts it. On a conscious level Joe and Molly had quickly decided that Arabella was a beautiful and unusual name, with a hint of Spain about it, and therefore of gypsies, rumoured (no doubt incorrectly) to be the source of those rose-and-castle motifs which adorned *Meadowsweet* and other narrow-boats.

As to food, Arabella's diet was soon sorted out. In common with a human baby she lacked any teeth in her mouth, and in her case probably always would. Thus a mash of rice and grains formed a good basis, though Joe and Molly needed to be wary of which grains, since nutritious barley proved not very palatable to Arabella and rye she rejected outright.

To this mash they must add protein such as white-fish meal, meat-and-bone meal, and skim milk; and let them not forget her mineral requirements. Steamed bone flour provided her with calcium and phosphate, while in their marble mortar acquired years earlier from a kitchen reject shop they were able to crush oyster shell and limestone chips for her calcium. They had long regarded common salt as a poison, causing bloating and high blood pressure, not to mention ruining the fine discrimination of the palate so that most people could only ever taste a meal if they first emptied a salt cellar over it. In large doses salt would indeed poison Arabella, yet she did require a moderate sprinkle.

Vitamins were essential, with the exception of Vitamin C which she ought to be able to synthesise herself. Thus: Vitamin A from greens, Vitamin B from wheat-germ, and Vitamin D from cod-liver oil. Lacking D, she might grow up weak in the legs, and precious little sunlight – source of D – entered the windows of *Meadowsweet* during that dull wet Spring. What sunlight did fall upon Arabella as she explored the inside of the boat was robbed of its precious ultra-violet component by passage through panes of glass.

Much of this nutritional fuss could have been circumvented by buying a proprietary compound chicken feed in the form of meal or pellets, yet Molly felt this would be subtly demeaning of Arabella, ranking her as an absurd pet rather than a biologically wayward infant.

Of course Arabella did possess concealed teeth, after a fashion. Her "back teeth" were located in her gizzard, the strong muscular organ deep in her which milled her meal and crushed grains before sending them to the intestine, the walls of which absorbed the nutrients. To fuel her gizzard she required grit. Daily Joe gathered a fresh bowlful from along the towpath, or else he ground up flints in the mortar. He also cleaned up Arabella's moist smelly squit from the floor and from their now tarpaulin-covered bed. Yet they were happy together; and their child was thriving on her diet. Within a month, fulfilling Molly's prophecy of growth, Arabella was a twenty-four pounder, a giant of a chicken; for that matter, a giant of a human infant of similar age. They began keeping the curtains closed across the windows in case any impertinent passer-by looked in.

Enough of her diet. What of her psychological development? To what extent did she relate to her parents as a human infant might?

Rather more so than any human baby! A very young human

73

is fully employed in simply getting its mental and bodily act together. It'll be a long haul through the stages, so it spends much of its time asleep and wakes to squall for more food; whereas Arabella was brightly alert most of the day and could certainly forage. No insect long survived being on board *Meadowsweet*.

Arabella certainly knew Molly and Joe. They weren't simply detachable extensions of her own body to be smiled at if compliant, screamed at if recalcitrant. She would readily feed from their hands – though this might draw blood – and roost on their laps, crooning. At such times of family affection she seemed inclined to control her loose bowels, a feat which became easier for her to accomplish once her parents realised they should cut out the bran and fibre from her mashes. Aside from laxative properties (which Joe and Molly might value, but not she) fibre and bran bulked Arabella out without nourishing her. She would feel she was spuriously full. Once fibre was drastically reduced, she grew more apace. Ultimately her comb and wattles swelled red and smooth, hot to the touch.

Enough about her diet, enough! We speak of her personality: which was clucky, warm, inquisitive, perhaps a shade scatterbrained, though nervous only to the extent of her not trying to flap her way up on deck in the absence of specific parental encouragement.

Soon lusty, busty May arrived, when new-sprung leaves first cloaked bushes and trees overhanging the waterways. Green, floral June followed. Arabella was almost three feet high, from claws to the top of her comb.

By now *Meadowsweet* was on the lower Leicester leg of the Grand Union canal. Joe and Molly intended to keep on the move a little a day rather than settling in a favourite spot for a month or more. Since Arabella's birth neither parent had managed much by way of art work. A turn at the tiller allowed each a rest from supervising their child, wiping up her squits, dealing with spilled grain and grits and water.

Molly popped up on deck, shutting Arabella below, to join

Joe.

"I've been thinking," she announced. "We oughtn't to bother tidying the grain and grits all the time. And why put it all in bowls? Why not scatter her food on the floor? We want her to be free-range, don't we? We want her to fend for herself, not be cared for like a poor spastic."

Was Molly fraught? On the contrary! She sounded quite a jolly Molly as she went on, "Now that Arabella's growing up she needs more experience, don't you think? Otherwise she'll believe the world is a long, curtained box we live in with her!"

These words stirred several lines of thought in Joe. Yet he kept his counsel, and she hers, while they were passing alongside another narrow-boat, its roof laden with girls in bikinis, a couple of young chaps in yachting caps chattering at the helm. Third boat in the last half-hour. Tourists were infesting the waterways.

"Maybe we're feeling a bit crowded." He jerked a thumb at the receding holiday-makers. "It'll be okay once we pass Market Harborough. We'll be on broad waterway then."

Molly gestured at the cow-grazed meadows, the rolling grassy hills around which the weedy, reed-lined canal was wending, the steeple-poke of a village in the distance. None of the scattered villages actually lay on this stretch of canal, though you could walk to them, a mile away or more. "I'd have thought we're okay now."

A warbler flew by.

"How about letting Arabella out this evening to see the world?" she said. "Let her peck ashore? Tourists will all have moored near some pub. We can't carry on as if we're ashamed of her."

"Still, we ought to be discreet, don't you think? It isn't everyone who has a child-sized chicken on their boat."

"*Unlucky* them. And we mustn't worry about not getting much work done to sell."

"I'm not worrying!"

"We can call this our holiday year. Remember," and she giggled, "we do have a bit of a nest-egg."

True enough, not all of her inheritance had been sunk in acquiring *Meadowsweet.* Joe and Molly still kept some money tucked away in the Post Office Girobank. Their needs were simple; perhaps a shade more complicated of late in view of Arabella's eager appetite for her own special diet, of which enough, enough.

Our holiday year, he thought. Arabella was shooting up fast towards, presumably, full-size maturity as a human chicken, whatever size that might be. Might she, not so much "outgrow her strength", as possess the same brief life span as an ordinary chicken? Did Molly fear that this year – and maybe one or two more – might be their only allotted time with their chicken daughter before she grew scraggy, lacklustre, and died of old age?

How long *could* an ordinary chicken live naturally, if left to its own devices and not slaughtered? Joe had no information on the subject. Farmers didn't maintain retirement wings in their sheds for grandma chickens, for pensioner poultry.

If the worst came to the worst, how would one dispose of the corpse of a giant chicken? Hide it behind a hedge, hoping that foxes would home in? God no! Bury her decently in a field at least.

The prospect, and the puzzle, sickened him momentarily. Arabella would not, must not, die after a brief span on Earth. Yet could she plausibly continue living with them year in, year out? Hidden in the boat by day? She herself might wish to leave home. Maybe she already did, though they couldn't interpret her cluckings. The notion that she was akin to a disabled child offended him. Here was a healthy human chicken, perfectly formed, with no sign of lice, mites, worms, or salmonella – she hadn't grubbed with other infested poultry. Yet in regard to her human aspect, did the chicken suit she wore spell a species of disablement? If so, might Arabella one day learn to read and write and by dextrous use of her claws or beak might she scratch or tap out her autobiography, which might win a literary prize to reward her courage in overcoming the obstacles of whimsical nature? To which end, she must surely need more experience of the big wide world to write about, including encounters – perhaps unsettling and feather-ruffling – with human beings other than her parents. Joe shied away from the implications.

However, he agreed with Molly. "Yes, let's take her ashore this evening, if we're moored alone. It *is* quite like paradise here. It'll be as though she's emerging from her shell, pecking her way out, seeing the sky and the hilltops – "

Or was their daughter short-sighted? Birds of the air such as that warbler must enjoy excellent distance-vision. How about fowl, which had to spot tiny specks of food on the ground at close quarters? Yet hens could flap aloft, could they not? Could, after a fashion, fly. Unless Arabella's wings grew disproportionately to pteranodon size, how would they ever buoy up her body weight? His mind was drifting again. Joy had entered their life, accompanied by doubts and anxieties such as they had not suspected the year before.

Yet maybe here was an encounter with *reality* – neglected (temporarily) by those bikini-clad girlfriends and their boyfriends who were pretending to be the Captain Cooks of the waterways. In spite of the rose and castle image, canal life in the olden days had not been an idyll for everybody. Only a few days earlier, *Meadowsweet* had navigated the bat-infested Braunston tunnel. During the nineteenth century "Ben the Legger" had spent the fifty years of his working life lying there in stygian darkness with his back on a board a foot wide and a yard long, while he legged one boat after another through the two thousand yards of the tunnel to and fro all day. He legged his way the equivalent of twice round the world, till his thighs must have been as plumply proportioned as those of a chicken, no less, from gross excess of muscle.

Just today, *Meadowsweet* had passed the village of Crick, home in his later years of George Smith, ex-brickworker from Coalville, Staffordshire, who had first crusaded on behalf of underage labour, issuing his *Cry of the Children from the Brickyards of England,* and who had finally exposed the plight of pre-legislation canal folk, slaving in wretched immoral misery, hot, soaked, stinking, drunken, and bug-ridden, tens of thousands of their kids illegitimate and illiterate . . .

"Let reality be transfigured!" Joe exclaimed to Molly; and she nodded her full-hearted agreement.

So, that evening, as the golden sun melted behind the hills under crimson banks of cloud, as a kingfisher darted from bank to bank, wings vibrating like a humming-bird's, as cows settled in their meadow perhaps anticipating rain, Joe heaved Arabella – squawking and flapping somewhat – up the steep steps into the open cockpit to parade herself aloft and blink over the side, raw, at a deserted towpath and at the wide world.

Out went the gangway on to land. While Molly went ahead to receive and encourage, Joe hoisted his daughter on to that narrow plank ribbed with shoe-grips.

As if trained to the occasion, Arabella waltzed ashore to be preened proudly by her mother. Guarded by Molly and Joe, Arabella pecked her way happily hither and thither till it was time for bed.

Later, in the curtained and grain-strewn cabin, Joe recollected his earlier vision of a chicken authoress receiving a literary laureate, and at last he took out from a cupboard the small pile of illustrated children's books which they had rashly, prematurely, far-sightedly bought during the later months of Molly's pregnancy. Two of these books seemed appropriate to Arabella: *The Little Red Hen* and *Chicken Little*, stirring tales – realistically anthropomorphic – of humanistic hens, chickens of articulate consciousness in full control of their affairs, with which she might identify or empathise.

"It's time to read stories to her," said Joe. With a minimum of struggle he settled Arabella's fussy bulk upon his lap, using both hands to keep her steady. Molly sat opposite, holding out the large-print *Little Red Hen* in front of Arabella (and Joe), and the first bed-time story commenced.

Alas – how should Arabella know any better? – their daughter apparently mistook the black marks, the regular printed letters on the page, for some line-up of unusual insects, at which she pecked vigorously. Her beak was big now and she tore the page again and again till Joe desisted, and Molly withdrew the gashed, punctured volume. Clucking vigorously, Arabella insisted on being let down on to her own legs on the floor where she set to, desultorily, at a drift of grain before turning to the boiled potato, a recent favourite of hers.

"Perhaps she's trying to tell us something?" said Joe. "She mightn't identify with chickens – she mightn't wish to! Maybe we're insulting her. Maybe she'd prefer stories about little boys and girls."

Though disappointed, Molly adopted a more practical approach. "I think the old grain and grit's getting a bit small for her to deal with, don't you? I think she'd prefer nuts, and little pebbles for her gizzard."

By July they were on the not-so-frequented Macclesfield canal. Arabella was the size of a ten-year-old schoolgirl – fat-bodied and seemingly stout-necked in her sumptuous fancy dress of feathers, her diminutive head bonnetted and a-dangle with rubbery adornments of a garish, blood-red lipstick hue. When Arabella bobbed her head zestfully, they sometimes heard pebbles tumble in her gizzard deep inside, rattling faintly like muted maracas. By now she was accustomed to stepping ashore of an evening when the coast was clear – of which they made certain – and she would return aboard when told. The gleam in her eye indicated that she saw eye to eye with them and understood not only the general sense but the very words they uttered, even if her own vocabulary of *tuck-tuck-tuck* remained opaque to her Mum and Dad.

Late one afternoon, when Joe had just hammered home the steel mooring stakes fore and aft and tied up with half hitches before rejoining Molly in the cockpit, a barrage of concerned cluckings erupted from below. As if a fox had sneaked into the cabin! Surely Arabella was well beyond any vulpine mugging. She could have kicked a hungry fox to kingdom come, trampled it, pecked holes in it; though hitherto she had shown no signs of aggression.

They hastened below to find Arabella flapping in a fine flummox upon their bed; and behind her tail . . .

"She's laid an egg!" cried Molly. "There, there, Arabella dear, don't fuss on, poor thing. This must be like her first period. She doesn't know what's what, or where it came from. Fine parents we are! We ought to have prepared her, we ought to have told her."

"I suppose it was bound to happen," agreed Joe. "Looks like a big egg. I wonder if it hurt her."

Bigger than any normal size-one egg! Bigger than any goose egg, though in proportion to Arabella's body-size the egg was probably no prodigy. It might have slipped out easily. Their daughter had simply been . . . taken aback by the event. The egg was russet brown with sepia speckles; warm to the touch, of course.

Arabella had calmed. Perhaps she had known what was due to occur and when she laid her egg had simply been proud of her achievement and wished to draw immediate attention to it.

"I wonder if we should let her keep it, to sit on?" mused Molly.

"Use our bed as a *nest-box*? Look, that egg can't be fertile. She hasn't met a cock. I don't know it would be much use if she ever did! Like a golden retriever with a chihuahua. Anyhow, she's too heavy. She'd burst the egg, she'd flatten it. Splootch, all over the bed. Terribly disappointing, that could be."

"What I meant was, keep it as a sort of souvenir. For us too! We could hard-boil it . . . I guess it would go off. Or else pickle it in a jar! Or blow out the contents and keep the shell."

"Sort of like baby's first shoe? She isn't a baby any more; and here's our proof! Parents don't exactly hang up their daughter's first sanitary towel, do they, eh?"

"*Tuck-tuck*," said Arabella; or was it "tut-tut"?

"Hmm. Maybe we should ask her." Molly crouched to face Arabella. "Darlingest, what shall we do with your lovely egg?"

Cumbersomely Arabella squirmed around upon the bed to scrutinise her product. Her beak descended and she tapped it gently a few times, rolling it in Joe's direction.

"I think," said Joe, "she's saying we can eat it. It's her gift to us. And why not? She can eat some too. We can all share it. Is that all right with you, Arabella?"

"*Cluck.*"

"Whip up an omelet? There's three eggs-worth, I'd say."

"*Cluuuuckk.*" With its rising intonation assuredly this was a different word from "cluck" – maybe it was a whole sentence, of approval.

"An omelet, it is!"

Which is what they made; and Arabella pecked her portion with gusto from a plate of her own.

Duly encouraged – no doubt she had little *choice* in the matter – Arabella went on to lay another egg a couple of days later. Presently she was producing an egg a day, and they were enjoying not only regular omelets but for variety scrambled egg, fried egg – some of her offerings were triple-yolked and divided up nicely – not to mention egg en cocotte, bacon and egg pie, egg à la florentine, egg friture, egg à la maison, and archiduchesse.

They felt they were enjoying a kind of holy loving communion with their daughter, part of her substance transubstantiated into yolk and albumen – a sort of suckling of the parents by the child. Arabella could hardly be regarded as indulging in auto-cannibalism any more than a cow that licks up its own milk. What a clever trick, to create some of your own food from out of your own body, thus recycling what you ate.

"Weirdest thing oy ever did see," declared a voice across the bar of the Sunrising Inn at Claydon.

"Oy tell you, Bert, it were like a massive great yellow *turkey* struttin' about over by the old railway line, only that weren't no turkey. The sheep were scatterin'."

"Dusk light plays tricks when you've had one too many,

Harry."

"Talk sense. How could oy have one too many by dusk?"

"By havin' one too many at lunch to start with, eh, same as today?"

"That's for me nerves."

"Maybe your monster came out of a yoofo, eh Harry?"

Joe took a nervous swig of his Hook Norton ale, which tasted buttery. By now it was well into Autumn, the tourist trade was slackening, and *Meadowsweet* was heading slowly southwards again. In this northernmost of all Oxfordshire villages, goats roamed the churchyard and the church clock might strike the hour but it lacked a face. The canal skirted the village itself – yet Arabella, now the height of a fifteen-year-old, had been spotted.

"We'd best head down beyond Cropredy this afternoon," Joe murmured to Molly. They supped up and sneaked away from the Sunrising.

Fortunately, with the decrease in sunlight, Arabella had grown a tad broody so she wasn't restless for her nightly jaunts in the open air. Still, she needed exercise; now there was more of her than ever to exercise, and to be seen. She had also quit laying and was moulting, which Molly and Joe at first feared was a disease – her feathers littered the floor of the cabin.

The acceleration of Arabella's childhood – the fact of their child maturing at the same speed as a barnyard chicken – made Molly and Joe feel prematurely middle-aged, as if in the course of a single summer fifteen summers had flown by. Surely Arabella's body incorporated some growth hormone which could prove of inestimable value to science, though possibly only in the rearing neither of persons nor of poultry but of the hybrid, a human chicken – product perhaps of some game of cat's cradle played with Molly's genes and Joe's at the behest of some narrowly focussed though happenstance bombardment by cosmic rays at the time of conception, so that Arabella, their creation, was "midwifed" by the explosion of some distant sun.

Should her vigorous form be a response to a tight beam of radiation rather than to, say, pollutants in the environment which must surely have affected other parents' offspring too – and neither the *Sun* nor the *Star*, those luminaries of the gutter press, had said a word about this to the best of Joe's knowledge – might military scientists be even more interested in Arabella as an ideal post-nuclear survivor?

Suppose that a nuclear war swept away civilization and humankind, clans of Arabellas might well rove and forage the irradiated, mutating landscape, carrying forward into a faceless future submerged within themselves a protected germ of humanity which might one day in a cleaner, fresher world a thousand years hence give birth once again to Homo – the cat's cradle unknotting, the DNA string pulling out straight and true – though goodness knows how those future human chickens would rear their slow, helpless, featherless, maggot-like babies when born, or hatched. Possibly those future parents, appalled and forgetful of human history, would peck their offspring to pieces or simply suffocate them under their feather-pillow rumps whilst squatting upon those babies in an effort to keep them warm.

The prospect of Arabella being spirited away for study – in a manner possibly insensitive to her feelings – did not appeal. Yet should not the world know *something* of Arabella, if only for the sake of her own liberty and fulfilment? She did appear to be developing her own opinions and desires, in so far as they could interpret these.

What's more, if Molly and Joe were in a sense growing prematurely "old" – emotionally, psychologically – due to their rushed experience of her childhood, who would care *for them* – care about them – when Arabella was fully adult? Who but her? Yet how?

Joe and Molly had distanced themselves from the workaday world, and the birth not of a child but a chicken had at first seemed to increase that distance. No longer! Arabella's presence, blessing that it was, now began to thrust them back towards the world they had left, both for her sake and theirs.

Without settling on any plan whatsoever nor having in any way resolved the ambiguities attendant upon their prodigy and wonder, they were heading back down the South Oxford canal towards Arabella's birthplace, and beyond.

Locking into the River Isis – the baby Thames – through Duke's Cut (yes, *Meadowsweet* did carry a licence from the Thames Water Authority) they moored abutting the common land of Port Meadow, Oxford, on the opposite shore from the footpath commonly used. Herds of cattle roved a mile and a half north and south from Medley to Wolvercote and back. Horses galloped. Geese honked. A mile away to the south-east the spires of the university dreamed. Being Autumn, every evening dense white mist sublimed from the sods of the huge meadow, veiling the view to a height of eight or nine feet. Though the city was close by, Arabella, restored to full plumage, eager and boisterous and five feet tall, could sprint about the wide midlands of the meadow, deserted except for beasts, herself unseen, clucking, gizzard rattling, wings flapping as if here at last was a runway long enough to lift her jumbo body form, even though visibility was atrocious beneath the moon-lit mist bank which hid her.

Unseen . . . till one night around eleven, when against the advice of her parents – did she fully comprehend? – she deserted those safe midlands for the southern neck of the meadow where the rough path crossed from Fiddler's Island over to the railway bridge and canal bridge, thus to Walton Well Road and into town.

Intuiting something amiss, Joe and Molly were already out searching for Arabella in the chilly mist when they heard discordant singing from a group of undergraduates staggering back drunk from the Perch Inn at Binsey by way of Medley boat station and long thin Fiddler's Island.

Before long, a series of screeches floated to their ears upon the mist, followed by cries of what sounded, at first, to be terror. Hearts in their mouths, their feet risking tussocks and hummocks and squidgy cow-pats, Joe and Molly hastened towards the source of commotion through the obscure fluffy murk. Had Arabella decided to prey upon travellers? Wooed by the sozzled songs, had she assaulted those beer-pickled undergraduates, racing down upon them from out of the mist and the night as if out of prehistory?

We must now pull back our focus and adopt a bird's eye view of events, as well as fitting an X-ray or infra-red lens to cope with the night and the mist. We must borrow Arabella's viewpoint.

Source of such squawks and cackles and crowings, these undergraduates were interesting to her. She meant them no harm. After their initial surprise, they perceived this. They grew, well, intoxicated with Arabella. To take a five-foot-tall intelligent chicken back to their college with them struck them as the most splendid notion. She certainly appeared to be bright and willing. One student, Jeremy, offered his arm gallantly. Arabella stuck out her wing. Thus linked arm-in-wing Arabella and escort marched up over Walton Well Bridge. Destination: Worcester College, where cricket field, lake, and gardens backed on to the final cul-de-sac of the Oxford Canal below Louse Lock.

Mist had infiltrated Walton Street yet not obliteratingly so. Would those undergraduates sneak Arabella through the maze of back streets known as Jericho, so as to enter their college via the cricket field, heaving Arabella over the gate if need be? Not at all. Adopting a full frontal approach, Jeremy and friends strode along past the University Press to the Porter's Lodge of Worcester and crowded through it. The long-suffering night porter eyed them sceptically yet he did not intervene. Oxford colleges had long since become co-educational. This couldn't be a scheme to smuggle a girlfriend in for the night. If a young gentleman, or lady, chose to costume themselves as a chicken, that was their problem.

Split screen: Joe and Molly had trailed Arabella and party, slinking along the misty pavement a couple of hundred yards to the rear. Thus far and no further; they weren't members of the university.

What to do? How to retrieve their daughter? Would she return of her own accord, clucking her way along Walton Street in the wee hours of the morning, and manage to steer herself all the way to the *Meadowsweet*? Molly and Joe returned to their boat and waited sleeplessly in vain.

Next morning, they untied *Meadowsweet* and chugged onward down the Isis to Louse Lock, locked through, and moored opposite the gardens of Worcester to keep vigil, by now praying that Arabella would not try to retrace her route to her vanished base in Port Meadow.

Through the Autumn-denuded branches they watched a few undergraduates jog along to the tennis court for an unseasonal foursome. Water hens trod the dying lily pads on the lake. A few Canada geese squabbled on shore. No sign of any dramatically larger bird. Down at the gut-end of the canal, up against Hythe Bridge, some vagrant alcoholics were stirring amidst a litter of empty flagons. Locking up their boat, which Arabella would surely spy if she and her hosts decided to take a turn in the gardens, Joe and Molly headed along the towpath to Hythe Bridge, declining the privilege of providing the raggy gentry with the price of a cup of tea. They mounted Hythe Bridge – by now it was late morning – and hurried round to the front of Worcester College . . . in time to see Arabella and her escorts of the previous night setting out boldly garbed in gowns.

"Arabella!" Molly cried, distressed by her daughter's exposure in full daylight. Actually, Arabella had been lent a long black scholar's gown which she wore with panache, her wings jutting through the short capacious sleeves – her friends were walking her to a lecture! Well, she would hardly have been able to ride a bicycle to one, would she? Thus the others walked too. Distances are short enough in Oxford.

Their daughter eyed her parents, and clucked reassuringly.

"Excuse me," Joe addressed blond, fresh-faced, bleary-eyed Jeremy. "She's . . . I mean to say, we're her . . . She's our . . . You can't!"

Yet they could, and they would, those frolicsome

undergraduates: all the way through the centre of town, even by way of the covered market with its rows of gutted, plucked chickens hanging upended from butchers' hooks, down to the Examination School at the end of the High Street where lectures were held, admittance to anyone wearing a gown, even including a human chicken. Arabella's new friends were reading English. The lecture that day was on Shelley, which seemed appropriate.

Of course, Arabella's progress through town and her return attracted attention. Though it was clear that she was *different*, acceptance of her was remarkable (perhaps less remarkable, this being Oxford). Many people must have supposed she was a dwarfish person – perhaps a thalidomide victim of genius – whose eccentricity it was to dress up in a chicken suit. Others better appreciated her absolute uniqueness but they kept mum.

And so time passed. No zoologists or brigadiers arrived to distress her. She fast became a mascot, an honorary member of college. Its esteem sky-rocketed as much as if its crew of oarsmen had bumped ten rival boats on the river. The Master and Fellows of Worcester more than condoned her presence.

Nor were Joe and Molly exiled from their daughter. Moored by Louse Lock, they could visit her in college where she shared rooms with Jeremy, who tipped his college servant handsomely to adjust to new circumstances. Each morning Arabella would trot around Worcester gardens as far as the tennis court, flapping her wings to Molly and Joe across the water and clucking, horrifying the Canada geese but gladdening her parents, who felt at last, through her, a sense of belonging.

Oh yes, Arabella had taken to college life. Although largely unschooled – apart from her abortive encounter with the tale of *The Little Red Hen* – she who had raced through her childhood had now gone straight to university. Could she possibly have capsuled not only her tender years but her whole educational career, proceeding directly from *The Little Red Hen* to a degree in English Literature? Could it be, mused

Molly, that their daughter might actually become Arabella, B.A. (Oxon)? – by an honorary nod, such as was bestowed on public figures who received doctorates of law without the strict requirements of passing an exam?

Not exactly. Fate had a rarer destiny in store. In this universe ruled by caprice, where the award of a fellowship at All Souls was rumoured to hang ultimately upon how well the candidates dealt at dinner with a dish of cherries for dessert – did they spoon the cherry stones out of their mouths onto the side of the dish? or use their fingers to extract the stones? did they *swallow* those embarrassing mini-marbles? or did they nonchalantly spit them upon the floor? – here, the honorary office of Chancellor of the University was newly vacant. For the first time in history the election was being hotly contested, tooth and claw, by several politician-alumni representing doctrinaire Tory, moderate Tory, and the splintering wings of the hectic, power-hungry minority party known as the "Alliance". What happened in the Oxford election might well be writ large upon the land.

Electors consisted of all Masters of Arts of the university, who must vote in person on election day. Many potential electors did not very much appreciate this once sedate, geriatric ceremony being turned into a political rumpus, a cock fight with substantial sums of money spent upon mailing propaganda leaflets to all living M.A.s of Oxford, whether they were currently residing in Manchester or Madagascar, to enthuse them to make the trip to Oxford.

Consequently, once Jeremy wittily persuaded sufficient senior members of the University – mainly wayward Fellows of Worcester College – to sign a proposal form for Arabella, who was by now a famous sight of Oxford, a campaign on her behalf rapidly gained momentum by sheer word of mouth.

Dons and graduates of the university, in their black gowns and other academic finery, had always somewhat resembled processions of penguins, had they not? Why not elect as their Chancellor . . . a giant chicken? (What's more, a female chicken – Arabella could surely rely on the feminist vote.) The formal duties of the Chancellor were slight: a Latin oration to be pronounced once a year, which only two or three people in the audience ever understood – with coaching surely Arabella could cluck her way through this?

Election Day in early December was crisp and cloudless. Joe and Molly were out in Broad Street most of the morning and afternoon to watch long queues of penguins, young and old, tailing back from the Divinity School, the ancient stone polling station. Tucked behind the Sheldonian Theatre guarded by its semi-circle of bearded stone heads, the Divinity School was part of the Bodleian.

Several colleges including Worcester had laid on a buffet lunch with wine for any old members returning to Oxford to vote. Late into the afternoon many voters were still trying to recognise, and hail, former acquaintances, often with little success. Some electors drank champagne as they shuffled towards the polling station; others concentrated on their walking sticks. Coachloads of vicars had arrived from the countryside, their transport paid for by the liberal-democrat candidate, or was it the democratic-liberal? These vicars would vote as the fancy took them, and as Arabella paraded back and forth along Broad Street she must have reminded them of eggs and chicks and Easter, high point of their calendar.

Some doddery voters seemed to be arriving by bathchair, invalid carriage, even perhaps by hearse as if disinterred for the occasion, almost resurrected.

The wintry sun gilded spires and roofs and gargoyles. The line inched along. The university police, the bulldogs in their bowler hats, stood sentinel by the door to the Divinity School, as in filed the M.A.s to bow to an exhausted Vice-Chancellor and to be bowed to by him before receiving their ballot paper. . .

At eight-thirty that evening, from the steps of the Sheldonian, the result was declared to a still-thronged Broad

Street, brightly lit. Applause broke out.

What a night for Joe and Molly.

Almost log-cabin-to-White-House! Well ... narrow-boat-to-ivory-tower. What might the future not hold for their daughter now?

"Rejoice!" cried Molly.

Jeremy popped open a bottle of champagne.

"The human chicken! The human chicken!" chanted Arabella's supporters.

She fluffed herself up. She did not cackle. For the first time in her life, quite rooster like, she crowed a resounding doodle-do.

The human chicken had been elected Chancellor of Oxford University.

MICK FARREN

FUN IN THE FINAL DAYS

ILLUSTRATED BY SAVAGE PENCIL

IN LOS ANGELES the asteroid's next rising would be just before sunset. That's what the weatherman on the Channel Two Noontime News had said and Carter had no reason to doubt him. Now the orbit had stabilised, the damn thing had become wholly predictable. Timing the phases of the asteroid was about all that TV was good for in what he'd started to think of as these Final Days. There were now only three broadcast channels left on the air and two of those were being run by teams of ghoulishly demented technicians. Channel Five had just completed a forty-eight hour marathon of disaster movies without commercial interruption. It had started with *Panic in the Year Zero* and concluded with *When Worlds Collide*. Prior to that, they had played the same Cal Worthington used car commercial over and over again to the point where Carter, watching in morbid fascination to see how long they'd keep it up, had feared for his sanity and finally changed the channel. "Buy a new car for your wife/She will love you all your life/Go see Cal, go see Cal, go see Cal." The jingle had gone relentlessly on, hour after hour, until the only people left watching were three cracked out cholos somewhere in South Central.

CBS alone still flew the flag of the people's right to know. The kind of millionaires who owned local television stations had long since abandoned the business of business, turned the asylum over to the lunatics and were busily trying to buy and bribe their way into one or another of the alleged safe spots – Australia. Lapland, Nepal or maybe Java. The rumours of places that might survive changed almost daily so the millionaires had their work cut out. One Tokyo property baron had attempted to set up a consortium to send a highly exclusive refugee rocket to Mars until the scientific community had pointed out that being stuck on Mars with no home-planet backup would probably be a worse fate than to be on Earth when the asteroid hit. At least that would be fast. Better than waiting until the last oxygen tank ran out.

Despite all the "what ifs" and the "maybes" and wishfully thought out avenues of escape, humanity knew, somewhere

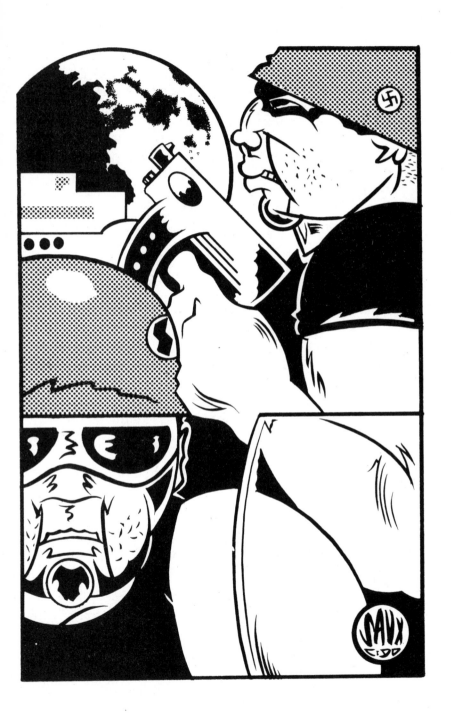

deep in its gut, that it didn't have much chance of recovering from this one. The asteroid was big and dense and it had been coming seemingly straight for the Earth ever since it had first been spotted some ten months earlier. The damage that it had caused already was bad enough. After the earthquakes, LA was a mess, San Francisco was worse and Mexico City was history. New York was still recovering from the tidal wave, half London was under water and Athens was under martial law. Cairo was still burning and Calcutta didn't bear thinking about. This wasn't a movie. Sean Connery or Paul Newman wasn't going to strap a bunch of H-bombs to this baby and blow it back into the deeps of space whence it had come while the world held its breath and Shelley Winters freaked out. This time it was for real. About the only consolation was it was a purely random, freak of nature, disaster. In no way could man seriously claim that he had brought it on himself. For Carter, there was a peculiar, if grim, satisfaction in this knowledge.

The gut feeling didn't stop humanity hoping, however. One of the favourite "maybes" was "maybe it won't hit the Earth at all. Maybe it'll just go into orbit and we'll have an extra moon." When it did what appeared to be exactly that, a wave of relief swept round the world and the tabloids trumpeted that we'd all been saved. Then Carl Sagan went on TV with the bad news. Everyone's favourite pop astronomer seemed almost to relish telling how the reprieve was purely temporary and that, with the asteroid zipping around the planet in a mere seven hours, its orbit was far too fast and, by the standard of moons, far too low. Ultimately it would decay and the asteroid would smash into the Earth, probably stripping off the atmosphere as it took the final plunge. It was after that broadcast that things began to get really bizarre. Just one day later, an astro-physicist who had been brought on to explain the facts and figures behind the bad news, had been torn to pieces live on the David Letterman Show, by an audience who apparently held him personally responsible. That incident had closed as many TV stations as the fleeing millionaires. There was a rumour that Letterman had shot himself after the show in a fit of bourbon and remorse but nobody knew for sure.

The naming of the asteroid had been an early example of prime farce. A nationwide TV poll had come up with the name Bluto, with Caligula running a close second. Bluto was starting to catch on until a conference of world leaders got together, headed by the venerable Margaret Thatcher, and, for once acting as one, declared that the designated official title of the asteroid was Damocles. Apparently naming it for the arch-nemesis of Popeye the Sailorman wasn't sufficiently dignified. Privately, Carter still tended to think of the asteroid as Bluto.

Carter went out onto the third floor terrace of the house in the Hollywood Hills to watch the asteroid come up. All but one of his neighbours in the apartment building, along with maybe two thirds of the population of greater Los Angeles, had fled the city after the five nights of rioting and looting, leaving it to the fatalistic, the ambivalent and the weird. The other tenants: the two lawyers, the cocaine dealer, the rock and roll manager, the movie director and his German girlfriend and the blonde with Porsche were all gone, headed out for the imagined safety of the mountains or desert. Only he and Leiberman were left and the two of them had the run of the building. Leiberman had also come out to watch the rising of the asteroid. The two men nodded to each other but didn't speak. Leiberman was a very private individual who showed signs of nervousness when anyone engaged him in anything more than the most cursory of conversations. Carter suspected that he was probably a solitary drunk. The third floor terraces looked out over lowrise residential Hollywood towards the cluster of downtown towers, the abandoned monoliths of banks and insurance companies that had lost their glass in the fury of the big shake. There had been quakes all round the Pacific Ring as Damocles' gravity began to stress the Earth's tectonic plates. The one in LA had come close to nine on the Richter scale and eyewitnesses told how the glass of downtown had cascaded like a razorsharp rain and the streets had run with blood.

From where he was standing, the asteroid would come up from directly behind the towers. No matter how many times Damocles rose from the haze on the horizon, there was always a first chill of fear, if for no other reason than that the thing was so damn big. At first it was a shimmering blob of white light, distorted by the heat and dust of the atmosphere. As it mounted higher, however, it seemed to completely fill the eastern sky, ten or twelve times the apparent size of the sun or moon. It seemed to bear down on those who looked at it as though it were coming directly for them. The surface details were frighteningly clear like a huge overhead relief map, circular impact craters, deserts of grey-white ash and mountain ranges of jagged black rock, airless and desolate and bent on remaking the world of men in its own image. When it eclipsed the sun, as it all too regularly did, the city was thrown into a twilight of blue shadows, an unavoidable portent of the coming end. The sunset sky behind Carter was blood-red from the huge quantities of dust that hung in the air in the aftermath of the quakes, the volcanic eruptions and the hundreds of fires that burned unchecked. Another chilling reminder that the end of everything was all too probably at hand.

On the other side of the canyon, someone was playing their sound system cranked to the max — "Fun Fun Fun" by the Beach Boys. Carter muttered to himself.

"Yeah right, Fun in the Final Days."

Carter had discovered that one way to maintain his sanity was, as far as humanly possible, to ignore the onrush of destiny and the threatening grandeur of the skies and concentrate as much as he could on the small everyday details. These at least had a certain comforting consistency. Right at this moment he was out of beer. He had to go out and get more. This, on its own, might prove a suicidal exercise. The streets were in the hands of the violent and the homicidal, dogpacks of psychopaths, running unchecked except by the random helicopter sweeps by the police and the National Guard. Carter had decided that, deep down, he must be a fatalist. If making a beer run meant that he ran the risk of being stitched full of high velocity bullets by some twelve year old with an assault rifle, or blown away by mistake by the trigger-happy door gunner of a Cobra gunship, so be it. It'd be quick and clean. Lately, he'd been thinking a lot about quick clean exits.

Since everyone but Leiberman had gone, Carter had taken to driving the immaculate black Thunderbird that had been abandoned by the coke dealer, keys in the ignition, in his hurry to get on the last plane to Lima. Carter had wondered why the coke dealer had picked Peru as a refuge. Maybe it was the time honoured instinct of heading for the high ground and Lima was the highest ground known to his profession. The T-bird was certainly a hell of an improvement on his own beat-up Monte Carlo.

He drove down Crescent Heights and made a left onto Santa Monica Boulevard. A police Huey had ploughed into the Security Pacific Bank on the corner and exploded and burned. There was debris covering half the intersection. He had heard a bang during the previous night but there were so many bangs in the night these days that he hadn't even bothered to go to the window and take a look.

The Nazis had marched last night. A five-block-long procession of fanatics in lockstep shadowed by helicopters above the palm trees that watched but chose to do nothing. The flames of the Nazis' torches had been clearly visible from his vantage point in the hills. Their signs and burned out flares and torches still littered the streets. The majority of the signs bore a single word: *Ragnarok*, the twilight of the gods. They seemed to be using the event of the asteroid as an excuse to add a twist of nordic death mysticism to their more mundane hatred. They treated the impending disaster as a visitation from Wotan that demanded blood sacrifice. They came with a crash of marching drums and engineer boots, singing the old SA beerhall songs they'd learned from limited edition records bought mail order through *Soldier of Fortune* magazine. Skinheads with swastika tattoos, uniform freaks in neat black and red, wearing visored motorcycle helmets and carrying plexiglass riot shields, Aryan Brotherhood jailhouse trash with Gary Gilmore eyes and camouflage jackets, toting pump shotguns and AK47s; they all roared out the traditional German lyrics probably without understanding a word of them. Their plan had been to move east, criss-crossing the area between Santa Monica and Hollywood Boulevards, driving out what they perceived as the scum, the mud people. A night of final solution before the apocalypse.

Fortunately they were stopped at Vista Street, in front of the Okie Dog, by an army of heavily armed gays, bronzed hustlers in tank tops and cutoffs with M16s at the ready, lesbians with .357 magnums and dragqueens with Uzis slung like shoulderbags. The street was still half blocked by barricades of burned out cars and the Astroburger on the opposite corner had been totalled by what must have been an anti-tank rocket from the Nazi side. Carter thought that he saw bodies in the shadow of an overturned *LA Times* delivery truck but he didn't look too closely. There was still a knot of defenders around the hotdog stand keeping a watchful vigil with guns over their shoulders. They eyed the T-bird suspiciously as he drove by. It was a hell of a context for a beer run. He turned on the radio. KRAM was still on the air. Talking Heads' "Burning Down The House" was followed by "No No – Bluto" by a cowpunk band called Hank's Skull. At least there was someone else who thought of the asteroid as Bluto.

So far, he'd seen hardly any traffic. It was still daylight and most of those who'd elected to remain in the city tended to live like vampires, coming out only after dark or not coming out at all. Not that there would be much darkness even after the sun had gone. With the asteroid climbing in the sky, the world would be bathed in the ghostly monochrome of its reflected light. He was actually quite surprised when the convoy of pickup trucks came racing towards him down Santa Monica, going in the opposite direction. There were four of them, jockeying for position, running what traffic lights were still working at speeds close to a hundred miles an hour. They were packed with bikini clad or naked teenagers, drunk out of

98

their minds and howling mindlessly. The lead driver spotted Carter's T-bird and decided to play chicken. The truck was coming straight at him, a candy orange, metalflake monster with chrome crashbars and giant oversized wheels. Carter spun his steering wheel. He had nothing to prove except that he was well aware that multiple vehicular suicide was a popular way of going out in a blaze of glory. His front wheels mounted the sidewalk and he jammed on the brakes. The truck flashed by with only a couple of feet to spare, leaving a slipstream of screaming laughter. Carter sagged back in his seat.

"This is getting fucking ridiculous."

The power was on at La Brea and a handmade sign on a lamp-post read "BEER THIS WAY". An arrow pointed north. It was almost certainly a rip artist selling off the load from a hijacked truck. It would be expensive but it was better than driving around, hunting for a supermarket or liquor store that was still intact. The beer dealers had set up shop on the parking lot of the gutted Mayfair Market. Two semi-trucks with Mexican license plates were drawn up side by side and cases of Corona and Dos Equis were being sold directly off the back for quadruple the regular price. A individual beer was five bucks, a six pack sold for twenty-five while a case went for eighty. Carter had always imagined that, in a time of disaster, money would hardly matter. Who needed cash if Godzilla was eating Tokyo? As it turned out, he couldn't have been more wrong. In these final days, money seemed to be everything. Street inflation was running at around four hundred percent. Money was the means to the end, the grease that it took to do all those things you'd never done before. The transactions were monitored by a security goon squad of burly biker types with ball bats and shotguns and the beer sale was an orderly affair by the standards of the time.

It had also attracted a very strange gathering of people. An LAPD cruiser was pulled up at the curb. There were two cops inside but, instead of protecting and serving, they were drinking Scotch straight from the bottle and pawing a couple of women who were all but out of their clothes. Since the arrival of the asteroid, casual sex had come back in a big way. Who gave a damn about catching a retro virus if you weren't going to live long enough for it to incubate? A roller-skater in shorts and a headband circled glumly, sucking on a half gallon of cheap Chablis. The speed at which he was drinking made it something of a miracle that he could maintain his control. Stooped figures were picking through the debris in the dark interior of the supermarket.

Carter had no idea why the girl picked on him. Maybe it was because of the car or maybe it was for no reason at all. He'd bought his beer and was getting ready to drive away. He'd gone for the full case plus a bottle of very dubious Scotch. It was hardly the time to economise. She was a California sun baby with one of those tans, not at all unlike the one with the Porsche who had lived in his building. She left nothing to the imagination with the short leather miniskirt, cowboy boots and a bike jacket unzipped to expose bare breasts.

"You want to give me a ride?"

"Where to?"

"It really doesn't matter."

Her eyes were glazed as though she'd been stoned on something or the other for longer than she was capable of remembering. She was chewing gum as though her mouth was chronically dry. Carter patted the case of beer on the seat beside him.

"I was planning to go home and drink this?"

"You want company?"

Carter nodded.

"Why not."

As he transferred the beer onto the back seat, she opened the passenger door and climbed in beside him. He gunned the T-bird out of the lot and turned up towards Hollywood Boulevard. On the radio, the Rolling Stones informed them that rape and murder were just a shot away. Carter glanced up at the huge disc of the asteroid. It was now about halfway to its zenith and the Earth's shadow was just starting to creep across it. Everyday was full moon madness with that sucker around. He turned to the girl.

"What's your name?"

She looked at him blankly.

"Morgan."

She seemed to be having trouble focussing but she did have exceedingly nice breasts.

"My name is Carter and I live up in Laurel Canyon."

She nodded. "It really doesn't matter." She eased back into the red leather of the passenger seat stretching herself like a cat. "Do you have any speed?"

Carter shook his head. "I don't."

Drugs had also come back in a big way. With only weeks to go, nobody said no to anything.

"I've been doing speed for days. I never want to sleep again. You know what I mean?" She stabbed an index finger at the asteroid overhead. "If that thing's going to get us, I don't want to miss anything. I want all the life I can get. You think it's going to get us?"

Carter nodded. "Seems that way."

"I've got to get some more speed."

There were crowds on Hollywood Boulevard, moving aimlessly in the grey Bluto light. It made them look like the night of the living dead. Morgan insisted that they drive down for a few blocks. There were armed guards in quasi-military uniforms outside the Scientology building. Even in the Final Days, the children of Hubbard were protecting their own. A metal band had set up a mountain of equipment in front of the Roosevelt Hotel and were blasting out hundreds of decibels of uncontrolled feedback. Jimi Hendrix would be turning in his grave. Morgan leaned close to Carter and yelled in his ear.

"You want to pull over and stop?"

Carter shook his head.

"Not really."

The kids basking in the noise in front of the makeshift bandstand looked to be totally out of their minds. One bunch had their clothes off and were group fucking and doing the soul fry right there on the Walk of the Stars.

"I have to get more speed."

"We'll figure something out."

Crude pentagrams had been daubed all over the outside of the Chinese Theatre. Morgan looked at the mess as though it was the most natural thing in the world.

"Satanists. They've been busy in the Valley already. I even heard that they sprung Manson out of San Quentin."

"Great."

"I heard they were holding human sacrifices out in Malibu. You think being a human sacrifice might be the way to go? At least you'd be the centre of attention."

He wondered if he should drop her off right there and then. He didn't want to be alone but he didn't know if he could handle her potential amphetamine mood swings. Self-protection was of primary importance. In the end, he opted for the company and the possible fantasy of sex. He hoped that he wouldn't regret the decision. The problem with allowing

himself to be picked up by strange women was exactly that. They were strange. It was the Groucho syndrome. He wasn't sure that he wanted to go home with any woman who'd want to go home with him. Since the coming of Bluto, things like that tended to go double.

He parked the T-bird in the garage and steered Morgan toward the elevator. She was telling some long and impenetrably complex story about the sexual convolutions of three people he didn't know and probably didn't want to know. When he'd first discovered the abandoned T-bird with the keys in it, he'd also found that there were keys to the guy's apartment on the same ring. Carter had taken a look round the flat on that first day but since then, he hadn't been in there and certainly hadn't used the place for anything. Now seemed to be exactly the right time to break it in. The pimp-chic decor, the big Sony projection TV and the extensive library of porno and junk-movie tapes seemed the ideal setting for the kind of brief and twisted liaison that was all he could imagine taking place between Morgan and himself. He had also discovered a small stash of left-behind cocaine in a silver cigarette box on a bookshelf. That would probably be of help to the girl in her bid to beat the world free fall record for staying awake.

The apartment was deliberately dark, decorated in Bat Cave dark blue and purple. As he opened the drapes on the Hollywood night, the first thing he saw was the asteroid, now a broad, thinning crescent in the western sky. Morgan took one look at it and turned her back with a shudder.

"I hate that fucking thing. It sucks out my brain."

Carter's first move was to cut out three long lines on the glass cube of a coffee table. After that, it was inevitable that they should make love. It happened on the big, circular waterbed with the black cover and canopy. It was impersonal to the point of being robotic. Her mouth tasted metallic and her movements were so detached and disjointed that Carter wondered if she was there with him at all in anything but body. Afterwards, he started drinking Scotch so he'd be drunk enough to fall asleep. She sat crosslegged and naked, wearing a pair of black Raybans that the coke dealer had left behind, staring as though hypnotised at the enormous TV screen.

"Carter?"

"What?"

She was inscrutable behind the sunglasses.

"Aren't you afraid of dying?"

"Sure, terrified."

"How do you keep going?"

He held up the half empty Scotch bottle.

"I drink and I console myself that, as far as death goes, there's only one per customer." He rolled over, spilling Scotch on the waterbed. He was already quite dizzy. "Actually, I'm happy to be seeing all this going on. If you gotta go, a rogue asteroid certainly beats the hell out of brain cancer."

Soon after that, he passed out. When he came to again she'd gone. The cocaine and the Raybans had gone with her. The TV was still running. It was the Channel Two early news. The entire congregation of the First Church of Pentecostal Redemption in Santa Ana had taken themselves out in a

Jonestown-style, poisoned Kool-Aid mass suicide. He crawled painfully from the waterbed. He turned off the TV and stepped out onto the terrace. The day was breaking but the now black shadow shape of Damocles/Bluto was already casting a pall as it once again rose from behind the skeletons of the downtown towers. Jim Morrison was singing about the "bloody red sun of fantastic LA" from the open patio doors of the house with the loud sound system on the other side of the canyon. Beneath the song there was a cacophonous undertow of other jumbled rock and roll from a dozen different sources. Ten or more columns of dark smoke rose from various points in the city. One of the tallest and most dense hung, as far as he could estimate, right over Hollywood Boulevard. Maybe the satanists had teamed up with the metal kids for a day of boogie and sacrifice, head banging, throat slitting and arson. Maybe Morgan had gone down there to volunteer as a sacrifice. The Doors were temporarily drowned out by the slapping rotorblades of a pair of police gunships flying low and south on a seemingly pointless dawn patrol. Carter sighed. The Beach Boys had started up again on the sound system across the canyon. "Fun fun fun."

"This is the way the world ends. Not with a bang, with a party."

He went back inside to see if Morgan had also taken the Scotch.

JAMIE DELANO

THE HORROR IN OUR LIVES

ILLUSTRATED BY JOHN HICKLENTON

THE TREE BUTCHERS were at work.

It had been a perfect, clear, November morning; rich sunlight shaved gold-leaf thin; a shining gilt of frost, foot-stamping cold, beneath a domed sky of deep ceramic blue. An illuminated-letter day in the bible of a life.

A clean white fluttering of doves whirred, beating upward into the rare air, circling the woodyard. A single, pristine snowflake-feather, looped down; a pamphlet of peace-propaganda or a coward's mark, perhaps; dropped into that charnel-house to be trodden into the flayed, scabrous skin of trees that was their carpet there.

Over beyond the towering stack of limbless carcasses that waited, occasionally groaning and shifting uncomfortably; for the eventual screaming kiss and cleaving lust of the saw's fierce steel, Death gave voice to hunger. From their kennel just up the road, the fox-hounds howled, knowing that butchery was being done; that even wood must bleed.

Chains rattled, steel cables hummed; a huge, horizontal shadow threatened the yard workers. For a moment they cringed, like mice overflown by hawks, then the crane laid out the great tree's sighing corpse and they advanced with keen axes raised to expose the slick, white, wooden flesh for the impassive gaze of that sharp winter's day. For a second, Jeremiah paused, attention trapped like an insect in prehistoric amber, by a sudden ruby gem of sun-ignited blood which oozed from a scratch on the back of his hand. In this minute wound's sanguinary crystal encrustation, he caught a fleeting glimpse of truth; a flicker of the multi-faceted mathematics of life.

Then fell the axe and wonder died.

The trick was to drop the axe just heavily enough to cut through the thickly crenellated bark but not let the steel tooth bite into the secret wood below. Then, a deft flick of the wrist to split this skin and it would fall away to litter the floor. If you hit it just right, the bark would flake and peel under its own weight and the trunk would slough its skin in hugely satisfying lengths. But Jeremiah rarely found the knack.

Usually his axe was too blunt, or his wrist too weak and he would peck, like some geriatric woodpecker, to break the tree's tough, fibrous grip on modesty. Today though, that was not the case at all.

His stroke was perfect; he chopped and flicked, the bark ripped softly along the tree's rigid spine and laid it bare. It was a startling metamorphosis. Jeremiah half expected the living wood to unfold leathern wings and stretch them into the cold light, pumping them erect, filling veins with muscular sap. Then, a timber dragon, it might stand into the winter sky, chilling them with the wind of silent wings. Jeremiah reached forward to touch the wood, to lay hands upon the corpse; a gesture, no more; as if to absolve himself of guilt. Sometimes he felt like a guard at Dachau or Auschwitz; somewhere on the borders of Inferno. Just another dumb fucker following orders.

The tree-flesh was cold; a dense, timeless cold; damp with a sickly mucus sweat. His fingers traced its smooth contours, looping and whirling with its surface grain. Jeremiah leant his face close, smelling the sweet strong wood. Then his caressing fingers found the wounds; a group of holes, clustered, as if made by a firing-squad. Around them, the wood was soft, punky, gangrenous. The holes were just big enough for a finger, so he slipped one in. He felt guilty, excited, as if engaged in some mild depravity. The hole was deep, accepting his questing finger to the hilt. Then something moved down in the dark.

As if he'd touched wild electricity, Jeremiah pulled out with a startled shout. Trembling gently from the core of his being, he took up one of the heavy steel wedges, still rimed with frost and, hefting the twenty-pound hammer in his other hand, turned back to the prostrate tree. Like a surgeon excising cancer perhaps, he placed the biting edge of the wedge along the grain where it bent around the tumour and let the hammer drop.

The wood screamed sharply as its muscle ripped. The tumour tore free and fell, barking his shin and bruising his toe, but his mind had no room for pain. His blow had exposed the tree's ancient heartwood; poxed and rotten; riddled with decaying catacombs. Jeremiah bent to investigate these secrets. His nose tingled with the assault of deadwood dust which, like some mouldering snuff, drew tears from his eyes. He fought for control of his impending nasal orgasm and peered into the gaping mouths of carved tunnels.

The first one nearly stopped his heart.

Purple, four inches long, as fat and ugly as a miller's thumb; shiny black-horned jaws scissoring wildly at the air, stiff hairs springing from its trunk, it reared, thrusting and flexing its ribbed body towards him, like some grotesque, prehensile prick.

Desperate, fearing it might make a sudden lunge for nose or throat and force its way into his body's soft sanctuary, Jeremiah recoiled. Off balance, he put out a hand, scrabbling for purchase amongst the litter of the woodyard floor and felt, pressed beneath his weight, another of the squirming grubs. Small jaws gripped his calloused skin firmly, but not hard enough to draw blood. Appalled he looked down. There were hundreds of them, wriggling, writhing and lashing, as if the light were acid to their puce rubbery skins.

Panicked, a hot pale sweat prickled Jeremiah's scalp. He shook violently, cracking his arm as if it were a whip to detach the nauseating thing. In the corner of his eye he saw Wink, the shrivelled, dwarfish, charge-hand, curled up laughing fit to shit his pants. Jeremiah whirled his arm faster, feeling the blood collect in his hand, swelling and tightening the skin. Then the vile thing let go and, describing a perfect parabolic arc, sailed through the air to strike, with a soft plastic plop, the side of the charge-hand's grinning face.

Leering like a devil's clown, Wink stopped and picked up the twitching grub between thumb and forefinger; momentarily considered it with manic eyes; then, unbelievably, popped it into his beard-rimmed mouth, bit off its disgusting head and chewed contentedly, as if savouring a rare delicacy.

Jeremiah spent the rest of the day alone, operating the

crane from its high cabin, hoisting the corpses of trees one after another to the jaws of the rapacious saw to be cut into pit-props or pallet-boards. As he worked, the cold climbed slowly up his body, numbing his flesh, lulling his mind to dormancy. The early magic of the day seemed now as vague and distant as a childhood memory.

When the work was done, he crammed into the back of the foreman's clapped-out car with three other burly axemen. Together they stifled in a fog of Golden Virginia and Old Holborn smoke; blind behind breath-steamed windows. As they headed back into the wet, grey, despondent winter town, Jeremiah decided that he wouldn't be going back to the woodyard any more.

That was when it had started. He was sure now. Until then everything had been alright. Not great, admittedly; but OK. Jeremiah's life had always been steady away.

The rain was heavier now, the wind lashing it in rippling sheets; like theatre curtains in the spotlights of the taxi's dripped beams. The wipers thrashed, panicking helplessly, to clear a sudden blinding spray as he slipped into the wake of a Tesco juggernaut which, in its turn, struggled, wallowing in the centre-lane to overhaul a marginally slower Italian road-train.

It was a bad situation but Jeremiah didn't really think about it. The sulphate coursing coolly through his brain matched reaction perfectly to control. He pushed down harder on the gas, squeezing the needle up to ninety-five. Briefly, imagination flashed a red warning light. There was no guarantee that through the blank opacity of spray the lane would be clear of obstacles. One strand of logic told him that it was just the sort of joke God loved; to place a contra-flow, warning signs unnoticed in the speeding night, sudden and solid in his path. The other said, faster, pass the danger quickly and enjoy the momentary thrill of uncertainty as; encased in loose steel armour; six giant threshing wheels to the left and the crash-barriers steel ribbon to the right; you catch your breath and plunge headlong through the wave.

Jeremiah made it through this limbo and out into the open night. Steadying the wheel with his knees, he reached for his tobacco-pouch to roll a fag. The sulphate sharpness at the back of his mouth demanded nicotine.

The Rizla stuck to his finger tips. He was sweating, conscious of his heart's shallow rapidity and the nagging, intestinal ache, which, since he took up this mobile, restless occupation had become a more or less constant companion.

Was it excitement, or the drug? Quite frankly, Jeremiah didn't give a shit. Sulphate was a part of his life now, a necessary fuel, like food or oxygen, or the four-star petrol which his taxi guzzled like a drain.

Addicted? He supposed he was; but it was vital medicine. He needed it to kill the *dream*.

Ahead now, the sulphurous ochre glow of Birmingham oozed into the saturated sky. Another sixty miles; less than an hour would see him home and dry.

Fag lit and smouldering in his mouth, Jeremiah reached out and stuck a tape in the machine, jacked up the volume, and inhaled deeply as the dense tropical electronics and cracked poetry of Lee Perry's 'Super Ape' massaged his brain with music. But, as always, it was a losing battle. As always when he sought to put his harassed mind at ease the memory of the *dream* reared up its ugly swollen head and leered lasciviously. Each day now, more of Jeremiah's world was crumbling into the void. Soon he would have to surrender; take the final dive; let go and merge into the sordid squalor of the Pit.

Jeremiah's flat was underground; a cavernous, damp, basement at the bottom of a decaying, three-storey, Victorian town-house opposite a draughty park.

Arriving home from his last day's work at the woodyard; the deathly depression engendered by the weird grubs slowly growing throughout his being, like fungus; Jeremiah had kicked open the door and clumped, work-booted, up the long, orange, corridor to the kitchen. Tiredness weighted him and filled his hollow bones with a cold, uranium ache.

He sighed as the smell of the kitchen pushed noxious fingers into his nose. He hoped that there was a clean plate left. Washing-up was an endeavour for which Jeremiah required the incentive of dire necessity. He could only bring himself to face the chaos of encrusted crocks and proliferation of grey milk-bottles, each harbouring its own unique bacterial culture in a sludge of mould-skinned waste, when visited by an almost mystical energy, somewhat akin to the Wrath of God. Then, driven, he would descend, a destroying angel and wallow in an ecstasy of sterilisation. It was as if he were purging the slate of his life of all the accumulated grime and grunge; the tenacious spoor of decay that signified the failings of the past.

Such times were very rare and today was not one of them.

He placed the tepid, grease-specked, paper bundle that contained his dinner on the table; clearing a space with the sweep of an arm amongst the littered wrappings, shrivelled chips and old, dried bones; remnants of a score of previous, identical meals. The thought of food almost made him retch. But he was hungry.

Jeremiah lit the gas and clattered the battered frying-pan over the blue-flame blossom, watching in fascination as the frozen lake of fat resolved slowly into hot clarity. Two pallid, thin-shelled eggs cracked, spluttering, into the pan. Then, half a scrawny chicken; pale, puckered skin; a gleam of cartilage and bone; and a mound of stolid chips dumped onto a cold plate.

Jeremiah briefly regarded this repast then, feeling suddenly close to tears, turned off the gas and walked away. It would be a week before he summoned the resolve to enter the kitchen again.

Stretched out on the musty candlewick bedspread, soothed by the gas fire's constant sibilance, Jeremiah sucked on the teat of a long, strong, calming, joint. An abrupt erection pushed up from its nest of torpor and cried out, "Comfort me". But even as his hand moved down, a tired mother answering a child's familiar wail, sleep claimed him – or some similar state.

The hot, sweaty Night was smothering him, gripping and twisting his aching body, shaking him with fevered epilepsy. He felt himself mauled, picked up from the bed and slammed against the walls; the ceiling. There was no pain, only the dull sensation of brutality masked by anaesthetic, like dentistry. Fear mounted as he struggled to control the frantic flapping of his limbs. It was dark, a deep red darkness and his ears were filled with a hot asthmatic roar which steamed his mind, bathing it in a sweat of terror. In desperation he mustered his fleeing will and rallied to force open his eyes. Vision gave form to Nightmare and he felt himself recoil, cowering, to the deepest bunker of his being. From this retreat he watched, helpless and despairing, while the Horror had its way.

Jeremiah was a big man. The thing was bigger. And it was purple. Its fat body; plastic, oiled with a damp pungency; was ringed with ribs which held taut its tubular skin, glowing with lurid translucency, over a slop of innards. From this clammy hide, obscene black hairs jutted from puckered craters, like huge, shiny, thorns.

113

It had arms; or things like arms; that reached out and coiled behind his neck, pulling his face towards its awful breast.

It had a head which nuzzled its black glossy carapace over his shoulder, butting up against his skull.

It had a mouth, framed with seeping blue jaws, and it had a tongue. Oh God it had a tongue; a ghastly caterpillar tongue which squirmed noisily, like a creaking rubber finger, forcing a passionate passage deep into his ear.

But worst of all, he realised on looking down, it had a prick and it was *fucking* him.

Jeremiah screamed a scream that should have shattered windows, punched holes through solid brick. A force, like snapped elastic, grabbed and propelled him through a vortex of confusion. He wrestled like a swimmer with a tide which denied his senses access to clues of light and dark and gravity. He felt as if he overtook himself. He was caught for an eternity in that blackly thrilling limbo of uncertainty where Future is the vague whim of Chance.

Then his body slapped against a solid plane, like wet meat on a slab. His eyes jarred open, wide lenses photographing a scene which could have been an alien world.

Jeremiah was lying across the room from the bed where he had lain down, huddled at the foot of the wall with cheek pressed to the cool blue plain of floor-tiles, across which draughts hurried dust-bundles, like tumbleweed, or giant spiders.

For several hours he could do no more than lie there trembling, until his shell-shocked mind crept out from hiding and once more took nominal control.

Nothing would ever be the same again.

Junction sixteen, nearly home. Jeremiah eased left and let the engine's power fade, relaxing in a coasting deceleration up the exit ramp. He turned onto the dual-carriageway and headed east. On auto-pilot he let the car follow the street-lights; ropes of amber beads, fading against the new red fluorescent glow of the dawn sun; gliding down into the dying nightmares of the town.

It had been almost a year since the Dream Demon raped him. A year crammed full of portent, through which Jeremiah had swum, immersed in a wash of tawdry ambience.

After recovering a semblance of composure, Jeremiah had crawled out of his basement cavern, locking the *dream* into the echoing rooms behind him. He walked down town and sluiced out his system with cheap gin and warm tonic in the tacky fug of the Black Pig's back bar. He spoke to no-one except George, from whom he purchased ten, ten-pound wrappers of amphetamine sulphate. He dreaded sleep that would awaken the hard ball of solid fear that now nestled in his gut.

The next day he had gone out and got a job as a taxi-driver, working nights; happily slipping further toward entropy.

Each evening, as the tired sun dropped thankfully out of

sight across the park Jeremiah would begin his shift with a strange, numb excitement humming inside him, like a lost chord. Switching on his two-way radio to call in for work he was a sly nocturnal predator sniffing the airways for food. Then, off on the scent, the night would be spent guiding the taxi from kill to kill; taking a little nibble here, a little there; sampling a feast of flavours from the anarchic menu of life.

The world of cabs and cabbies was the *Naked City* cut-up with the *Naked Lunch*.

At first, Jeremiah liked the life; but it took its toll. For some reason, happy people rarely seemed to ride in taxis. Or, if they were happy when they got into the car, as soon as the meter was switched on, angst and depression came spilling out.

Jeremiah began to feel that he was selling indulgence by the mile. Sometimes he was like a policeman and others a priest. The transience of contact between driver and fare seemed somehow to imbue the torn seats and ash-greyed interior of the overworked Ford Cortina with the aura of a confessional or Interview Room. Often unprompted, the full range of human hope and fear would be paraded in short, intense bursts. Like holiday romances condensed into five-minute quickies, the stuff of life was drawn in vivid, impressionistic line; each journey a comic-strip between pick-up and put-down. Even the silent passengers would leave a little of themselves; a few molecules, an essence, no more; adhering to the loose change of a tip, smeared on the door-handle, or smouldering in the ash-tray.

The more they spilled their miseries, the harder Jeremiah worked at becoming part of the machine; a robot driver, faceless, invisible even. But this only served to encourage them to greater excesses of confidence.

The standard cabbie defence against this suffocating miasma was humour. When they met together on the rank in a dead spell; perhaps after pub closing-time, while the punters were winding themselves into reckless frenzy in the clubs; they would spill out their frustrations in a lightning repartee of brash, brutal hilarity. They stroked each other with outrageous tales, polishing their calloused hides to proof them against the acid assault of tormented humanity.

"D'you hear about Ken Bolan? Picked up this old boy to take him to his kid's house for Christmas. Well they get half-way up to the new estates and the old boy – who's sitting in the front – flakes out into Ken's lap choking and moaning, like. Fucker's having a heart attack.

"Anyway, old Ken near shits himself, but he swings back round and shoots down the dual-carriageway to the hospital. They wheel him into casualty, but it's too late, the poor old sod's a dead 'un. So, Ken's a bit put out by this – there's twelve quid on the meter, it's Christmas remember, double-fare – so he hangs around, waiting for the relatives to arrive and then hits them for the fare. Even got fucking waiting time off of them."

"He's a right hard bastard, that Ken. Was probably his mad driving that give the bloke the heart-attack in the first place."

Then out would come all the known dead-people-in-taxis folklore. If Trevor were there he would tell of the time he picked up an elderly couple from Gatwick. They were coming up through the City, heading for the M1, when a querulous, aged female voice from the back announced, "Oh Lord, 'es gorn."

Rather than be delayed by complex formalities at a strange hospital in a strange town, Trevor persuaded the bereaved spouse that it would be better to take the remains of her loved one on to their destination. Apparently she sat, silently shocked, propping the stiffening corpse upright with her shoulder for fifty miles in the back seat of the car. There were hold-ups on the motorway that day and, when eventually the porters tried to get the corpse out of the car, it was grotesquely frozen in a seated position with one eye open and one shut.

Jeremiah would laugh with the rest of them, but often the laughter had the bitter taste of bile. More and more he felt himself like some thick, pale worm, turning in the rotten heart of the world; sifting his fingers through rank ordure to find hard bright coins. He was sickened by himself but did not wish

116

it any other way.

Jeremiah checked the time; six-thirty, still too early to go and fetch his day-driver, Jimmy. Jimmy was about fifty, an ex-Glasgow axe-boy who told stories of nineteen-forties gang wars. Berserker streetfights; Vikings on Benzedrine; mortal combat for the tall tenement territories. Jimmy had the scars to back up his tales. While he was working he always stowed beneath his seat a sharpened screwdriver; for protection; and a half-bottle of Smirnoff; for relief.

Jimmy was dying of cancer and an alcoholic, spending his time between jobs alternately sipping from his bottle and coughing blood into a handkerchief. On the whole he was a bit of a liability to have driving your taxi but Jeremiah was past caring now. Anyway, Jimmy's wife June, who was twenty years younger, wanted Jeremiah to screw her.

Jeremiah thought he might as well; but it would be safer to know where Jimmy was at the time.

Jeremiah thought that he was probably hungry so he tooled on round to the bakery next to the dole office. He knocked on the back door and the guy sold him hot, black-market rolls; oozing with melted butter and folded round thick, pink steaks of ham. These he ate, swallowing them hurriedly in unchewed gobbets, as he guided the car back round to the taxi office. Briefly he was conscious of his swelling belly. He was getting fat and these days nausea was a constant part of his life.

Sometimes he worried about ulcers; or worse. Jeremiah considered a visit to the quack, but by the time he pulled onto the office forecourt the idea had escaped.

The taxi-office was hot and airless, stale with cigarettes and farts. Four or five drivers sat around waiting for the shift to end. Their eyes were dark and bleared; faces white and stubbled in the bright, flickering neon. Jeremiah expected that he looked the same. It was certainly the way he felt.

Rocked back on a battered chair, Concorde was holding forth, entertaining the crowd. They called him Concorde on account of his excessive nose.

"Yeah, I picked her up from the Club LA. Said she wanted to go to Daventry. Real classy piece, y'know?"

They knew, at least, four heads nodded their assent. Jeremiah fed coins into the fruit machine and Concorde continued with his story.

"She tells me she's just had a row with her boyfriend then sits there in the back bawling. I can't take that crap, so I turns up the stereo and just gets on with the driving.

"Anyway, we're well out of town, about five miles from Daventry; there's six quid on the meter already; when I look in the mirror to check if she's alright."

He paused, the tension was too much for old, toothless Ron. He squeezed too hard on his plastic coffee-cup and it split with a sudden spurting, crackle. Concorde let the general laughter subside.

"What d'you reckon then? The bird's sitting there with her skirt hiked up around her hips, legs spread, knickers around her ankles and there it is in the mirror; just *winking* at me."

118

"What, y'mean the old vertical smile, mate?" interjected the drooling Ron. "Blimey, what did y'do then, kid?"

"Pulled into the next lay-by and screwed her, of course. Twice in fact. What would you have done?" Casually, Concorde sent his empty cup sailing, like a shuttlecock into the open mouth of the stained bin. "I had the meter running all the while, too. She paid up without a murmur when we got to her house. Fifteen quid; cheap at the price, I reckon."

Jeremiah took a second cup of thin, bitter coffee through to the back-room and emptied his change bag of ten-pence pieces into the video-game machine. He numbed his mind shooting endless streams of little, bleeping spaceships which swarmed across a hissing screen, like insects. It passed the time and postponed the inevitable need to sleep.

A couple of hours later, he was nosing the taxi through the maze-like courts and alleys of the *barrio* of new council-houses which sprawled on the far, cold, edge of town. The roads were lined with sparse rows of weedy infant trees, lashed leafless by the bitter wind. Kids in thin clothes were trudging off to school, weaving slow passages through the stripped shells of abandoned, burnt-out cars which littered the parking-bays. Up on the hill the walled order of the private estate looked down like Legoland; nose raised in superior disdain at this cheap imitation Betta-build.

Jeremiah turned into Jimmy's court, passing the house where Big Myra, June's raucous mate, lived with her three perfect half-caste babies. His stomach felt bloated and swollen now. His guts squirmed and bubbled, pushing hard against his belt. He pulled up outside the house and hauled himself from the car. From the house next door, where Sally and her simple, teenaged husband Craig lived with their infant and a scabby, crippled cat, a faint flurry of shouts and slamming doors pushed vainly out into the deaf, grey morning.

Then Jimmy, with his tottering, dypso's walk, came up the path to meet him.

"Chraist, mon, wha's up wi' ye? Y'luk laik shite!" He wiped a thin lash of spittle from his pale lip with the back of a mottled hand.

"Bad guts, Jimmy."

"Get awa' inta th'hoose then, pol. Tell wee Junie ta gi'ye braikfast. The bairns are awa' t'the school just now, so it's good an' quiet. I'll see y'later."

Jeremiah hesitated for a moment, feeling the tentacles of conspiracy coil around him. Then, too weak to argue, he nodded and turned toward the chipped blue door. Well, what the hell? If that was what the man wanted, he thought; then so be it.

In the bathroom, Jeremiah cleaned the soapy stubble-scum from an old razor-blade. With mildly shaking hands, he cut a line of vague pink speed with a dab from his precious half-gram wrap of pure white coke. Judging by the desperate look that June had flashed him as she burned the toast, he would need its instant electricity.

A sharp bolt of pain pushed upwards from his groin, towards his heart. He groaned and gasped involuntarily as the pain repeated. He ran the tap into the small, toothpaste-smeared basin and splashed his face. The water was luke-warm; the walls in these houses were too thin for it ever to be truly cold. He stared at his ravaged, drawn features in a soap-flecked magnifying-mirror. His pores looked like volcano craters; his eyes were shattered with red veins and underhung with sacks of soot; his stubble was the blasted stumps of trees.

Again the pain scourged through Jeremiah's seething belly. A pressure which felt for all the world like constipation distended him. He thought back. No, it couldn't be that. He clearly remembered stopping at Chorley Wood services. The toilets had been flooded. He'd had to paddle through a lake of piss. He remembered how its surface had been broken here and there by the swamped grey islands of discarded paper towels. The cubicle had been covered in Fascist graffiti and there wasn't any paper. Jeremiah was forced to use his handkerchief.

There was a movement behind him in the mirror and Jeremiah looked down as he felt June's thin hand scramble up under the waist-band of his sweatshirt to tangle with the sparse hair of his chest. The other one walked into view, chipped, red-varnished nails plucking anxiously at the fastening of his belt.

"Don't think bad of me, please. But I need a fuck."

Passive, he let the urgency of her need drag him into the bedroom, struggling to match it with his own. Their kisses were dry and thin, as was her body, pushing hard-boned corners against him. His stomach churned again and nausea fattened his tongue. Despite the coke, it wasn't going to work.

Near frantic, she gripped him by the hair and forced down his head inside her open dressing-gown. For a moment hope stirred as, in the hollow of her hip, a tattooed butterfly fluttered nervous scarlet wings. He moved upward, cheek against her flank, to where her tiny breasts swelled from a grid of ribs. His tongue snaked out to circle a nipple, silhouetted against the pale window gauze; and froze. Her purple aureoles were puckered with stout, bristly hair which waved like tentacles above the horizon of her skin. All thought of sex died then and there, as the gross memory of the Dream Demon writhed back and choked it.

Another spasm of agony wrenched him. The belly pains were getting worse. Jeremiah gritted his teeth and gripped her arms. June moaned with transferred pain. But the sudden piercing screams came from next-door; drilling through the fireboard walls.

Everything was in uproar. Commotion; running footsteps; slamming doors; a woman crying, screaming in the street. Then someone was pounding on the front-door downstairs, rattling the frail house like thunder.

"June. June are you there? June you've got to help me, please. He's bleeding everywhere!"

Jeremiah swung from the bed; the room swayed dizzily. He wrestled to pull up his jeans but they seemed too small. He could not get them to fasten at the waist. June was already jerking hurriedly down the steep stairs. He heard the front-door open and a bubbling flood of explanation; the voice receding as they went back next door.

"Oh June, thank God! It's Craig, he's finally gone and done it. Just like he always said he would."

"Somebody told him I'd been carrying on with the Corona man. But it isn't even true!"

Jeremiah's belly was hard, protruding. He dragged the belt around it as tightly as he could stand. It seemed the muscles were twitching now but in his haste to catch up with June he put this down to nerves. He was always a bit kinky for emergency and this one sounded wild.

The house next door was quiet. The front door stood ajar. He stepped inside. From the corner of the living-room a baby, penned in a cage of toys, gurgled and threw a half-chewed chocolate-biscuit at his feet. The air was edged with the sharp, pungent smell of cat.

Upstairs there was a renewed outburst of wailing and scuffling. Doubled against the, by now, almost constant midriff pain, Jeremiah hauled himself up the bare-wood stairs

121

and stumbled into the main bedroom. As he raised his whirling head he knew, suddenly and without doubt, that finally the Horror had caught up with him.

Tall, thin June and small, plump Sally both stood, aghast with dumb-struck awe, staring at the room's grotesque centre-piece.

Craig; it had to be he; swung from the knotted light-flex. Ridiculously, the ceiling was so low that his bare, rope-veined and blood-engorged feet, down-pointed, almost brushed the floor. Jeremiah assumed he must have jumped from the rumpled bed; the side of which now steadied the body's sway.

The corpse's face; for corpse it surely was; swelled black and shiny-tight above the biting ligature. Eyes bulged like those of insects and a bloated tongue stuck, purple, from the froth-roped lips.

Not content with merely hanging, the man had used a craft-knife to trellis his chest with stripes of flapping red, and lay open the flesh of his arms. The frantic slash of steel had filleted dull, grey, bone from tangled hawsers of muscle and vein.

Blood ran in a constant stream, dribbling from hands, half-cupped in some last, vain regret, to pool below in a spreading crimson lake.

Speechless, Jeremiah drew near in awful fascination. His skin tightened, stroked by a cold blade of déjà vu.

There was a scent here, a deep, sweet smell, which he had smelled before. Outside, as if a million miles away, a street-dog howled, giving tongue to the taint of butchery.

Jeremiah was a marionette, trembling in the hands of a palsied puppeteer. His body now moved outside of his control. Hoisted on strings, his arm swung out; fingers like jointed, wooden worms, wriggling to insinuate themselves into the empty wounds.

Something turned slowly in his gut; pushing and scraping; while outside, the edges of his world began to crumble in.

This was where it had waited this last year. While he had raced the night-time highways in his cab; trying to lose it amongst the confusion of the lives which his work shuffled all around the town; the Fear had sat here, waiting.

Circling the tediously familiar streets, from pub to club to lover, hospital or home, he had re-crossed his trail a hundred-thousand times trying, he realised now, to forestall the inevitable day when he would look in his mirror and see it winking there.

The pain in Jeremiah's belly was now urgent agony. He jack-knifed, clutching at the wet, swaying body for support. His hands slipped. He pitched forward to his knees. Pincers wrenched the muscles of his gut.

A blow of realisation toppled him like a tree. Black light exploded in his mind.

Peering into the scarlet ocean's mirror surface, Jeremiah saw it beckon him with terrible arms. It was the Dream Demon, come to supervise the birth.

There was no choice any more. Jeremiah surrendered and squirmed, wallowing down to embrace the Horror; his tormented body lashing furiously in the slick of blood as now the contractions began in earnest.

R M LAMMING

WASP SONGS

ILLUSTRATED BY DUNCAN FEGREDO

THERE'S NOTHING QUAINT about it.

I've never been able to ignore trapped wasps, panic-stunned and dithering on a window, looking for out.

There is no out. None they find, at any rate.

I've always hated them.

To deter wasps, I have louvre windows, and I keep them shut — or correction: I need air as much as anyone, so I ration myself with little cracks between the slats; and every summer I've watched wasps squeezing in (as we all squeeze in, bruising ourselves, forcing ourselves into where it would have been so much better for us if we hadn't come — the analogy is obvious.)

In comes a wasp —

Buzz.

— Threatening a sting. For me, it's pure outrage, that gratuitous menace from an uninvited creature which may be trapped certainly, but, if it is, am I its keeper? Must I answer for it? Did I encourage it?

I ask you.

As I say, they seem incapable of ever finding the crack again, and squeezing out.

And for the wasp, whether or not it knows it, my glass slats are the outrage, those hard, shaped divisions of air, wallings of light inexplicably cutting off where it is from where it was.

Buzz. Buzz.

I kill them.

I've killed them in their thousands because they're filthy, because they sting, and — more than that — because they promise to sting and buzz their song of promise instead of humming it. A hum might be ignored. Possibly. But that buzz — get me before I get you —

Oh, I get them all right.

Mostly.

You could heap them to the ceiling, all my dead wasps.

And you could joke about them if you wanted to — Death, where is thy sting? etcetera — but there's nothing to celebrate. Slaughters and wisecracks have never altered truth much,

and, believe me, behind the filth, the provocation, there's a truth busily at work in each wasp which you may have sensed (I always have) but you haven't known.

Wasps are terrifying.

Listen—

It was last June. I was working on my tax return. I'm always late with my tax forms. I was concocting those troublesome little figures, deposit account interest, higher interest account interest, when—

Buzz.

There it was, a fat one, its bright, yellow-striped belly trembling on the glass, somehow inside and frantic to get out, its black head zizzing in the sun and dust—

BUZZ

A particularly loud one.

I keep a rolled up newspaper at the ready. I swept this up and lunged. I missed. Buzz. Lifting itself, it circled and came down again on a higher slat. There it lay pinioned by its longing to get out. I stood poised with my arm raised. Silence. It was waiting for me. It was weeping on the pane. Wasps weep silently. I know all about it. If you hate them enough, you develop sensitivity: you know all about the moment when the wasp understands, even if it doesn't know it understands, that you're after it. Without tears, with no sound the wasp weeps, filthy victim with its pack of stings—

No clumsy swiping this time. I took my aim tenderly. My arm stole like a panther . . . Just as the wasp began to rise, I got it.

Whack! A hit! Whack!

It staggered. It dropped to the windowsill, belly sizzling, wings blurring, its grotesque head swelling (they can look like that), and it was just about to heave itself upright when—

Whack! I got it. Whack!

Silence. It had curled up on its side, quivery legged, belly twitching.

I stopped breathing to listen.

Silence.

I poked it with the newspaper. All the tremblings suddenly went out of it. It was as dead as cigarette ash. One more speck on the universal rubbish heap. I left it where it was and went back to my tax forms. Corpses should be left where they fall for a while, I've always believed that. What has lived doesn't die easily. You should wait and see. Even cigarette ash, when you think about it, may be something more than just ash.

So I worked on my figures with that debris, when I raised my eyes, darkening on the windowsill.

At least they seem to darken, and their darkening says Dead dead

This one wasn't.

Nothing fakes as well as a wasp can. Sometimes, the very darkest of them manages to crawl away when you're not watching and recuperate somewhere, or it drops to finish dying where you can't get at it, jammed in a crack beneath the skirting board, and sometimes —

Buzz

This one was up. It came at me. I had a flash-glimpse of the windowsill dazzlingly spotless, and I batted with my hand — instinct. A small, pelletty body banged against my fingers — it was knocked back to the light, the hard, snared light of the glass. And there it clung on a slat, stunned, silent, praying for out. Oh they pray yes. Or you could say they're simply prayerful, spread like that against the glass. It's a question of interpretation.

Out Out

No chance.

I was on my feet, reaching with the newspaper —

And it knew. Up. A distinct whine rose inside its buzz as it came soaring over me, then turned —

I ducked. I parried.

A neat tap sounded on the newspaper —

Another silence.

What could be more hideous than the creeping secrecy of wasps across a carpet? I stood still, analysing several square feet of the floor.

But it was on my desk. I have antennae of my own, and suddenly they detected it moving like a drop of oil down the desk's side. The top drawer was a fraction open: I saw it yellowly making for the lip, and the possibility of slipping in, into the darkness, covering up its sting among the papers, where it could lie until my hand came blundering – all that was falling on the wasp, whether or not it registered the fact, as the thing to do.

I went for it.

Whack!

It gave me only one chance, and I missed. It howled past – there are as many buzzes in a wasp as there are snows to an eskimo – back to the window.

Buzz

Whack! Whack!

That second swipe got it.

Whack!

It dropped so heavily, it bounced clean off the windowsill and landed on my stack of bills and bank statements, shrivelling, unshrivelling

I'm dying I'm dying

No one takes me in twice. I picked up the paper weight. It's one of those globular, glassy masses that enlarge a few fanciful flowers set in its base, a work of *multi fiori* with tonnage of death enough for six wasps. The sun sang. I got a good grip on that weight. The wasp had curled like an embryo. It buzzed faintly as the globe came over it. I ground it to pieces.

That takes some doing, actually. Those succulent-looking bodies are astonishingly resistant. But the good thing about a paper weight is that the job can be done with sun glinting off a pretty shape and patterns, and you don't have to look beneath until you really are quite sure, this time.

What was left was still more than you might have thought, but its belly had burst, all its filth had spilled out and smeared across the paper, as colourful as piss, and its black head was smashed.

Done for.

This time it couldn't be left to corpse. Curling on a window sill – that's one thing, but pulped across the present state of my current account – that was blasphemous, so I tore the whole mess off. I missed the final balance by a hair's breadth, and only left a faint stain yellowing it.

Then I chucked the wreckage in the waste paper basket, and snapped shut the window slats. A wasp-free zone. Sometimes, it's better to stifle.

I have no dependants. Nor am I dependent on anyone. When I fill in tax forms those parts about dependants need only a few scrawls: N/A N/A. But my expenses are a headache. It can take hours, justifying allowances. The whole list has to ring true.

So I was working hard.

Buzz

I didn't hear it.

Buzz

I was imagining things.

Buzz –

It rose from beside me, a blur, a smudge – and came to rest by my hand, bright, so bright, posterpaint perfection of blackness and yellowness, a great wasp, the fattest with the strongest looking wings I ever saw. It seemed more than hornet-sized – that's what the advantage of surprise does for you – a wasp so crammed with itself that all its stillness, all its silence there on the desk outbuzzed the loudest buzz.

HERE I AM

I dropped my pen.

They sneak in sometimes; they can hide for days –

I grabbed the newspaper. The wasp rose, arcing. It roared, I batted. It arced again. I jumped up. I brushed against the wastepaper basket and felt that go slowly rolling over. The wasp was shrilling at my ear. I windmilled wildly, even though nothing beats a wasp's persistence once its tactics turn to kamikaze, not unless its own instincts call it back to the sun.

This one chose the sun. It hissed past my eyes, turned for the window and arrived there clamouring.

OUT OUT

It spun with buzzing. It was drill-like with buzzing so that I half expected to see a hole form in the glass.

OUT OUT

No sneak ever had such fury.

OUT

Sneaks weep. Sneaks panic. This demanded, and, suddenly, I found myself perpetrating the unthinkable. I pressed the lever, opening the slats wide. This wasp and no other I let go.

Into the blue yonder.

Out into the teeming world of wasps that would know it as I did, even before I was down on my knees bundling rubbish back into the waste paper basket.

Their Messiah has come.

Here's the proof: as unsullied as a new-born soul, the torn off corner of my bank statement – but you won't believe that, naturally. It's one-shot evidence. I myself hardly believed it. I'm as keen as anyone to shrink from this miracle, discredit this revolution. What are Messiahs for? Don't they bring regeneration to the masses? And if so –

It's true. I count. I watch. Fewer corpses stay where they fall on the windowsill. There's that for a start. More of them vanish. More of them re-vitalise. They can't all be sneaks and fakes.

(As for resorting to the paperweight, if I have to – it's quickly out with the remnants to the dustbin. Let them piece themselves together in the garbage, if they can. I don't wait around to see.)

There are also pilgrimages.

Sometimes at night, when it's dark, I hear buzzing on the windows. I know of two huge nests in the garden, two at least. Assemblies of the faithful. And if I'm working late and haven't closed the curtains with a physicist's precision, the bright slats attract them. That's to put it logically. What in fact they do is fly

132

up in swarms crying
　　Holy Holy
pressing eagerly against the glass, behind which I sit in the aura of a miracle.

I've even found them in my bedroom. Once, when I switched on the light, they were crawling down the flex singing jubilations. It exhausted me, swatting them, and then a few again, and one – again. Only one had that much in it: faith is so difficult.

And recently in my bath, a stray devotee. I found it resting sluggish on the white enamel where my own body has to lie, so that I couldn't bring myself to pulp it. Instead, I turned on the hot water tap and let a seething tongue rush out, lick it up, and draw it down the plughole.

There, horrors, it hung. The belly went down all right, but the dark head somehow wedged itself between two spokes, and so it hung as though in a bracket, submitting to its boiling and mutely singing a victims' hymn, until I beseeched it to let go. I scorched my face in the steam, watching. I screamed my beseechings – and even then it took time.

133

NEIL GAIMAN

WEBS

ILLUSTRATED BY SIMON BISLEY

IN THE WEB-COVERED halls of the King of the Spiders, Lupita spent a most memorable year. She had servants in attendance upon her, and a jerkin covered in chryolanths, a present from the King. Lupita was a guest of one of the Dark Lords, although nobody seemed to know which one; it was the subject of much court speculation:

"Today, milor' Lupita abased herself perhaps a trifle too low before Lord Caryatid."

"Ah, but yesterday she was seen publicly to ignore Lord Tistatte, and on one of the dark days: surely there is a sign of favour?"

"Or of other protection. Perhaps she is in lien to one of the Lords of shifting position . . . "

And all would be silent, and watch Lupita as she walked across the hall, strands of webbing adhering to her cape and drifting behind her like fronds of plants from the slow zone: old man's folly, perhaps, or tiger-whiskers, a plant spoken of in the classics as possessing certain unusual properties, although no one today knew nor cared what they were.

It was the uncertainty about Lupita's status that had kept her safe from court intrigues; for, after all, no one would dare to risk their status on a cheap guess. Blood was the Dark Lords' tithe from those who worshipped them, and few were overly eager to hasten the communion by involvement in the complicated and shifting game the Lords played. Instead they mirrored it, or thought they did, aped what they presumed they saw, with their petty little cliques, and their treacherous little factions.

Although the webs did much to mute sound in the endless corridors of the Palace of Spiders, there was always a soft susurrus, a sly whispering as alliances were formed, the hiss of betrayals discovered and bought, the kiss of character assassination (and possibly of assassination of another kind, for sometimes bodies could be seen lolling high in the webs of the halls, wrapped around in pale silken strands like empty insects in some old larder, although no one ever climbed the webbing to find out who it was that had been left there. The

bodies were always gone in a week, or two at most).

In her time in the palace Lupita formed a number of oblique liaisons, but took no sexual partners, something which somehow was no surprise to anybody.

There was much that Lupita did to surprise, however.

She once went out hunting, and brought back a mammal, alive.

The King, before whom it was unveiled, said nothing, but signalled with a staff to the Chamberlain, who enquired:

"It is?"

"A cat, my Lord Chamberlain."

"And does it make good eating?"

(There was a ripple of appreciation at that: the Chamberlain had punned most elegantly, such that her words had also meant, *And is it given to men to eat their gods?* and also, *Unravel this and we shall rejoice.*)

"No, my Lord Chamberlain, I do not believe that it does."

The animal stayed with her after that for many weeks. Then one morning, when mist hung low on the banqueting chamber and formed beads of moisture on the crouching iron bodies of the Dark Lords, the body of the cat was to be seen hanging some forty feet above the ground, in the webs, not far from Lupita's chambers.

A small crowd gathered.

Lupita rose at her usual hour. She came out of her chambers, but when she saw the crowd, and when she realised what they were looking at, she turned, with no expression, and went back in through the door from which she had come.

When she returned, about thirty minutes later, the crowd had swelled to almost a score of courtiers, and an equal number of others.

Lupita carried with her a basket containing a filled waterbladder, several small dry rolls, and some crystallised fruit. The black of her cloak had been replaced by a rich crimson, and she had placed a knife in her belt.

She took a crossbow from one of her servants, and aimed it at the mammal's wrapped body. The bolt made no noise when it struck home, trailing a thin thread behind it.

Lupita tied the thread around her thumb, then sat, cross-legged, on the floor of the corridor, and waited.

The crowd stared at her, enraptured, waiting with amazement for her next trick. It was all so new, so daring. Someone at the back began to applaud, swallowing gulps of air and belching loudly, but the noise was quickly shushed.

By the time the stone was struck for evening meal, the last onlooker had given up, and wandered off. Lupita was still waiting, sitting in the shadows, pale eyes gazing up at the shrouded body.

When the last stone was struck for deep night a servant came by and replaced the food and water Lupita had consumed on her vigil.

On the third night it seemed to Lupita almost as if the servant were about to speak to her, but the servant did no such thing. So Lupita spoke to the servant.

"Do you know what I will find?"

The servant shrugged.

"Do you care?"

"It is," admitted the servant, "not something that will affect my lot one way or another."

Lupita nodded dismissal, and the servant backed away.

It is said that at that time Lupita slept, and dreamed a dream. But a dream is a private matter, and we shall not concern ourselves with it. Be that as it may, Lupita was either woken, or not woken but alerted, an hour after this, by a tugging on the thread about her thumb. Looking up she could just make out the cat-cadaver lurching up the web. She let out loops of thread from her thumb, like someone coaxing a nervous kite to fly, until she saw the shape vanish in the webbing, pulled inside by a dark and spindly limb.

It was then that Lupita hand-over-handed up the web (which would have caused apoplexy, and perhaps a chorus of eructation, had an audience been there to observe), trying, and not altogether failing, to move at random, as if she were merely a rip in the net, old bones and gnawed skulls slipping

139

and shifting from the turbulence in the web caused by the recent passage of the cat.

She waited near the spot where the mammal's body had vanished until the thread was tight around her thumb (which she could feel was losing feeling) then she let out the last couple of loops, and pushed into the web. Strands of the stuff stuck to her eyelashes, her face, her hair. She screwed her eyes together tightly, then pulled her cloak in front of her face, and moved forward into the space.

She had expected a tunnel.

Instead she found herself disoriented, moving through something that felt like a waterfall, but which was composed of light and something else, not matter. It seemed like something was brushing her lightly from the soles of her feet to her head. It tickled, but it was a tickling inside, not outside, not on her skin.

Her eyes were still tight shut, but colours formed inside them, seeping like river mists of blue, of green, of peach and viridian, then exploding like fire inside her head.

She said nothing, and was still. When her inner world had calmed down she lowered her cloak, and opened her eyes. The world had turned silver: lights shone silver from mirrored panels, illuminated silver switches and buttons, cast silver reflections on silver surfaces and spilled to the silver floor around dark grey shadows.

In a corner, next to a vast metal ship, its silver sails fluttering in a non-existent breeze, sat two huge spiders, white spots on splotchy brown abdomens; angular knobbly-jointed legs waving gently in the air; emerald eyes gleaming with hunger and greed.

They had divided the cat between them, and were eating it in a most unpleasant fashion.

Lupita pulled her knife from her belt, and threw it at the largest of the spiders, hitting it in the abdomen. White stuff began to ooze from the cut, dripping onto the metal floor. The creature ate on, not noticing the wound, not even when the pale substance (in appearance, Lupita observed, somewhere between pus and jelly) oozed as far as the cat, and the spider continued its meal with itself as sauce and condiment.

Since her knife attack had done no apparent good, Lupita slowly began to circle the spiders, walking as quietly as was possible. She circled them once, twice, three times, then she ran, hard, as fast as she could toward a far wall.

She turned around, and winced. The thread had performed its function, but while one of the spiders – the one with the wounded belly – had been neatly sliced in two, yellow organs swimming in mucus now slipping and spilling onto the floor, the other had been less fortunate. The thread had slid down, so that, instead of encircling the body, it had merely noosed the legs. The final tug had pulled seven of the eight legs off, and they lay stiff and ghastly on the ground, stacked up like dreadful brushwood against the spider's shivering body. The last leg twitched and spasmed, spinning the spider around on the silver floor.

Lupita went close enough to it to retrieve her knife, then, keeping well clear of the mouth, which was opening and closing in impotent and silent fury, she slit the creature's belly wide open, with a cry,

"*Haih!*" and jumped back, pulling up her cloak as she did so to avoid the tumbling organs splashing it.

She tried to untie the thread from her thumb, but it had been too tightly wound for too long, and her thumb was blue and cold. The thread had been pulled too tight to untie and was too tough to cut, although she produced a respectable amount of blood in trying.

In the end she had to cut the thumb off. She cauterised it in spider-spit, which took away the pain and stopped the bleeding, although it made her feel strangely distant, as if she was not participating in her life, but was merely an interested spectator, watching her own actions from over her shoulder. This feeling, which was new to her, was to recur several times in later life.

She wiped the knife on her leg, returned it to her belt, and climbed out the way she had come.

141

The next day it was observed that neither the King nor the Lord Chamberlain were to be found in the palace environs; however this realisation was rapidly overshadowed by the discovery that a certain antique Dark Lord had gone into fugue, and was apparently blown out.

It was widely assumed that Lupita had cut off her thumb in order to appear mysterious, and the court, unable to cope with further mysteries, agreed to find this in faintly bad taste.

Worse was to follow:

That evening Lupita left the palace. Before she went, as she passed through the hall of the Dark Lords, she was seen to stroke the casing of the Lord-in-fugue.

The court gathered in an observation tower to watch her leave; they stared after her until she had crossed the border line and was lost in the mists; but the sky remained curiously free from lightning, there were no awful screams or terrible cries, and the earth did not part and swallow her up.

They went back to their halls feeling slightly let down. Later they polished the Dark Lords: Iliaster and Baraquely, Zibanitu-tula, Ettanin, Bodstieriyan, and the rest.

It was then that one of the lesser courtiers was foolish enough to be heard praying that Lupita be punished for her lack of respect. Prayers of any kind were anathema to the Dark Lords, and he was turned to twisted stone where he stood.

The people waited for their king and his chamberlain to return to them.

The webs collapsed and rotted in the halls near to where Lupita (now just an enigmatic memory) had had her chambers. But other webs were being spun; they were all over the palace, if you knew where to look for them.

STORM CONSTANTINE

DID YOU EVER SEE OYSTERS WALKING UP THE STAIRS?

ILLUSTRATED BY STEVE YEOWELL

WHAT A HELL of a day that was. Rain like you've never seen before, pink lightning . . . Yes, pink lightning. Tara said it was an omen for strangeness and, looking back, I know she was right. Simon and Dominic moved in that day. They were taking the top floor and Tara and I were all eyes watching their delectable male behinds struggling up the stairs with a less than delectable sofa. Becky was off work sick (she had the other, smaller, middle floor with her boyfriend Al), so she joined us, sniffling, on the stairs to watch the scenery. "Funny coloured light out there isn't it," she said to the boys. They made one or two smart remarks which we all laughed at. I don't remember what they were.

Tara suggested the six of us have dinner together that night, a sort of getting to know each other party. Of course she was overjoyed at the prospect of having two unattached, attractive males around. As our flat was the largest in the building, we would play host. All afternoon, I was shifting junk into the studio from the living room where a lot of our tools and sketches and even half-finished pots had strayed to. Tara was looking forward to telling Simon and Dominic about how we were successful businesswomen. Successful? Well, we kept our heads above water, that's about it, but we had a good life. Both of us adore freedom and working for a big pottery would have stifled that for ever. I shook out the coloured shawls that covered the sofas and Tara dragged a duster round the place. We shoved a mixture of mince and vegetables and spices into a pot, called it bolognaise, and hey presto, we were nearly ready.

Eight o'clock and everybody was banging on our door. Thank God they'd had the presence of mind to bring wine; we'd forgotten completely. Becky, by daylight a decent sort, had turned into the clinging, whining limpet she usually was when Al was home. Tara and I made faces, recognising the signs straight away. "Al, why didn't you get Riesling? You know I hate this one!" Al this, Al that. All we could do was roll our eyes and watch her smother him. He was a nice guy though, thin like a hunter, dark and lissome-looking, so we

used to put up with night-time Becky because of that. He was a systems analyst which I thought sounded like some kind of cyber-punk psychotherapist. Computers are not my line really, so it was a relief Al was not the kind of guy to rabbit on about the things out of work's time.

Tara and I swapped glances across the room when Simon and Dominic arrived. I reckoned we'd both made the assessment of ten out of ten, although I didn't go for Simon's slogan T-shirt too much. Dominic, altogether lither and darker, impressed me more with his designer-rips, although Tara remarked to me in the kitchen as we prised meat from the saucepan, she thought that was a little passé. I let that go without argument, relieved my voluptuous friend appeared more interested in peroxide Simon. The boys hovered around looking awkward for a while, until we sat down to eat, and then praised the meal beyond all reasonable requirements; it was pretty foul after all. Tara and I eat to carry on living, not for any particular pleasure in the act. After the meal, Dominic produced a bottle of Jack Daniels, the sly beast, and we all proceeded to dilute the soggy spaghetti in our guts with good liquor.

146

Tara, with her usual gift for diplomacy, soon managed to scrape out the information that neither Simon or Dominic were romantically attached at present. They were both students and, oh joy, Simon was a *poet* too. Perhaps that was what first made my hackles rise about him. I've had many bitter experiences of men who thought they were poets, and many subsequent embarrassing experiences of learning how much they certainly weren't any such thing, generally while they were expecting favourable critiques of their earnest outpourings. I actually cringed when Tara cooed about how much she'd like to see some of his work. Dominic must have been psychic. He said "'Fraid I don't write", to which I nearly responded, "Oh good" but caught myself in time and said, "No, me neither."

"Do you like poetry, Al?" Simon drawled, leaning back on the green sofa. Luckily, it was not the one with three legs. Al looked positively cornered, poor thing. I began praying Simon wouldn't offer to nip upstairs and fetch some of his efforts down for us.

"Um," Al replied. "Well, I – er – read it at school." He shrugged. "You know."

"Yes, well I think you'll find styles have changed since then," Simon said. His tone was quite sarcastic. I couldn't understand why on earth he'd want to get at Al, who was such a pussy-cat.

"You prefer horror books, don't you Al?" Becky put in, quite courageously I thought, although I doubt whether the put-down was intentional. Simon sniffed. A *horror book* had clearly never sullied his shelves. He decided to change the subject.

"This is a great house. I love it! It was so lucky we got a place here!"

"Yeah, we like it too, but I wish we had it all to ourselves," Tara said, "I keep hassling Mrs Cryer to let us use the ground floor as a studio. It's full of junk down there, but she won't have it. This must have been one hell of a place when it was all one house."

"I like old houses," Becky said.

"Well, there's hundreds of them around here," I said. "This must have been quite a hoity-toity area at one time. Now, people like us live here."

"Who lives in that green place down the road?" Simon asked. "Looks pretty run down. More students, by any chance?"

"Don't think anybody lives there," Tara told him. "Last we heard, it was going to be knocked down and they were going to build pretend houses there. You know, the ones that are all red brick and patio and last about twenty years before the cardboard goes soggy between the rooms. The ones that sell for risible amounts to young executives."

"What a waste! It's enormous. And the silly bits on it – it looks like a Victorian wedding cake!"

Tara sighed. "Ah, that's progress you see. Destroy the

country's heritage and smother it with disposable eyesores."

"Is it haunted, do you think?" Al asked, rolling his eyes and making ghoulish faces.

Tara laughed. "Honey, any house that big and old is haunted! At least, I bet anyone going in there will be scared shitless whether it is or not. It must have seen so much, so many lives . . . "

I recognised the warning signals that Tara was about to become philosophical; a state of mind unsatisfied unless it provoked arguments. One glance at the nearly empty Jack Daniels bottle confirmed my fears.

"Why don't we go and see?" I said, brightly. They all looked at me; sprawling around, stuffed, lazy and warm. Nobody wanted to move. It would be cold outside. "Oh, come on!" I cajoled. "We could do with some exercise. I can hardly move."

"Neither can I, nor do I want to," Tara said.

Becky pressed closer to her beloved Al, pouting prettily for the benefit of the attendant males and mimicking the shivers.

"I'd like to," Simon said. At that point, I had to concede he was certainly the better looking of the two and I saw Tara and Becky stir themselves towards him like sun-glutted lizards. Suddenly house exploration seemed like a good idea.

It *was* cold outside and damp too; streets all wet and shining. Tara took hold of Simon's arm, marching into the lead. Dominic and I looked at each other assessively for a moment before deciding we'd forego the bodily contact. He hunched into his leather jacket, I hunched into mine and we walked behind the others, feet apart. "I can't believe we're doing this," he said. "It's like something out of a cheapskate horror movie."

"No, it's not," I replied, rather stiffly. "Everyone goes in that place, I'm sure. It's fuck-city. Nobody has ever disappeared or even been scared in there to my knowledge."

"Have you been there before then?" A double-edged question, I felt.

"No," I fixed him with a gorgon stare. "Always meant to. I was curious but never got round to it."

He stared back speculatively, wondering whether all that was a double entendre or not. While this sparkling repartee was going on, we'd arrived in front of the empty house. Becky started going on about how she wished she was rich and could afford to buy such a place etc. The front gates, gowned in dead convolvulus and rust, were padlocked, so we all had to scramble over the wall. Tara and I went first and headed off up the drive. We knew what eruptions could be expected from Becky playing helpless female and didn't have to say a word to each other about wanting to avoid it; we just vacated the area swiftly.

Lamp House, it was called. Lamp House. Why? It had a rakish look to it; knew it was past it, didn't give a shit. This is me, it said, uncompromising. Half of the external woodwork had gone. It would have cost several fortunes to restore the place. Simon and Dominic came scampering up behind us; further back Becky was complaining to Al about some ravagement to her tights.

"We could be in the middle of nowhere," Simon said, clearly impressed. A fat, waxing moon illuminated the scene but we had still been organised enough to bring torches. The grounds to Lamp House were flat and, if once lawns and borders and all that business, now only weak scrub. Trees formed a thick border round the edge but grew nowhere else. Clearly, the garden had never been landscaped properly. Soon it would all be cheerful estate populated by middle executives and their cosmetic families. I experienced a deep, resonating pang of sad frustration, sharing Becky's desire to be rich, to be the saviour of this grand old folly. Behind us, I could still hear her going on about what she'd do with it, if she had the money.

The blistered front door was impenetrable and the lower windows all boarded up against the soulless attentions of the local youth. Naturally, such obstacles had been overcome some time ago by determined explorers and we found a back door that was open a few inches. It was a gap just wide enough to squeeze through; the door wouldn't move a fraction either way. Simon went in first and switched on his torch, the rest of us piling in behind rather tentatively. It had crossed my mind that Lamp House might be regularly occupied at night by characters I wouldn't want to stumble over, and I don't mean supernatural ones. We were in the first of a series of rooms that had probably been domestic-staff territory in Lamp House's days of glory. The presence of illicit occupants, either present or past, was evidenced by the fact that all the woodwork had been ripped away, even the floor-boards here and there. We guessed it had all been used as fuel by tramps or lovers seeking warmth. In single file, we ventured further into the house. Wounds upon the passage walls, revealing gouged plaster, showed where the panelling had been torn away. We had to be careful where we walked because of the vandalised floors. It made me think about how it wouldn't be easy to make a fast getaway from Lamp House. I wasn't scared though; it was all rather depressing. I'm sure no ghosts could have stomached such a raped and ransacked environment. The place was dead.

We gathered in the front hall and shone our torches around. Cleaner patches on the yellow walls showed where furniture and paintings had once lived. The tiled floor was mostly intact, surprisingly, but the banisters had gone, the stairs leading up into a predictable, sepulchral gloom. Tara came and took hold of my arm. "God, it makes me want to cry," she said. "Just imagine if the guy who'd built this place could see it now!"

"Bloody kids and vagrants!" Becky exclaimed.

"No, antique dealers, dear," Tara said drily, and went to stand at the foot of the stairs, looking up. "The panelling and banisters alone must have been worth a bit."

We took a look around the ground floor rooms. It wasn't mentioned aloud, but no-one felt like going upstairs. What had promised to be an adventure back at the flat now felt as if we were examining a vandalised family mausoleum. All that was missing were the blackened bones kicked carelessly around the floor so that whoever had come for profit could get at the mahogany coffins. I wanted to go home. This wasn't fun at all. We were a sensitive lot; we all *cared* about poor old

Lamp House.

"Now, I wonder why no-one took this," Simon said. We were in a room at the front of the house with french windows at the far end. There was a huge, black, empty hole in the wall where a posh fireplace had once stood. It must have been beautiful at one time, perhaps a dining-room, for there was a fairly large table standing in the middle of it on what remained of a carpet. Even to me, and I know nothing about furniture, it seemed an interesting piece; carved legs, sturdily built. Hopelessly mauled, of course, and covered with the detritus of previous visitors; yellowed newspapers, remains of crisp packets and beer cans, various lumps of unrecognisable material and an undeniable dried dollop of faeces that looked uncomfortably human. Al wandered over to take a look, shining his torch up and down the room, while Tara, Dominic and I hovered near the doorway. Becky was still poking about in the hall. "Think this is worth something?" Simon asked Al.

"How should I know?" Al replied touchily. I thought, ah, he's not that impressed with boy wonder either and immediately felt justified about my slight antipathy towards Simon.

"Doesn't everyone recognise something worthwhile when they see it?" Simon continued undaunted. At that point, Becky came noisily through the door. When she saw the table, she gave a twitter of delight and danced over to it, like some disarmingly gauche heroine out of a American teenage movie. "Al, *look!*" she squealed. "It's divine. It's unique!"

"It's still here," Tara said to me, and her look was more cynical than usual in the light of the torches. Al, brightening up with his usual goofy, self-effacing humour (the life-saving trait which Tara and I were sure was responsible for him being able to put up with Becky) started cracking jokes about how it was a *crap table*. Ha, ha. From Becky's enthusiastic noises, it seemed logical to conclude the dizzy bitch wanted to take it home with her somehow. Simon, Dominic, Tara and I had unconsciously started to back towards the door.

"It's just what I want," Becky said, "and we can't afford to buy one. Those second-hand stores are such rip-offs! We could put it under the window, you know. Al. Al!"

"Beck, it's *filthy*!" Al pointed out to her. "And how could we get it out of here anyway? The only open door's stuck and everywhere else is boarded up."

"Don't be such a wimp!" Becky replied and shouted over to us, "Come on, you lot, give me a hand." Nobody moved.

"Al's right, Becky," Tara said. "And not only do we have a door problem, but the gate is padlocked too, remember? I don't fancy hauling this thing over the wall. Anyway, people would see us and I suppose it's a kind of stealing, isn't it?"

"From who?"

"Property developers?"

"It's been left here," Becky insisted. "Probably isn't worth much to a dealer or anyone, but it's just fine for me. Oh, come on, help me, *please*?" She can be charming when she wants to be. Sighing, Dominic and Simon went over, rubbing their hands. Tara and I went into the hall.

152

"She's mad," I observed. We could already hear her calling out instructions and the rattle, rustle and crash of garbage sliding to the floor.

"They won't get it out of here," Tara said. "Come on. Let's leave them to it. Let's go home."

We went back and put the coffee-pot on. Tara lay down on the best sofa and described what she'd like to do with Simon if given the opportunity. I cleared the plates from the room and put milk into mugs, deliberately refraining from comment on that score. "I wonder where they are? It's nearly half past one."

"Probably trying to explain to a policeman why they're nicking fire-wood," Tara replied. "If they got that table over the wall at all, I strongly doubt whether it's still in one piece. Must have weighed a ton. Christ, they could be at the hospital for all we know!"

"That girl is an ass-hole."

Tara sat up, grinning. "Don't be stupid. Nice young ladies like that don't have ass-holes."

"Unless you count Al."

"True, but he's more of a masochist with a self-image problem than an ass-hole!"

With such banter, we started to drink the coffee, adopting one of our favourite late night topics; what Al saw in Becky and why. At two o'clock, Becky swept triumphantly into our front room and announced, "Well, we got it."

They certainly had. It had taken the men an hour to haul the damn thing out of the house, force the back door open wide, stagger down the drive and drag the table over the wall. Luckily, it was not as heavy as it looked and in the unflattering light of our downstairs hall, did not appear to be very much of an antique at all, but a recent copy of something older. The surface was stained and scratched, all the polish gone, bits of the carving were missing and it didn't smell too sweet either. Becky seemed oblivious to its shortcomings. In the morning, she planned to have another day off from her job and start work on restoring it. After examining her haul, the rest of us retired back upstairs for a quick coffee before bed. Much to Tara's displeasure, Simon and Dominic didn't stay for long and Simon made no intimation at all about wanting to get to know Tara better. The evening ended on rather a sour note.

The next morning our landlady, Mrs Cryer, turned up. She's a decent sort; rich, old, a bit scatty, but generous. She has agents to handle the property and rent collection but likes to drop in from time to time to see how the old place is getting on and to have a chat. We gathered her family used to live here. I was in the front room, working on a new design with the door open because Tara had just popped out for some supplies, when I heard Mrs Cryer's unmistakable fluty voice come wavering up the stairs. "Tara, Jo!" She always shouts out to us when she arrives. Tara says it's a trait left over from when her people used to have servants or something. I called out a hello, but her voice came back more urgently, "Tara! Jo! Please!" I thought she'd hurt herself and came hurtling out of the flat still clutching pencil and rubber. I leaned over the banister.

"You alright, Mrs C?" I could see her wrinkly, powdered

face looking up at me all confused.

"Jo, hello darling! There's something *horrid* down here in the hall!"

"Something horrid? Hold on a min., Mrs C. I'll be right down."

The horrid something turned out to be Becky's table. I did a quick explaining job. "She's going to clean it up today, don't worry. I'll get them to move it upstairs."

"But what does she want it for and where did she get it?" Mrs Cryer was still puzzled.

"She thinks it's unusual. It came from Lamp House, the old green place down the road."

Mrs Cryer made a strange dismissive, half disgusted, half disinterested noise. "I've better tables than this in my attic," she said scornfully. "Rebecca could have had one of those if she'd asked."

"I don't think she knew she wanted one until she saw it," I said. "But if you've got any going spare, we could do with another table."

"Of course, dear. I've a lovely old piece with little lion feet. A bit marked, but you could put a runner on it."

Feeling pleased with myself, and not a little smug, I invited Mrs Cryer up for a coffee. She sat down vaguely on the rickety sofa, so I had to move her, wondering whether I ought to enquire whether her attic stock ran to sofas as well as tables.

It didn't look right, Mrs Cryer sitting there, gripping a big, thick mug in her dainty, papery hand, but we haven't any fancier crockery. She didn't appear to notice though, still holding out her little finger and asking, with a roguish, naughty-girl glint in her eye if I'd mind if she smoked. Shaking my head and even accepting one of her black, Russian, horribly vile but posy, cigarettes, I asked her about Lamp House.

"Family went under," she said in a condescending tone, nodding and winking. "They were never *people to know*, the Ruttickers. When I was a girl, the daughter, what was her name, oh, *Celia*, was always trying to *get in*, but we'd have none of it, of course."

"Why was that, Mrs C.?" I hoped that wasn't an indelicate question.

"Suspect background," she answered darkly. Tara came in then. There was a flutter of greetings, more table talk, and Mrs Cryer said, "I'm not sure if I approve of *Rutticker* furniture in my property," but from the way she said it, we knew it was a bit of a joke.

"Tell us about the scandals then," Tara said.

"Scandals, dear?"

"Well, there must be some."

"We never talk about *that* family," Mrs Cryer said firmly. "The last Rutticker left Lamp House about forty years ago."

"It's been left to decay since then?"

"I think it was rented out for a while. It's been empty for a long time though." We couldn't get much more out of her than that. She wanted to tell us about the latest antics of her neighbours, an on-going soap opera. We felt we knew them as well as she did, although we'd never met the people. Before she left she made us promise to get Becky to move the table from the hall as soon as possible. Tara went straight over and knocked on Becky's door. Somehow, she was roped into helping clean the relic up and I spent the rest of the day in glorious peace, lost in the euphoria of a creative surge.

Two weeks later, Becky and Al invited the rest of us in for a meal, to be eaten off the recently completed table and to celebrate Becky's success in restoring it. When we arrived, we found it had been pulled into the middle of the room, where it gleamed seductively beneath the light of a dozen candles. "Wow!" I said, genuinely impressed. "You've done a great job on it, Beck!"

"All thanks to my help," Tara added, breezily, and swept into the kitchen to open our bottle of wine.

"She didn't do that much!" Becky said sharply, and with a touch of venom that was most unlike her. I wondered if she and Tara had quarrelled. It happened occasionally, mainly because Tara took a sadistic pleasure in flirting with Al, knowing how it wound Becky up into a frenzied ball. Becky was an irritant and, I thought, rather stupid, but she wasn't spiteful at all. Tonight, she wore a definitely mean look. Perhaps not Tara then. Perhaps Al had done something we'd all be praying for and been unfaithful or answered her back. Miracles might happen.

So: Simon and Dom arriving and then down to the meal. Bare arms in the candlelight and soft, witty conversation drifting across the glossy surface? Hardly. For a start, Becky whinged and bickered at Al all evening and hardly spoke to Dominic and Simon, so the atmosphere wasn't exactly congenial, until everyone had drunk enough to ignore her. The meal wasn't that great either. Perhaps eaten off knees in front of Al and Becky's TV as per our usual habits, it wouldn't have tasted so boring. Perhaps we should only have eaten venison and consommé off Becky's elegant restored furniture; I don't know. Anyway, Tara, never one to mince words, pushed back her plate half-finished and said, "Not up to the usual standard, chef." Normally, Becky would come back with the nearest she could manage to a smart remark. This time, she merely glowered at her plate. Her face went bright red, but she said nothing. Tara didn't notice. She was up to her usual trick of trying to allure Simon. It seems Al had changed his mind about Simon. Now, he was almost as bad as Tara, sucking up to the insufferable jerk as if he was Apollo Incarnate. Heaven forbid, he'd even been reading some of Simon's work, which certainly put one over on Tara who hadn't been offered the privilege. "And is he a genius, Al?" she asked.

Al shrugged. "I'm not an expert." He smiled into his wine. "But I can honestly say it doesn't make me cringe."

"What more splendid praise could an artist hope for?" Simon cried, throwing arms all over the place. Tara giggled, batting her eyelashes like the rollers on a car-wash.

"Simon is going to be famous one day," Dominic told me in mock serious tone.

"Don't be such a philistine, Dom," Simon said smoothly. He

looked at me, which didn't happen very often. "This boy reads nothing but comics. Sometimes I worry about him, although I have it on good authority it's merely part of his image."

"You talk to *me* about image?!" Dom cried, but I could tell there was never any real bad blood between these two. Becky made an odd, grumbling noise and stood up to gather the plates, which were still half full of food. Seeing as nobody else was going to offer, I helped her carry the remains out to the kitchen and junked it into the bin. Even Becky's cat didn't stir itself to come and investigate. Becky looked tired so I asked her if she was OK, a perfunctory query. Personally, I'd found her moodiness rather tedious. "I'm not a cook," she said.

"Oh hell, Beck!" I exclaimed. "Don't take it to heart! Since when have you or Al been able to finish one of our efforts anyway?"

"But I wanted it to be a good evening. It all looked so nice, didn't it?"

An alcoholic, emotional surge took me over. It happens. Poor, forlorn little thing, I thought. What could be bugging her? She was normally such a *frothy* girl. "It *has* been good, you idiot!" I said and, overwhelmed by this brief wave of sympathy, not to mention several glasses of wine, I went and put my arm around her. She started to cry.

"Why, when I try so hard, do things go wrong?" she asked. I was stumped for an answer. I had no idea Becky thought that way, or that deeply come to think of it.

"Oh, come on, who's complaining?" I said, shaking her a bit. "We've had a laugh, a performance from dear Simon, and plenty of good wine. Cheer up, love, it's not that important."

"No, I don't suppose it is," she answered and wriggled away from me, slamming plates into the sink.

And that was the beginning of Rebecca Jane Olson's decline. Her personality changed so dramatically that, to begin with, we wondered whether she was putting it on. She became unapproachable, no longer dropping into our flat all the time for a gossip, and once even avoided me in the street. Tara caught her hanging about on the landing one night and

157

she almost jumped a mile when Tara asked what she was doing. There was some excuse about hearing noises on the stairs, but Tara was unconvinced. Al, on the other hand, seemed unaware of Becky's aflictions. We had to admit we'd rarely seen him so cheerful. After several sessions of deep discussion of the matter, and because Tara and I are artistic, imaginative people, it didn't take long for us to confess a mutual suspicion. Could Becky's marked change in behaviour be something to do with the imposing, shiny mass of the Rutticker table? It became quite an obsession with us really as Becky's sunny personality sank progressively deeper into an irritable moodiness. Some nights we could hear her whining at Al, and his exasperated responses. We concluded that the main problem was an increasing decline in self confidence on her part; introspections that the dizzy Becky of old wouldn't have had time for. After only a week, Tara told me she thought we should tell Al what we suspected and that he should get rid of the table. "It must be that," she said. I couldn't imagine being greeted with a favourable response coming out with such an idea however, so Tara suggested that we mention it to Simon and Dom first to see what they thought.

"Not Dominic!" I said quickly, because I cared enough about my friendship with him not to want to look stupid in his eyes. Maybe he hadn't come anywhere near declaring his raging lust for me, and OK, we'd never even touched each other, but I was growing to like him and despite his penchant for fantasy comics, he didn't strike me as an impressionable sort. On the other hand, I felt sure the poetically-inclined Simon would love our theory, even if it did sound like something out of one of Al's tacky horror books.

Tara bounded up the stairs straight away (any excuse) dragging a rather bewildered Simon back down with her to hear our suspicions. "What's all this cloak and dagger stuff?" he said. "*What* can't you tell Dominic?"

"Just listen!" Tara told him, pushing him into a chair. He brushed that glorious, gold hair off his face with a gesture that seemed almost nervous. Tara began to explain in great detail what Mrs Cryer had said but he interrupted her story-telling with, "So who's haunting the table then? This Celia person?"

To be fair, he didn't sound utterly sceptical or even that amused, but there was a light in his eyes that showed a certain amount of reserve. He was sounding us out.

"Seems likely doesn't it?" Tara replied, who'd concocted romantic theories about the socially spurned Celia Rutticker cutting her wrists over the table or something.

"Perhaps you'd better find out a little more about these people first," he said. "For all you know they might have gutted a local child on that table."

He snickered at his own joke and Tara pulled a face. "OK, don't take it seriously, but you have to agree Becky has changed dramatically for the worse and it started happening since she got that table."

"Do things like that happen in real life though?" Simon asked. Something about his posture was irritating me like mad; a certain smugness, his awful tolerance. It reminded me of a teacher I used to have. I wondered again why Tara found him so attractive. OK, he was positively beautiful, but also undeniably furtive and calculating. I took a swig of wine. Perhaps I too was being affected by the vibes in the house.

That night I dreamed of Becky, duster in hand, leaning over her beloved table and polishing and polishing. Her movements were sinuous, her face creased into a frown of despair. I woke up thinking, that table has to go, terrified things could get worse. That day, I intended to start investigating seriously. The situation had gone beyond the analytical discussion point. We had a huge order on that week, so really neither Tara nor I had the time to drop work, but I couldn't let the matter rest. I scraped a breakfast together and went to telephone Mrs Cryer. She sounded overjoyed to hear from me and began to relate a tale concerning her neighbour's teenage son. Carefully, I wheedled my way in to her monologue and asked if she'd mind popping round that day. There was a silence. Never, in the two years or so that we'd lived there, had we ever asked our landlady round before. She smelled trouble and began to fire questions at me. No, we hadn't had a fire. No, the windows were fine. I managed to calm her. "Look, Becky's not too well and I really need to talk to you," I said. She said she'd pop in around lunchtime.

I went across the hall and knocked on Becky's door but there was no answer. She must have gone to work, although she'd had a lot of time off recently. I'd tried talking to her several times, but she didn't want to know. Each time I'd asked her how she was, she'd flown off hysterically at a tangent, as if desperate to avoid talking about herself. I'd said to Al, "Becky's not looking too grand, is she?" and he'd shrugged.

"She's going through a phase," he'd said. "Tough time at work, you know? Personality clashes or something. She'll work it out. She always does." I sensed a brush-off and backed off, bowing. Why couldn't they confide in us? Wasn't that what friends were for? I was a bit put out and Tara said they obviously thought I was just being nosy.

"They know I'm not like that," I said, all wounded dignity.

"Oh, come on, everybody's like that to a degree," Tara replied.

Mrs Cryer arrived just as Tara and I were taking a break, which was good timing. We offered the usual coffee and settling down talk and I said, "Mrs C., would you tell us about the Ruttickers, please? It's very important."

She gave a little laugh. "You look so earnest, Joanna. Have they come back from the dead to sit around their table or something?" Whether that was intuition or coincidence, we'll never know.

"Mrs C, we think there's something . . . not quite right about that table. Becky's not been the same since she got it."

"So we were wondering whether there's anything we ought to know about the previous owners," Tara put in, "to help us work out what might be bugging her."

Mrs Cryer gave a little shrug. "I think it'll disappoint you, but there's not that much to tell, really. The Ruttickers were an ill-bred bunch, rather coarse, though they pretended to airs and graces. I think the parents were disappointed that they were never accepted around here. They must have moved in, hoping to become acquainted with their influential neighbours. That was how they were, you see; social climbers." She sneered delicately. "They moved out when the father bought a country estate further north. Happy as pigs in muck then, of course! I really can't see them leaving any . . . *psychic* mark on their furniture. They weren't those type of people; totally insensitive. Anyway, the table might have belonged to someone who rented the property off them after they left."

"Does the family still own it?" Tara asked.

Mrs Cryer took a sip of coffee. "As far as I know. They've let the place run down, which is sinful and probably deliberate. Ruttickers have cold business heads on their shoulders. They'd know that land would be worth a fortune for development one day and must just have been waiting until they needed the money for something else to sell it. That would be just like them!"

Tara leaned back against the sofa, sighing. "Well, it wouldn't seem as if the spirit of a despairing Celia Rutticker is haunting the table, would it?"

Mrs Cryer spluttered. "I should think not! She married very well in the north and as far as I know, now has grandchildren training to be nuclear physicists and God knows what else, and a successful dress-shop chain of her own. She's not even dead!"

"No, but her youth is," Tara said, which made me shiver.

"Do you know who lived in Lamp House after the Ruttickers, Mrs C?" I asked quickly, thinking Tara's remark might have offended her. She was no virgin girl herself after all.

"Can't remember, I'm afraid," she answered. "Nobody memorable." She frowned. "I have a feeling the son stayed on for a while." She shook her head. "No, he was a bad sort. Ended up in jail, which caused an awful stink for a while. I'll wager the old man turned purple over that!" She laughed with delight at the image.

"Aha!" Tara said, raising a finger. "So there *was* a scandal!"

I clapped my hands with pleasure. "Mrs C *do* tell!"

She shook her head with a strange smile. "No, what happened wasn't anything to cause a haunting, and it's over now. An ugly business at the time, but . . . " Another head shake, strangely regretful. " . . . times have changed girls. People look at things differently now." She came back into the present. "Now, if you want to know about who lived there after the Ruttickers, you might try Capt. Lonsdale who lives at no. 6, supposing you can get any sense out of him. I believe he's rather . . . past it, now."

Tara and I exchanged a glance. Capt. Lonsdale was a local character, completely batty, who sometimes walked the streets with his flies undone. He lived on the ground floor of his old house and rented the rest of it to students. He was a typical old-timer who liked to talk to everyone he met and tell them about the war and things. He was also a filthy old goat who stared at your tits and your arse and occasionally was brave enough to invite you for tea. Nobody ever accepted.

After Mrs Cryer had gone (we'd had to assure her it would be no help if she had a word with Becky herself), Tara paced the room, tapping her lips with a pencil and frowning. "Are we going to beard the ancient perve in his den then?" I asked.

"I still think it's something to do with the Ruttickers," Tara replied.

"Really? Why? You heard what Mrs C said."

"She's biased, Jo. Remember the social gulf. I still think poor old Celia with her less than blue blood sat at that table sometimes wondering what the hell she'd done wrong and why nobody wanted to know her. It makes sense. That's what Becky's like now. She feels totally inadequate. People don't have to be dead to leave feelings around, especially if they were strong feelings. Maybe Celia's parents tried to make her think it was her own fault she had no friends around here. Perhaps she ended up blaming herself."

"Well, it didn't appear to leave an indelible scar!" I said. "She's a successful woman now."

"We don't know her," Tara insisted. "How can we tell what she's like. I don't trust Mrs Cryer's judgement for a start. No, Celia's the answer, I can feel it."

"What about that business with the brother? Shouldn't we investigate that? I wonder what it was."

Tara wrinkled her nose, unwilling to let anything sway us away from her convictions. "Oh, it was probably some financial shenanigans. That's generally the sort of thing that offends people like Mrs C. She *did* say it was nothing that could have caused a haunting, didn't she."

It seemed plausible. "So what do we do?"

"Tell Becky of course. Make her see what's happening. She'll have to fight it."

I had to laugh. "Tell Becky? Are you serious? She'll think we're mad! She hasn't an imaginative bone in her body!"

"So what do you suggest, smart arse?"

I shrugged. "Perhaps you're right."

"Shall we tell the boys?"

"Do we have to?"

"Faint heart!" Tara sneered. "I like people thinking I'm weird!"

That evening, before Simon and Dominic came down to see us, there was a commotion across the hall. Tara and I leapt to our feet and struggled through the door at the same time. Outside, Becky was crouched against the banisters, screaming, really screaming. Her nose was bleeding. "Becky! What the fuck's happened? Becky?!" Tara's voice was high with panic. Simon and Dominic came belting down the stairs. Becky wriggled round and yelled at them. "Hate it! Hate it!"

She tried to get away from Tara, stumbling, hitting out, making for the stairs. She had no shoes on, no coat, her hair was wet with blood and tears. When the boys tried to help us calm her, restrain her, she went wild.

"Where's Al?" I cried, to no one in particular, running into Becky's flat. It was empty. He wasn't home.

Tara managed to drag Becky into our flat and the boys lingered on the landing. Their presence clearly made Becky worse. I thought she'd slipped completely. "We have to find Al," I said. "This is going too far."

"She's nuts!" Simon said.

"Yeah?" His smug voice made me so angry I couldn't think of anything to say.

"So call a doctor, Joanna. Get involved if you want to." Simon went back upstairs.

"Perhaps I should," I said. "But we still have to find Al." Dominic was hovering. I was bored with the pair of them and turned to go.

"He's upstairs," Dominic said just as I was about to shut the door on him. "Al's upstairs." I wondered what profound meaning he was trying to inject into those words, hopping around on my threshold.

"Do you know something, Dom?" I asked, not meaning to sound quite so sarcastic. Dominic closed up like a fist. He shrugged.

"I think Al's had enough of that relationship, that's all. He's had enough."

Had enough? I was dumbstruck. His girlfriend was having a complete breakdown on the stairs and poor old Al's had enough! So much for responsibility. I went to tell Tara. She would probably be up to going up and bawling the spineless cretin out. I couldn't face it. Tara had forced a glass of vodka down Becky. Neither of us was sure whether that was a good idea but we were desperate to calm her somehow. I was afraid that Al had beaten her up or something but she burbled out something about falling over. Neither Tara or I could really see Al being violent anyway. We left Becky lying limply on our sofa, weeping softly to herself and went into the kitchen for a conflab.

"That's it," Tara said vehemently, "we have to do something. I'd rather take that wretched table outside myself, chop it up and risk not having Becky speak to me again than let this crazy stuff continue."

I told her about Al. "He's a pussy-cat, Jo. We know that. He can't handle this, so we must. Let's try and talk some sense into

Becky and then we'll get Simon and Dom to help us lug that table downstairs."

Becky was sitting up on the sofa when we went back in to her; hunched up, hair hanging in strings, looking thin and pathetic. She wasn't crying anymore and had tried to rub the blood from her face. Tara sat down next to her with a circling arm. "OK, honey, tell us about it," she said in a professionally kind voice. Becky looked at her with mistrust.

"Look, we've an idea what's going on," I said. Shock wiped the misery from Becky's face for an instant.

"*Do you?*" she said, truly surprised. I was relieved to see how well she'd pulled herself together. Or appeared to have done.

"Yes," I said.

"It's the table," Tara said.

"The table?" Becky's voice was bewildered. She obviously didn't know what we were talking about.

"Yes, we've done a little research," Tara said, and told her what we knew. Becky listened with a thoughtful expression on her face, not looking at us, not interrupting at all. "So you see," Tara concluded, "we reckon some nasty vibe is hanging around that table and it's kind of *infecting* you."

"Causing delusions. . ." Becky whispered and then more urgently, "Could that happen? Delusions? Even hallucinations and things?"

"Well yes," Tara said, backing off an inch, clearly surprised by Becky's seemingly ready acceptance of our theory. "I suppose it could. What you've been experiencing recently haven't been your feelings but Celia Rutticker's . . . probably."

Becky sighed deeply. "Oh, of course, of course," she said, and the relief in her voice was heart-wrenching. "I didn't think for one moment that it might be *me*!" She looked at us desperately. "And now I know, the . . . feelings will stop?"

Tara glanced at me. "I should think so," she said. "But anyway, we're here across the hall. We'll help you."

Becky set her face in a determined expression. "I think I

165

should get rid of the table," she said. "It may seem like cowardice, but I don't care. It's going, whether we need one or not."

"Hey, you can have the one Mrs C gave us," I said, not daring to look at Tara in case she disagreed. "We didn't really need another one. Everything's fine."

Becky sighed again. "I did such a lot of work on it," she said. "And this is how it repays me. With tricks, with lies. I hate it. I want to burn it."

"Then let's do it. Probably do you good."

Becky nodded. "I have to apologise to Al," she said.

Tara went upstairs to fetch the man. It all seemed like a happy ending. I thought I'd go over to Becky's and clean up. She was perfectly OK now. She'd been given answers. In the flat, I dumped papers, Becky's sewing and a few mugs off the table and left them on the floor. The table gleamed beautifully; its surface almost like a mirror. What a shame, I thought. All that work. What a shame. Becky must have gone a little wild before she burst out onto the landing. The place was pretty well messed up, things thrown around, so I started tidying. On the fleece rug by the hearth I found Al's little strong-box, the one he kept his birth certificate, kiddy photos and exam results in. Becky must have broken it open. The rug was strewn with the black flakes of burned photographs.

Almost like a religious ritual, the table was ceremoniously carried downstairs and into the back yard. Muffled in scarves and gloves, we beat the thing to bits and then set fire to its hacked-up body. Becky and Al stood close together, but with a definite barrier between them. Becky stared into the flames and her eyes were saying, "Burn you bastard, burn!" I was feeling strangely annoyed with Dominic and reacted badly when he came over and whispered, "Why the hell are you doing this?" in my ear.

"It's symbolic, that's all!" I hissed, not prepared to explain further. Obviously, nobody else had told him. By ten o'clock it was all over, just a mess of smouldering charcoal, and we went upstairs to hit the vodka.

God, how naïve we were! What wonderland did we inhabit where ghostly emotions could live on in a piece of furniture? Some wonderland, surely, for we just accepted that it could happen. In stories, in our story, the haunted table can be burned, burned and destroyed. A tidy ending. What we'd forgotten was that lives were involved; those complex things, beyond straight lines or analysis. And lives are real.

The house was on tenterhooks for a few days, testing the water, sniffing around, but nothing happened. Quiet prevailed in the flat across the hall and all we heard at night was the whirr of Becky's sewing machine. Al still spent a lot of time upstairs though. Whenever Tara or I called in to see Simon or Dom, Al was there with them, either curled over a chess board or else tapping his feet, listening to examples of Simon's infinite collection of cacophonous jazz records. It was true he always looked more relaxed away from Becky, hanging bonelessly over Simon and Dom's furniture and flashing his wonderful, dark eyes far more than he usually dared to. We half suspected he hadn't noticed that much going on. Dominic, in fact, began to spend more time down at our place (perhaps he didn't like the jazz either), offering to help out with our orders, which both Tara and I appreciated. He was no artist, but at least he could keep our coffee mugs topped up and offer encouraging remarks. One night he told me I looked nice which pleased me immensely. I revised all the suspicions I'd had about him being gay, and wondered whether he was just shy. A couple of nights a week, Simon would come down too and the four of us would get drunk and set the world to rights until 2.00 a.m. Sometimes Becky and Al would join us and we'd all stroll off to see a movie or go to a nightclub. Becky certainly seemed like her old self but perhaps it was only me who saw the real ghost, the real phantom; Becky's smile, Becky's laugh. I realised she hadn't forgotten whatever illusions the table had shown her but, because I truly wanted it to be over, I didn't even talk about this with Tara. I just watched and, God help me, I know I waited.

One afternoon, I was in by myself toying with an idea for a new line of dinner plates and Becky came over for a chat. It was a weekend and Tara had gone shopping with the upstairs boys. We'd planned to spend the evening in with liquor and a couple of new videos. Becky prowled round our front room until I told her she was making me dizzy and to sit down. She perched on the edge of the sofa and pushed back her hair. God, she'd lost so much weight, to the point where it was past becoming. "Want a sandwich?" I asked.

She said, "OK", in a tired voice and followed me into the kitchen leaning on the sink, looking like a schoolgirl. I cut cheese and slapped margarine around, uncomfortable and edgy. Becky never used to be such a looming presence.

"What do you think Celia Rutticker used to worry about?" she blurted out. I looked and and saw she was blushing furiously.

"No, Becky," I said, "don't." But it was for my benefit, not hers.

"Tell me. You asked Mrs Cryer. You know all about it, so tell me."

I blathered on, repeating Tara's theories about social rejection, inadequacy, self-blame, etc. etc.

"So you don't think it was to do with . . . a boyfriend, or anything?"

I furiously cut bread. "How the hell can we know that, Beck? Most of it is guesses. How can we know what Celia used to think about?"

She shrugged. "Just wondered. Whether Mrs C said anything about that or not. Do you think I should get in touch with Celia Rutticker?"

"Good God, no!" I cried, excruciating visions rushing before my eyes; the result of such a suggestion. "At best she'll think you're insane, at worst, dangerous and call the police. Leave it, Beck, it's over. You must forget it."

"It's cosy for you to think that, isn't it," Becky said quietly. She took the plate of sandwiches from my hand and went into the living room again. I took the slap in the face and thought about it for a few seconds. She was right. I followed her in. "You're still bothered then?"

She nodded.

"I am. It seemed so convenient to blame it all on what you said. I'm still not right, Jo. I'm scared."

"So what's wrong?" I sat down next to her. She was nibbling on a sandwich.

"I get these crazy ideas, really crazy. Sick too. I'm not sure what's me anymore. If I'm going mad or not."

"What ideas?"

She looked at me gravely and shook her head. "No, I can't tell you that, Jo. I really can't. Not that I don't trust you. I just don't want to hear them aloud, not ever." She took another bite. "I am fighting it, and I know I can be naturally paranoid over . . . certain things, so I am fighting it." We were silent for a while. "I've been wondering whether I should get away for a day or so," she said eventually, "but I know I can't do that because the fears, the *sickness* will just feed on that, making it worse when I get back. My head will be full of the *things*. I can't leave but I don't want to stay. What can I do?"

I put on a blank face. "Have you thought of seeing your doctor?"

She gave a small, bitter laugh. "Weeks ago, Joanna dear. The magic pills he gave me have kept me quiet these past few weeks.

"I'm sorry, I . . . " I shrugged helplessly.

"I've been happy for years," she said. "That's what makes me keep on thinking it's all to do with that damn table. It has to be, otherwise . . . " She shook her head.

"What does Al think?" I asked.

"I don't tell him. He goes upstairs to drink beer and play board games and listen to music. I don't want to bother him." She avoided my eyes. "I'd better go. I'm interrupting your work."

"No, no," I said.

"I don't want to stay," she replied and walked out.

If only she'd told me what was going on in her head. She

169

didn't. She didn't tell anyone until it was too late. A week later, Becky tried to commit suicide, cutting her wrists, inexpertly, on the floor of her living room while Al was upstairs with Simon. We only found her in time because Dominic was down with Tara and me, helping us with a rush order and we ran out of milk. Becky and Al always leave their door unlocked when they're in. Perhaps she wanted someone to find her. Perhaps she'd have locked it otherwise. Tara went over to scrounge milk and we heard her yelling and rushed across the hall to a scene from a horror movie. Becky had managed to spray a hell of a lot of blood around. There were ambulances and police and noise and panic and rushing about, Al wringing his hands in the doorway, Tara blaming herself for whatever reasons and Becky saying to me in a weak voice as they patched her up before the journey to hospital, "There were no faces in the picture, but I knew, Jo. I just knew." She never came back to live in our house, never. Her mother came and I helped her pack up Becky's things. "It's best if she came home for a while," Mrs Olson said.

Post script. About a month later, Simon moved out of the upstairs flat and in with Al. We guessed Al needed the company; he'd gone white and withdrawn, understandably. After a lot of self-denial and flirting disguised as sparring, Dominic and I realised we'd fallen in love with each other somewhere along the way. All that time I'd been thinking he didn't fancy me and he thought I wasn't the kind of girl who wanted proper commitment in a relationship. We'd both been wrong. I also decided that he was far more beautiful than Simon, and one night told him so. He laughed ruefully. "Simon sends people up, you know. He's not that bad a person."

I shrugged and rolled onto the other side of the bed, wondering at the same time, why those words made me feel edgy. "I don't like him," I said, relishing being able to say that out loud at last.

"I know. You hide it well though. That's a talent you both

have."

"What do you mean?" I did not like being compared with Simon.

"Hiding what you feel. Simon comes on like a hard-hearted bastard. It's a defence mechanism."

"You don't have to defend *your friend* to me!" I said, angrily.

Dominic sneered and laughed and grossly misinterpreted my words, which as usual, I'd uttered in all innocence. "Oh, *I see*! You thought . . . " He laughed again. "Is that why you hate him so much? I suppose I'm flattered. Shows you care. I like possessiveness in my lovers." He sidled up and nuzzled me, while my brain did a few somersaults.

"Hold on, dear," I said, fending him off. "Can you just elaborate a bit on that, please."

"Simon and I have never been lovers," he said matter-of-factly. I spluttered a little. "Does it make you feel better to hear that? Will you stop hating him now? Of course, you must still feel bad about your friend, but . . . well, I heard all the other side of it, I suppose. I know it's hard, but try to understand. He *did* try to talk with her about it, you know, but it was so difficult, she was so . . . well, straight, I guess."

I sat up in bed. "Dom, what are you telling me?" There was a huge silence. He lay there, looking up at me, his mouth half open.

"You don't mean . . . Christ, Jo, don't tell me you don't know!" He slapped his head. "Jesus! What have I said?"

Well, naturally, I made him tell me the rest. He said that Al and Simon had been having an affair from virtually right when the boys had moved in upstairs. The biggest jigsaw piece ever. I felt giddy when I heard that, not just because it was such a shock to discover that Al had gay proclivities never suspected before, but because it made me realise that us, with our stupid table theories, had probably fucked up Becky's life, if not forever, then for a long time to come. Everything became all too clear; the suspicions Becky must have had, the change in behaviour, paranoid prowling of the stairs, feelings of inadequacy. She'd known, of course she'd known, but hadn't wanted to accept such a horrifying truth. She and Al had been together for nine years, for God's sake! And we, little know-all occult sleuths, we'd taught her not to trust her instincts. We'd let her lie to herself, encouraged her to, until the overwhelming wave of evidence against her safety must have swamped her. Why the hell hadn't one of us had the sense to see what was going on? The start of Becky's trouble coincided not just with acquiring the table but when Simon had arrived too. Simon the seducer. It was obvious now the way he'd taken Al over, getting him upstairs away from Becky who was quietly going mad beneath them. But we'd ignored the signs; too fond of the mysterious, I suppose. We'd just made it easier for them. If possession exists, it's surely a human manipulation. "If you'd told me about your crackpot theories, I could have enlightened you!" Dominic said in a bristly way. "I just thought you must have known. I thought Becky would have told you."

"I think she tried to," I said, "and we kept insisting it was the table! God, were we fools!"

"It's not your fault, Jo. Like I said, Simon's good at hiding things."

"And you did pretty well too," I said coldly.

"I never gossip about him. We've been friends for years. I'm sorry. What else can I say?"

Well, he said plenty, and I forgave him eventually, but it still made me feel sick about the way dear Simon must have watched Becky disintegrate. If he'd been decent, he'd have confided in Tara or something. He'd had the perfect opportunity that night we'd called him down to tell him our suspicions. How he must have laughed at us. I'm not as generous as Dominic. I think there's a pretty hard heart beating in Simon's beautifully tanned chest, whatever my lover thinks. Tara and I don't have much to do with Simon and Al now. In her most generous, philosophical moments, Tara says this is because we feel piqued because we weren't in on what was going on. Perhaps she's right. Neither she nor I ever really liked Becky that much. I wonder. Are we all cold, cruel creatures under the skin? One thing still had me foxed though, and that was how Simon had managed to seduce Al of all people. That is, until . . .

Yesterday, I met Capt. Lonsdale in the street. For whatever reason, maybe because the sun was shining and it was a beautiful day, or I was just in a good mood, I stopped to listen to him. An idea struck me. "Tell me about Lamp House," I said. "Our landlady thinks you knew the people that lived there after the Rutticker family left."

He chewed his beard and rolled his eyes a bit. "Knew, young lady? Hardly." He leaned forward. "Knew *of* of course." A roguish wink. "But *knew*, never!"

"Really?" I prompted. "Why?"

He lowered his voice to a confidential level and came so close I could smell the whisky he'd had for breakfast. "Queers, you know," he said. "That Rutticker boy. He stayed on at the house after his people went to the country. Had some kid living there with him. Perverts! The police got 'em! Bloody good job too! Locked 'em up good and fast, but there was a hell of a mess." He grabbed my arm, which had frozen, despite the warm weather. "Young lad tried to kill himself, you know. Cut his wrists or something. Rutticker was done for it. It's like attempted murder when you think about it, isn't it?"

Tara and I are amateur researchers of the supernatural. I don't think we'll bother again.

LARRY NIVEN

THE PORTRAIT OF DARYANREE THE KING

ILLUSTRATED BY DON LAWRENCE

IT WAS A good game while it lasted. Jovan left the palace that night as a hunted fugitive, ruined by the mannerless sixteen-year-old daughter of a border nobleman; but at noon he had joined His Majesty's Thirty-Eighth Birthday Celebration as one of the most powerful men in Seaclaw.

The parades and games made pleasant cover for the real business of the birthday, as two hundred local and visiting nobles gathered to meet anyone who could do them good. By sunset all was circles of private conversation; an outsider might as well go home. The guests had eaten well and drunk better. King Daryanree was monopolizing the youthful Lady Silvara, to the discomfiture of many who coveted her attention, or his.

Jovan should have been watching them. But he had made an ill-considered remark to Raskad Mil, and the princes' brass-voiced teacher had backed him against a wall to lecture him on ghosts.

Jovan was flattered but wary. Old Mil had taught literature and history to the King as well as to his sons. He was treating Jovan as an equal. That could help Jovan's own reputation . . . unless Mil caught the purported artist-magician in some egregious ignorance.

"I only said that I have never seen one," he protested.

Mil would have none of that. "After all, where do barbarous peoples bury their dead? The ancient battlefields become the graveyards, do they not? And so they remain centuries later. You, Jovan, you hail from a war-torn land. Of course you see no ghosts!"

A young man at Jovan's shoulder asked the question Jovan dared not. "Why would it matter, Raskad Mil? Battlefields—"

"Ancient wars were fought with magic as well as swords. The sites are exhausted of the *manna*, the magical force. Ghosts give no trouble on a battlefield."

"But—"

"But Seaclaw's battles were all at sea, and even that was long ago. Our folk have always buried their dead on Worm's-Head Hill, with a view of land and sea for their comfort."

DON LAWRENCE '90

They were superstitious, the Seaclaw folk. Jovan's smile slipped when peals of laughter suddenly rang through the audience hall. He'd missed something—

Conversation stopped. Lady Silvara was easily the loveliest woman in the hall; but she was young and fresh from the border, untrained in courtly ways. In the silence her voice was clear, musical. "Majesty, I would have thought that a man of your age would find interest in less strenuous pursuits!"

The King's fury showed only for an instant. Give him credit, King Daryanree had learned self-control at the negotiation tables. He said, "But unlike many a lovely young lady, Silvara, I grow no older."

And Jovan was already working his way through the crowd, not hurrying, but *moving.* He barely heard Silvara's, "Dyeing one's hair does nothing for crow's feet, Majesty—"

At the great doors Jovan nodded to the guards and passed outside. A sliver of sun still showed at the northern edge of Worm's-Head Hill. An autumn chill was setting in. While an attendant went for Jovan's cloak, another stepped into the courtyard and waved peremptorily toward the line of coaches. Nothing moved. The attendant said, "Councillor, I don't see your driver."

Jovan knew about luck. Like wine: when luck turns sour, the whole barrel is sour. "Kassily probably went for a drink. Well, it's a nice night for a walk."

"We can provide you with a coachman—"

"No, I'll just go on down to the World-Turtle and send Kassily back for the coach." Jovan waited. Death for the price of a cloak? He could not leave without it. In this cold he would seem freakish.

The man returned with Jovan's cloak, and Jovan wished them both goodnight and strolled off into the growing dark.

Now what?

In any place that knew him, the King's men could find him. The King would be wanting explanations! Jovan had known that this might come. For eight years he had postponed his departure. The King might die, some fool might steal the painting for its powers; at worst he could be clear before the King's hairline began to recede; and meanwhile his wealth accumulated in Rynildissen.

Jovan turned left toward the World-Turtle, toward the sea, toward Seaclaw's ancient hill of the dead.

He dared not go home. He had not married; he had not left hostages for the King to take. His house and lands would be confiscated, of course, and the excellent painting of Jovan himself as a decrepit octogenarian . . .

But there was money to keep him comfortable for the rest of his life if he could reach Rynildissen. He would buy passage on a ship, if he could reach the docks. Had he enough coins? Never mind; he wore rings; that was what rings were for. He would sell the silver buckles on his shoes if need be.

He passed the tavern, walking faster now. He'd painted that sign himself: the turtle whose shell was the world, afloat in a sea of stars. Real stars were emerging, and the World-Turtle was noisy and bright with candlelight. *Kassily, we've lost our professions tonight, but you at least will keep your life.*

There were no houses beyond the World-Turtle, and Jovan felt free to run. He had a good view of the castle. Something was happening there. Mounted men galloping down the torchlit drive? But horses wouldn't come here, nor would the Seaclaw folk. He was passing graves already, though nothing marked them but bare rounded earth or thicker grass: the graves of those who could not afford better.

Jovan was panting now. He passed white stones set upright, with marks chiselled into them. Higher up the stones had been hacked into rectangular shape. He could see small buildings, crypts, a miniature city of the dead lined along the crest of Worm's-Head Hill. Already he was wading through thickening mist. The night fog might help him.

Hide in a crypt? He would need shelter. A man could go hungry for a few days. It might do him good; he had fed too well, perhaps, these eight years. Water would be a problem, but this was wet country. There would be dew to collect in the morning.

The crypt he was passing was shoulder-high, built of stone with a stone door barred on the outside. The next was like it. Children's tales spoke of a time when ghosts were deadly dangerous . . . but an outside bar meant that he could get in.

A miniature castle loomed to his right: the royal crypt, centuries old, with (reputedly) plenty of room left for future generations. No guard would enter there. Jovan circled, making for the great stone door that faced the harbour. The fog was thick, waist-high; it rippled as he moved.

Clothes would be a problem when he reached the harbour. He could hardly walk the docks dressed for a ball! But his cloak would hide him long enough . . . and Jovan had begun to think past the next hour of life. That was all to the good.

He slowed to a walk, and a grin began to form as he pictured King Daryanree dancing with fury. None would dare go near; how would they get their orders? Would the Guard even know what they were hunting?

Just before the door, the fog rose up and faced him.

Elsewhere the mist was rising to take other shapes, but Jovan didn't turn his head. This before him was enough: a burly man with a ravaged, eyeless face, six inches broader of shoulder than Jovan and a head taller, wearing the crown of Seaclaw. He leaned on the haft of a two-handed war-axe. The skin of the right arm flapped loose; it had flayed away nearly to the shoulder. The left hand looked soft, with every bone broken. Loops of . . . what might have been sausage hung below his torso-armour.

The ghost spoke in a voice that seemed to come from miles away. "I know you. Samal! Usurper! I would kill you slowly, but to what point? Time enough to torment you in the ages *after* you're dead," it shrieked, and the war-axe moved with supernatural speed.

Somehow, Jovan hadn't thought of moving.

The axe swung down, split him from crown to crotch and drove deep into the dirt. Jovan felt no sensation at all. The old King stared, aghast. He swung from the side, a blow that would have severed Jovan at the waist. Then he howled and hurled the axe away.

The axe was a wisp of mist. The King, turning toward the crypt, lost shape and became a whorl in the waist-high fog. And a voice behind Jovan said, "He's mad, of course."

"Is he?" Jovan turned.

Ghosts formed an arc around him. They watched him solemnly, like the audience that often formed to watch him paint. Some were only an unevenness in the mist layer, mere suggestions of human shape. Others showed detail: men and women ravaged by disease or age; the heads of children just showing above the mist; a burly man who hung back from the crowd, whose rope-burned neck hung askew and whose fingertips dripped big droplets of fog.

The nearest had the shape of a lean old man with pointed nose and chin, bald scalp, a fringe of long hair blurred at the ends: a very clear, precise image. That apparition said, "Zale the Tenth was tortured to death. He lasted ten days. It would have driven anyone mad."

Jovan got his own throat working, largely to see if he could do it. Could he get the ghosts talking? "I take it you got off easier."

"I think not. The plague is an easier death, but it took my family. Will you be here long?"

"A few days."

"Good. We'd like the company, and we won't harm you. Can't."

"The *manna* level's worn too low." Jovan sighed, perhaps in relief; he wasn't sure himself. "Over most of the world ghosts have no power at all. You're the first I've ever seen."

A child's voice asked, "Are you a magician? You talk like one."

"I am," Jovan said.

The old man's ghost drifted toward him. Jovan held himself from flinching at its immaterial touch. The ghost reached into Jovan's chest. Jovan thought he felt cold fingers wrapped around his heart. The ghost grinned (the teeth were missing all down the right side, and scarce on the left) and said,

"You're not."

"Why not?"

"A magician keeps some of the magic that passes through him. A touch of *manna* makes a ghost stronger. You don't have any. We all know about *manna* here, but how did you find out?"

Jovan sat down on a headstone. "The old woman who taught me to paint, *she* was a magician. She'd given it up long before I met her, when all the spells gradually stopped working. But Laneerda made her magic by painting. You know, paint a successful hunt, put hairs of the animal and the hunter in the paint. Or paint your own army winning a battle—"

A distant scream caused Jovan to jump. The scream of a horse? Two horses in chorus, down at the foot of the hill.

The spectre didn't appear to have noticed. "Hunters still did that when I was a young man," it said. "So you're a painter. Why did you say you were a magician?"

Jovan wore a guilty grin. "Well, the King thinks so."

"So?"

"Maybe he doesn't by now. But he did, for eight years. I came to Seaclaw just four days ahead of the King's thirtieth birthday. I got into the celebration at the palace by painting my landlady's daughter and bringing it as a present.

"King Daryanree wanted a few words with me. He wanted to meet the girl. She wasn't as pretty as I painted her. But I mentioned my teacher Laneerda, and Daryanree knew the name. Legend has her a lot more powerful than she ever was! We talked some more, and I saw how much Daryanree hated the idea of getting old. So I told him I could keep it from happening."

"That sounds dangerous," the ghost pointed out. "Not to mention dishonest."

"But they did it that way! Paint a portrait, put hair and fingernail clippings and blood and urine from the subject in the paint. Do it right, the painting grows old instead of the subject. Of course you have to guard the painting, because if that gets hurt . . . but the better the painting is, the better the spell works. It's not my fault if the magic isn't good any more. *I'm* good."

"Why didn't you just take the money and run?"

It was strange to be talking to a ring of ghosts as if they were any normal audience. Strange, and oddly pleasant, to finally speak his secret where it could not harm him. "Daryanree isn't a complete fool. He offered me a house and an annual fee. I couldn't see any way to turn that down without making him suspicious, and it was good money. So I told him it was just as well, because the painting would have to be tended – even Daryanree knows that *manna* fades with time – and when I told him about the old spell I added some details.

"I painted him naked, and I made him shave so more of his face would show in the painting, otherwise he'd get old under the whiskers. He wouldn't shave his head. He did agree to keep his face shaved for the rest of his life. It started a court fashion. I made him up a fluid to rinse his hair every few days, to maintain an affinity with the paint – "

"He'll still get old," the ghost protested. "Only the dead don't get old."

183

"Well, but I had him washing his hair in berry juice that turns dark, and there's no gray in his beard because he shaves it off, and maybe he's getting wrinkled, but who's going to tell him? Nobody says that to the King! As for the painting, I insisted on absolute privacy while I renewed the spells. Trust me, the King's painting did grow older!

"I did some good, too. Daryanree was due to execute a bunch of farmers for not paying their taxes. The hands in the painting showed bloody. I told the King, made him come see. He freed the farmers. When he was ready to declare war on Rynildissen, the painting sprouted a dripping red line across the neck, and his crown and robes turned transparent. That took days. I had to paint it in my house and smuggle it in. But the King signed a peace treaty, and he made me a Councillor.

"Then this afternoon the King made an advance to the wrong girl. Right about now he's staring into a mirror and wondering how he could have been so gullible."

"And you came here."

"I thought I'd be safe. I didn't really believe in ghosts. I was sure they couldn't hurt me."

"And now?"

The murmuring around Jovan didn't sound entirely friendly. Nonetheless Jovan said, "It's still the way to bet."

"Do you believe in a finding-stone?"

"Mmm? For finding a man?" Jovan had never heard of such a thing. "Well, it would be magic, of course. It wouldn't work except in a few places . . . why?"

The elderly ghost said, "I was second in command of Zale the Tenth's forces when I was alive. A lot of us joined the usurper, and that way a lot of blood wasn't spilled, but the plague that followed . . . maybe we brought that on us too. Killing a King carried a curse, and Samal's veins carried no more than a jigger of royal blood. But the Guard had a finding-stone spelled by the wizard Clubfoot himself. The Kings of Seaclaw still have it, even if it's lost some of its power."

184

Jovan felt a numbing fear flowing through his body. "Will they dare come here?"

A voice cleared its throat and said, "I did." It was clearly human and very close.

Jovan didn't turn. A clean swing of a sword through his neck? When the luck turns sour – "Companion of dogs," Jovan whispered to the old man's ghost. "You kept me here. You made me talk. You're dead! You're not an officer any more, you didn't have to – I didn't do any real harm – " He couldn't speak further, his tongue was too thick.

Something massive moved through the ring of ghosts, and their bodies swirled and steadied as it passed. Jovan stood up to face a man of the King's Guard.

Daryanree chose his guards partly for their appearance. The man was tall; he fitted his armour well. He carried a well-polished, well-honed sword in one hand and what might have been a large volcanic-glass arrowhead in the open palm of the other.

But he was alone. No horse would walk among ghosts and

no companion had followed, and he must be half out of his mind with fear. Jovan could smell chilled fear-sweat. And Jovan cried piteously, "I can't move! They've got me, but it's not too late for you. Run!"

There was a tremor in the burly guard's voice. "These spectres are my own people, barbarian! I heard what you said. The King wants to talk to you. Will you come quietly?"

A king cannot afford to look the fool. Jovan knew too much to live.

He said, "Yes! Yes, if you can pull me loose from this." He let his eyes roll; he stretched his arms toward the guard; he writhed on the headstone, then sagged in defeat.

"Liar!" the guard roared. He moved forward as if through glue. Jovan waited to see if the guard would break.

The mist surged up, and Zale the Tenth stood before the guard. The skin of his arm flapped as he moved. Massive, flayed and blind and tormented, the old King's ghost was a horrid sight. "I know you," it cried. "Samal! Usurper!" The war-axe rose and fell.

The guard tried to riposte. The axe wafted through his sword and smashed his naked shield-arm back across his chest. The guard reeled backward and smacked against the rough stone of a crypt.

Jovan shook his head.

The guard didn't move. And the fog had clumped above him, nearly hiding him. Ghosts surrounded the man like jackals feeding. Jovan remembered other legends, of vampires –

He forced himself to move among them, through them, feeling resistance and chill. He unlaced the guard's leather torso armour and pulled it off and placed his palm on the man's chest.

"His heart's still beating. I don't understand," the artist said, and sudden claustrophobic terror took him. He could see nothing; he was embedded in ghosts.

The finding-stone was shattered in the guard's hand. The magic in it could have made Zale's axe real enough to hurt, real enough to send a man flying backward. But there was no blood, no break in the armour or the tunic beneath or, when Jovan carefully pulled the tunic off, in the skin either. Not real enough to cut, then. A bruise was forming above the sternum, but Jovan found no broken ribs.

"Bumped his head," Jovan mumbled. He found blood on the back of the man's scalp, but no splintered softness beneath. "He'll wake soon. I've got to get moving. They think the stone will find me. They won't look for me at the docks – "

"They'll look," said the old Guard officer's voice.

Jovan stripped hurriedly. The touch of the ghosts was cold, and they clustered close. He donned the guard's clothing as rapidly as he could. The boots were roomy; he tore up his own shirt to pad them. His rings he took off and put in the toes. His cloak wouldn't fit the look of the uniform. He spread it over the guard.

He strode out of the mist of ghosts. The fog ran away from him downhill, to form a pale carpet over the harbour and the sea. The lighthouse on Seaclaw Point showed above. Jovan took it as his target.

The dead general took shape, striding alongside him, clutching something. It said briskly, "They'll look. I'll follow you and point you out."

Jovan stopped. He said, "You can't leave Worm's-Head Hill. You never could before and you can't now."

"Do you believe that?"

With the magic of the finding-stone to give them life, ghosts could harm him now. When the luck turns sour . . . but luck had saved him from the Guard. Push it, then!

He snatched at the ghost's clenched fist. The bones of his hand passed with a grating sensation through other bones, and tore away two shards of black glass, two pieces of the broken finding-stone. Jovan flung them far into the dark. The ghost ran after them. Jovan ran the other way, downhill towards the light.

DAVID LANGFORD

ELLIPSES

ILLUSTRATED BY RIAN HUGHES

PRELIMINARY CONDENSATION of statements for publication assessment. Text marks indicate omission of irrelevant, impertinent or classified material. Not for outside circulation.

1. John C. Cormill

Naturally I object to being asked, but I'm ready to avow — not admit — that I'm an atheist. I was only invited in as a sort of control, a token sceptic. As such, of course, I should have been consulted from the start and allowed to work with Elder on the experimental design. Any halfway competent [. . .] A hospital just isn't a controlled lab environment, even if it's university-linked.

Of course I doubt the claims. In spite of the alleged evidence I'm still highly dubious of the Messiter algorithm itself. Something which only one man has quote mastered unquote: what kind of reproducible process is *that*?

All right, I agree that the final incident is sort of inherently a one-off. Poor guy, we can't treat him to a big horse-laugh about repeatability now, but I reckon we still ought to be committed to aiming at some kind of objective truth. Dead fakes can do more harm than live ones. For example, look at [. . .]

I do admit that at the time it was impressive.

A million ways it could have been done. How did Messiter pull his communication tricks? I wasn't asked early enough; never had long enough to watch him in action. Professional magicians should have spied on him through concealed video camera . . . they did all that? Well, no one denies he was clever.

If you insist. For the sake of argument, I'll go along with the big names who endorsed Messiter. Remember, though, the spiritualists made fools of Crookes and Conan Doyle. I just want to mention it.

Even taking the Algorithm at face value, we're still left with the big unrepeatable of the last message. What can I say? It was impressive, incredibly impressive, at the time. I have to state that at the time it actually seemed to meet my criterion

188

pattern in your head. Sort of, you know, a huge mathematical mantra.

about information which must have an extraordinary source. Though, remember, Messiter *was* a brilliant thinker, and he *could* just conceivably have had that last bit about Fermat's theorem up his sleeve . . . I can't say anything until I see the unedited transcript I've kept asking for.

That apart, we're talking about a [. . .] computer output here. You've heard of viruses and logic bombs. All of us had the opportunity when we were keeping that endless creepy death-watch. Four days, three nights, meals and sleep. Even I had to sleep. Two minutes alone with the equipment would be enough to load something that did it all; erased itself; left no trace.

Frankly, you ought to be stopped from going public with [. . .] like this.

2. Marina Elder

I have no objection to the question and I quite see why you should ask it. I'm an agnostic. And whichever way the preconceptions tilt, I like to think I'm a trained observer too.

My role was really just the same as in all our past demonstrations of the effect. I felt very close to Dr Messiter after working with him over the years, and it was a terribly sad time for me. If the idea hadn't been his own, I'd have dismissed it as ghoulish. How could I deny him the chance of that one last experiment, though?

Of course I'll be happy to fill in the background "for the record", though you must know an open report won't be able to use most of the fine detail. In the beginning Dr Messiter was trying to refute the Sheldrake theory of morphic resonance, of which he didn't approve. So he tried to push it to the point of *reductio ad absurdum* collapse . . . you know, to extrapolate until you got some logical prediction about the real world that was so silly, the theory had to be silly too. The way he approached [. . .]

So there he was with the idea of a compulsive resonator pattern. Something which, if the morphogenetic field existed, would make waves in it. The Messiter algorithm is just a way to set up a working model of the pattern in your head. Sort of, you know, a huge mathematical mantra.

That's the "large" algorithm, the transceiver. I got my little share of reflected glory by programming the "small" pickup algorithm on a supercomputer. It only has [. . .] recursive steps instead of [. . .] for the large version, you see. You assume the morphic field can modulate the output of an indeterminate pseudo-random number generator, and [. . .]

I suppose any roomy enough human brain could take the large algorithm on board, but only Dr Messiter actually succeeded.

Yes, he gave me full credit for my part, when he was able to publish at all. He was always extraordinarily kind. I'm sure I remember it was the very last thing he sent, that little reassuring message that he *would* see me again. And vice-versa too. I remember that, but the transcript [. . .]

When Professor Steck tells you how he understood the Doctor's theories fifty times better than the Doctor ever did, you ask him about the year *he* spent trying to tackle the algorithm. The old goat. Where was I?

It's cruelly unfair, but I'm sure that's why the Nobel committee passed over Dr Messiter's work. Only he ever mastered the knack of sending data to a computer running the pickup routine. Even from that point it took 800 hours of supercomputer time for my program to decode his personal mental symbolism. All the same, the work was classified by [. . .] because they imagined computers doing morphic telepathy between themselves with zero transmission lag. Dr Messiter had already *proved* that the quantum effects [. . .]

I thought it was marvellous of him not to be so much more jaded at the end of his life. He hated Sheldrake's woolly notions and he found he'd vindicated them. Instead of an earth-shaking new scientific paradigm, he came out with what that horrible man Cormill calls a mentalist act. Who wants to transmit thought instantaneously when the receiver costs umpteen millions, you need close proximity to set up the

contact, and after separation the superlight link lasts for a
theoretical maximum of fourteen and a half minutes?

"Einstein was right," Dr Messiter used to say: "God is subtle
all right. But the old boy was wrong to add that He's not
malicious."

And then they told him about his cancer.

3. Jane Soar

I'm just a nurse – C of E if you must know, what a funny
question – and I'm sure I can't be any help. That whole
business, it really wasn't nice. Hovered over the old man like
vultures, they did. Even if it was his own idea, they shouldn't
have.

He should have had heroin, that's what. I mean, no chance
of addiction, was there, with only a day or two left? Fancy
taking pain like that, all on locals. Every hour on the hour, in
the stomach wall, and you could see it hardly helped. Wicked,
it was.

Yes, there was something about him being all wired up to
this computer, but *I* didn't see any wires. Maybe it was radio.
Stuff kept coming up in big letters, blue on yellow. Like he was
typing with his eyes shut and somehow not using his hands. I
remember this bit of poetry used to go past quite often, the last
few hours.

TESTING TESTING
JUST THE PLACE FOR A SNARK I HAVE SAID IT TWICE
THAT ALONE SHOULD ENCOURAGE THE CREW
JUST THE PLACE FOR A SNARK I HAVE SAID IT THRICE
WHAT I TELL YOU THREE TIMES IS TRUE

Of course I know it. Kids' stuff. I thought to myself, he's
wandering, but most of those observer people just looked
pleased and went on about "maintaining the link". Except the
little scraggy one – he kept hunting under the bed for wires or
something. I had to tell him off.

[. . .]

It was plain he didn't have long. You can usually make a

good guess in that sort of case. From my own experience I gave him till midnight, and the house surgeon thought that was about right. As it turned out, he went a bit faster, and so would you with that lot staring. I put him down as gone at 11.36: no pulse, no respiration. They could have pulled him back for a little while if the unit had been ready, but it was a firm NTBR on the chart.

Stands for "not to be resuscitated". Everyone knows that.

Well, I've seen some funny reactions from the friends and relatives when a patient finally goes, but nothing to beat this. I'd been told to wait half an hour before fetching the trolley. What d'you think: all that time they never even looked at him. Not once. Some last respects. Some friends.

No, they were all crowded round that computer screen, watching, watching . . . In the end I had to have a look, but it didn't make much sense. Something about a throne and a sea? It made me feel [. . .]

4. Professor Waldemar Steck   193

It is something of an insult for you to suppose that my Catholic beliefs could influence my judgement in this affair. One has a certain commitment to objective truth . . . when it can be found. Please do not trouble to apologize.

Certainly I am the person best qualified to report on the incident. Dr Messiter discussed his work with me at a level which I fear young Ms Elder could not attain. She, in any case, was distracted by her curious emotional involvement with Messiter. How do they put it: May and December?

[. . .]

Our late friend, when he spoke at all of last things, showed that blend of jaunty freethinking and muted hopefulness which sounds contradictory but is in fact rather common among scientists. Over the port he liked to venture cheap little digs about micrometer measurements of the pearly gates or making a spectrum analysis of the Real Presence. I grew bored with his reiteration of, "They *say* you can't take it with you."

Of course, a nonphysical communications link – the famous Algorithm – is precisely what he intended to take. If in fourteen and a half minutes he could come close to [. . .], he wanted the world to know.

My dear fellow, you mustn't think that real faith is so easily jarred. Since then I've developed some rather interesting speculations about informational levels; information and meta-information and the rules which govern meaningful signals. Suppose for example that in our "real" world it were not only impossible to express certain truths but actually impossible to formulate such a question as, for example, [. . .]

Malicious, no, but surely subtle. Consider the early section of the transcript which seems to impress you so disproportionately:

WHIRLING TUNNEL [. . .] IT IS AN ENDLESS TUNNEL VERY LONG AND DARK I SEEM TO BE MOVING ALONG IT [. . .] GIDDY SPEED WALLS OF SHAFT FLOWING PAST [. . .] ALL SEEMS SO REAL DEFINITELY NOT DREAMING [. . .] AND AT THE END [. . .] WHITE AT THE END [. . .] LIGHT BRIGHT LIGHT MOVING TO THE LIGHT [. . .]

In fact I can assure you that this is among the commonest of experiences at or near the point of death. Entire books have been written about it; we must not lend it an undue weight simply because in this case the information comes via an unconventional (as it were) medium. The parapsychologist Susan Blackmore has convincingly discussed the tunnel hallucination as a function of visual-cortical activity in the absence of other sensory input.

There again, we have only that one nurse's opinion as regards the actual timing which places this passage of the report at some two minutes *post mortem*. By no means do I unthinkingly reject the wilder interpretations; although I suspected that my old friend's "proofs" would always dissolve in ambiguity, I was severely shaken by the final part of what came through.

This appeared to be a species of ontological argument,

expressed in the terms of the propositional calculus. At the time it affected me profoundly; I still find it extremely hard to believe Dr Messiter capable of formulating such a proof. By then he was fourteen minutes gone. The details are blurred in my memory. It was most disquieting. I would prefer not to discuss the matter without seeing [. . .]

5. Dr Kevin Messiter (final unedited record from 6 min onward)

kk kkk;;;} [. . .]

6. Assessor's note

No defect was detected in any of the hardware. Nevertheless, the final transcript from the machine algorithm is unsatisfactory, and not easily reconciled with [. . .]. Hard facts should not dissolve in this ridiculous way. Earlier, it was clearly stated that [. . .]. Professor Steck's "cosmic censorship" analogy begs the question. If the witnesses' memories are really so absurdly hazy as to detail, can we not have access to [. . .]
   [. . .]
   [. . .]
   [. . .]

JOHN CLUTE

DEATH OF A SACRED MONSTER

ILLUSTRATED BY DAVE McKEAN

JUST PAST THE swinery, first-wife Elspeth came to a maze of roads and saw that she had gone astray. Waving her arm out of the window to warn second-wife Sahara, she brought the small convoy to a halt in a lay-by. Her brown head shivered like a rabbit's before the numbing. We must be half way to Felixstowe, she chastized herself. "Oh damn, oh damn," she said. Then she cheered slightly. "Nothing venture, nothing gain," she said to the giant male in the seat beside her.

Papa Bear's cheeks reddened and puffed. He was holding his breath in a stall of terror, because quite suddenly the world had begun to shrink, or he to grow.

In the car parked behind them, second-wife honked her musical horn.

Elspeth performed a thumbs-up gesture in the mirror, and quite soon the two vehicles managed to cross against the stream of lorries, and headed north again.

Papa Bear began to breathe, shallowly and fast.

"All's well that ends well," said first-wife Elspeth.

They were only an hour late by the time Elspeth steered her flock through the electrified gateway and across the narrow stone bridge into the property bequeathed to Papa Bear by his shrunken mother. He opened his lungs carefully, not to breathe too deeply the invisible flecks of oxygen. He got out of the front car. To stand upright against the washboard Suffolk sky was an exertion of a master's will against the terrible summer heat. Everything continued to shrink under the pounding pale pandemonium of the sun, even the surface of the planet. He gazed vexedly earthwards.

Parking her electronic Japanese car beside Elspeth's hand-bolted Rover, second-wife Sahara nearly reversed over his feet. Papa Bear gave a hollow growl from deep within his throat. One of their children gaped blankly upwards at him through the rear window, like a lab monkey awaiting the excision of its brain or sweetmeats or a limb. He leaned against the wall of the gnome cottage. Elspeth dodged past him, disappearing through the round door, but when he tried to follow her into the warren of tiny rooms he banged his head

against the black oak portal, because of the shrinking. Still, he forced his way inside. Windows rattled, dust sank about him, the sun spurred the dancing motes. He was smote.

"Sorry. Oh," said Elspeth, already at the deep sink. She exposed the side of her neck in a humbled, presenting fashion for an instant before ducking her head. She was beginning to rinse dishes for the first huge meal. Her elbows jerked. "Rub-a-dub-dub," she muttered absently.

"Fuck you, Miss Bianca," said Papa Bear, turning his great tufted body sideways to edge between her and the breakfast nookery, breathing closely and shallowly by her ear so that the fine brown hairs on the back of her lowered neck began to shiver, where the paw would settle; but he continued across the uneven tiling, which seemed to settle under the weight of his great slowly shuffling feet, and her hands, which had frozen shut, began to tremble. Then he stopped, as though his vast form were baulked by the narrow doorway into the old lean-to that Samsons, a local firm of indolent dwarf builders, had converted into an enclosed patio which was almost rainproof. Elspeth glanced upwards from the encrusted sink, furtively. Her face puckered with guilt and self-knowledge. She dropped a plate.

"Sorry! Sorry!" she mumbled, with venom.

But Papa Bear hunched his vast back and continued his progress into the patio, for he had heard nothing. First-wife Elspeth's face cleared, and, for a moment, became hurriedly sanguine, her lips pursing into the semblance of a whistle, though no sound came.

"Else?" said second-wife Sahara, from somewhere.

Elspeth looked up through the broken window over the sink with an expression of chuckling obedience and saw the much younger woman standing in open daylight with her golden tresses loosened, falling loose, et cetera. She seemed to have given up unpacking her little car.

"What is it then, mate?" said Elspeth, though she knew.

"I'm not really feeling very well," said Sahara through the window, in a tone of confiding urgency, as though imparting a scoop.

"You can tell me," said Elspeth. "Mum's the word."

"It may be my lymph glands, I think. Because of the pollen count. It's just hell. If Papa B wants me for whatever I'm taking a stroll, sort of."

"You poor thing," said Elspeth. "You go right ahead. Everything's under control here. Everything's just . . . "

But second-wife Sahara had already drifted out of sight, round the side of the vine-encrusted cottage, moving with an odd liquid pushing shrug of her youthful body, much as though she were floating on a kind of miniature barge, so Elspeth kneeled quickly to sweep up the valuable broken plate. Grief muscles pulled at the inner corners of her eyes. From outdoors there came a sudden descending descant of shrieks, like crows dying. The whites of Elspeth's eyes showed.

"Shut up, all of you," she murmured inaudibly at the invisible screaming children of her loins and second-wife's. Damien, Rain King and Jezebel. Kalahari and Bjorn.

There was a sound of car doors slamming, then horns. The elder children, like death-intoxicated samurai, continued futilely to defend their domain against the round eyes. Bristling with arrows, they would soon make their last haunted charge against the cannons of their adversaries thundering in the tattered morning, or dusk. Elspeth's face paled with the intense relish of her anticipation of severe psychological stress.

Halfway across the shrunken patio, Papa Bear noticed that the poison vine on its trellis seemed somehow to have twisted itself in his direction, so he ducked his head. He stood as still as possible, though he was continuing to swell. In the distance, a sound of insectoid screaming began to mount. It was the children fighting over *lebensraum* again. Soon, while he was in the middle of an important call, Elspeth would lurch casually through the patio quoting haikus about dead chrysanthemums out of the corner of her mouth. "Do you need them yet?" she would ask. "I mean, to run errands into Leiston

201

for Gauloises and maybe some yoghurt and maybe some aromatic soap to ease Sahara's poor dear skin?"

Through the French windows he could see into the secluded lower garden, and the rough trunk of the Lebanon cedar, and the duckpond whose waters exited under the stone bridge to become salt in three miles. A stone Narcissus gazed into the waters. Papa Bear's head began to touch the ceiling, though he had not moved. His shoulders were hunched like an orang-utan's. His round blue eyes were extremely remote. Sahara came into sight, kicking her way in silence down the velvet lawn on her expensive skateboard from Harrods, skilfully dodging the seven garden gnomes modelled after each child. He forgave her, he forgave her. He forgave himself everything. By the weeping willow she disembarked and began to disrobe in its shade, curtained and glowing like a lady in a lady shaver ad – the one she had made some months after the release of *Pa?* to selected film clubs. She hung her clothing on the Narcissus, draping it. Her breasts were whiter than lilies. He felt the burden of the umbrella of his love. She made a splashing sound, without actually splashing. Perhaps she had decided not to go into the water after all. Papa Bear envisioned that her eyes were beginning to droop, just as they had, so fatally, in the filming of *Pa?*, during the bondage sequence. She was behind the weeping willow now, out of sight, but there was no splash, she was not taking her swim. She was not drowning. Under a sun much hotter than it had ever been in the life of Papa B, she was getting a tan. The Narcissus gazed through transvestite gauzes into the unpenetrated waters. Papa B turned his eyes from the white spears of light. He could drink a gallon of milk. It might soften the crackling of his skin.

Somewhere in the sunlight, almost higher than a human ear could catch, the children were continuing to scream or speak a language. In the kitchen Elspeth was talking to herself of what was past, or passing, or to come. Where the ceiling had descended upon it, Papa B's hair was damp. If the room continued to shrink like this, he would soon have to get

202

entirely out of doors. Suddenly the vine wrapped itself around his neck. The trellis shuddered.

Slender brown legs dangled down.

"Bjorn?" said Papa Bear, lifting his great arm to free himself of the vine. There was a shrill giggling sound from the heart of the morose green tangle.

"Get down out of there and piss off," said Papa Bear.

Like a spider monkey, second-wife's younger child scrambled head-first down the trellis and skittered into the kitchen, chattering softly in pig-Latin or some other tongue.

"Elspeth," said Papa Bear loudly.

He did not move, for fear of the pain.

"Sorry? Yes darling?" said Elspeth in a high thin suppliant voice that affected a bear's ear as strangely penetrating. She stopped at the entrance to the patio. Any significance within Papa Bear's pale blue eyes remained hidden from first-wife, like eyots in a deep marsh far from the fields of home.

"Milk," said Papa B, "get me milk. It feels like the Sahara desert."

"Oh no, darling," said Elspeth, "she's just gone down to the pond to slumber. She'll be back soon to eat lots."

"Piss off," said Papa Bear. "And keep them at bay."

"Kalahari and Bjorn?"

"All of them, Miss Bianca. Tell them to go play martyrs behind a distant hedge."

"Ah so."

"But not too far. As soon as Sydney gets here I'm electrifying the fence."

Papa Bear glanced at the telephone by the minuscule *chaise longue*, and Elspeth trotted around him to retrieve it. Her delicate hands touched his, for an instant, before she fled. He began to punch numbers. He told the New York agent his precise location, in case there was any movement at all, on any front. The London solicitor gave him an update on the Hong Kong suit. The Swiss backer reiterated with slithery glottals the substance of his objections to the casting of Sahara as Princess Casamassima in a projected film about the tortured life of Henry James. "Then the film will not be made," said Papa Bear. "Not with me." The conversation ended.

From the doorway his son watched P Bear's stomach rise like Piedmont, fall like the adventure of the Hidden Valley. Papa rang his best friend, his dwarf roadie, his old mate, and said, "I feel like an embolism. Postprandial, like Saturn. Yes of course I'm in Suffolk, pay attention. No, they haven't all arrived yet. I don't know where Sydney is. Sahara is fine, considering."

The phone rang.

"Allo allo?" said Papa Bear.

"Puffy!" came a voice like mosquitoes caught inside an ear.

Tears started to his cold eyes.

"Teensie," he said. "Where are you?"

"Where are you!" screamed Teensie, quite clearly, given her difficulties with motor coordination.

"I'm here, little Teensie," said Papa Bear, softly and gently, with pathos.

"Puffy Bear is here!" screamed Teensie.

Bjorn stared savagely at his father's trembling mouth.

"Jimmy crack corn, and I don't care, Jimmy crack corn, and I don't care, Jimmy crack corn, and I don't care, my master's gone away," crooned Papa Bear.

Third-wife Sydney came onto the phone. There was a crash, and the sound of a child ululating. The sound grew. Teensie was perfectly all right, Sydney told. She had only fallen a short distance to the floor. Sydney only had this to say, that they were all leaving soon,and would arrive at dusk, or some time. Was the guest house aired, or should she speak to Elspeth, or was Elspeth only speaking to herself today? Was Sahara really very well? Had she managed to take her swim yet? Elspeth should know, and P Bear should know, that she was bringing along a new therapist for Teensie, and the double bed would do fine. A harsh boyish scream echoed down the line. Everything was perfectly all right, said third-wife. Percival was playing with matches and had discovered fire. There was no problem. Sydney cursed and hung up.

The phone rang.

She said, "Please would you hide any matches."

She hung up.

The sun descending struck sideways through the aquarium and ignited the goldfish, which soared bloating through its element, like an embolism. Papa Bear stroked the telephone with his index finger. It did not ring. He shrugged his shoulders, so far as he could still shrug, and drank the rest of the pitcher of milk. He picked the telephone up and dropped it to the floor. The telephone cord fell into a tangle around his massive leg. The house wrapped itself around him, his nostrils flared like a snake's in spring. Something like a spider monkey hid in a dark corner.

"I must have more milk," said Papa Bear. "I must get out of here."

He moved. The vine stroked his brow like a Nanny. The telephone cord pulled from the wall. Before the French windows shrank too far, he edged outdoors. He stood on the lawn, pressing into it. Suddenly he could feel himself expand. He began to fill the available world. It was as though he had shed a skin. He took some steps but his feet sank into the velvet lawn. Very slowly, like a sphinx relapsing into sloth after attempting to claw the sun from its rails in heaven, Papa Bear sank downwards, and lay prone upon the closely mown grass, under the shade of the Lebanon cedar. Small tremblings scampered across his body. His voluminous clothes were beginning to split. Bjorn stood by his head with a great jug of fresh milk; through his feet he could feel his begetter breathing, very slowly. Draped in sheets, Damien and Rain King and Jezebel, the wizened street-wise offspring of the first marriage, slunk around the side of the shrunken cottage, dodging the gnomes. They had been rummaging through the guest house, where the extra sheets were stored. Kalahari followed, moaning very softly. She was naked. In the shock of seeing her immense father in the shade of the Lebanon cedar, Jezebel sideswiped a musical gnome in the shape of the eldest child; they toppled together slowly to the soft grass, and the deck within the gnome began to turn.

"Damien," boomed Papa Bear.

The gnome began to sing "Some Day My Prince Will Come." Its lips, which were not synchronized, made a soft clapping sound.

"Pull off my sandals, Damien."

The first-born crouched down obediently and loosened the remnants of its father's sandals, freeing the toes. The low slanting rays of the sun lit his dark face and polished it. He raised his eyes to meet his father's ice-cold stare, which seemed becalmed above the terraces of his mushroom cheeks.

"Son."

The first-born inched closer to the great full mouth.

Bjorn edged away.

"I've told you before, Damien, that you must not bully Kalahari and Bjorn." His voice rumbled like the gods leaving Alexandria. "You'll break up the set. And there are plenty of sheets for all of you to play ghosts. There are hundreds of sheets, hundreds upon hundreds. So drape Kalahari in a sheet. And check with Sahara," Papa Bear added confidingly, in a whisper that shook. "She may need something in town. She's had a long drive and she hasn't been feeling very well." He sighed then, as though sinking slowly into a slumber.

But with each breath Papa Bear took, he grew.

"Dinner soon," cried Elspeth from the broken window over the sink.

"You heard your mother's ultimatum," said Papa Bear. "Bring my dinner here when she has decided it is fit to eat. And water. Gallons of water. And turn off the gnome."

"Everybody happy?" cried Elspeth. "Right!"

Her head retracted.

A momentary breeze of evening caused the cedar to moan softly above the great prone father lying prone and slumbrous, in the heart of his demesne, autodidact and cornucopia. From deep within the bark of the cedar came smells of sweet incense and healing resin, mottled odours of the deepest Africa of the first days, when man first set out, into the pomegranate dawn, into the solitude of the dreamwork, returning at dusk-down with gifts of seed and gab for all the women of the flock, the horn of plenty swelling then as now, without respite. Sweetly and shrilly in the growing dusk, the cassette deck continued to produce its song as Jezebel untangled herself, with Damien's help, from the embrace of his plastic twin. In their ghost sheets the five children on site linked hands while the plastic Damien continued to serenade the much darkened sky. Eyes lustrous, Damien and Rain King and Jezebel and Kalahari and Bjorn began to move their feet in a slow machicolated *chassé*, perfectly in tune with the thunderous pulse-beat of their owner's heart, who encompassed them, he framed them with his eye. It's a wrap, murmured Papa Bear. Very slowly the eyelids of the father began to drape shut, ghost sheets wrapping the magma. Each breath, like tides, changed the shore of the world. Surely we are encompassed, on all sides, by these waters. Like delicate tiny spider monkeys pawing for trove, the children inched their way sideways between the guardian topiary ribs, and came safe and sound, hands linked, into the brachiated resinous bosom of the Narrenschiff, upon the deep. He embraced the seedlings. He tasted salt. For a spell they gazed seawards, in total safety, for the great crammed chassis granted them handholds against the unending wind. But they could not keep their feet still! Slide skip shuffle pace. Slide skip shuffle pace. They filled the ark to overflowing. Bearing its load west, the heart of the dreaming monarch began to slow, each pulse a child's archipelago of porcelain hardening against the sea, then giving. Then giving. He was beginning to split apart, he was fully ripe. A tocsin, a tocsin, we all fall down. In the world outside, the gnome fell silent. There was only the tocsin of the pulse, the shore of the world rising. His eyelids lifted. Damien and Rain King and Jezebel and Kalahari and Bjorn and Teensie and Percival and Elspeth and Sahara and Sydney gaped through the rimed and glinting wounds in his roasted skin, which were scars of love, he had given birth to them all, steerage westward. Sydney seemed to be crying. Teensie stood terribly close to her father's blistered globular eye. There was a smell of resin.

"Ah Puffy," said Sydney, kneeling by the side of the beached monarch. "Everything's perfectly all right."

"Puffy Puffy," screamed Teensie, tight golden curls plastered to her bandaged forehead. "Big Puffy!"

Ignoring the pain, Puffy Bear edged his head sideways so that he could focus on his reliable third-wife, his rhinoceros bird.

"Sydney."

"Yup."

"Is the fence on?"

"Yup."

"Give me the key."

She placed the security key in the delta of his palm.

"Next, Sydney, ring New York. Tell them I want. I want no . . ."

His gums were bleeding into his throat, he could not talk. Someone reached up and bathed his eyes, and the lids shut very slowly.

Time passed, he strengthened again.

"Sydney?"

The audience could continue.

"Yup."

"Do Samsons do demolition work?"

Sydney nodded crisply, ominously.

Elspeth put her hand between her breasts.

"Tell them I have a job for them," said Puffy Bear. "Tell them to remember Jericho."

"I'll ring from inside," said Sydney, reaching across to touch his shoulder in what might have been a caress, or a houseclean. "No sweat," she said. "We'll sort the bastards out."

The wives stood at his midriff.

"Can I help?" whispered Sahara sotto voce.

"No way."

"I'll be glad to help sort of," whispered second-wife, fixing them with her slow black eyes.

"So unpack your car," said Elspeth, and stared suddenly into the distance, past the swollen habiliments of the owner, at the last flicker of sunset. Sahara nodded complicitly.

"Sure, sure," she said, and slid backwards on her skateboard until she was out of range of the larger wives, her face glowing like Snow White's. For now the heavens were dark. Puffy Bear turned his head slowly until his cheek pressed into the grass like a melon, but lost sight of second-wife by the Narcissus, in the dense shadows under the weeping willow. I forgive you, he thought, don't try to leave. Sydney passed before his eyes, disappeared behind his head in the direction of the patio. Somewhere beyond his stranded chest, Elspeth was speaking to herself, curtly, in iambic pentameters. Wisps of steam floated upwards from runnels of his body. Just this side of the weeping willow he could see the seven children. They were sitting at the picnic table. They were chattering. It sounded like pig-Latin. He could not understand a thing. There was treachery afoot. He had given life to them all, but they fled his cover. Now and then they glanced his way, flickeringly, their tiny eyeballs glittering like fireflies. Only Bjorn continued to stare unblinking at him, with absorption, rigidly, like a flayed bat. Your father is dying of thirst, thought Puffy Bear, but could not move his lips to cry out for a replenishing drink of cold water from the well, or to command his progeny to stay, the women scuttling hither and yon to stay. The air of night pressed down like desert sand, and he fell asleep.

After some time his mouth cracked open, and he screamed like a great tropical bird caught in the jaws of a leopard, and awoke with a mucusy snort. The children stared at their sire, then turned their eyes to other things. There was no telephone beside his body in the darkness of the night, no way he could ring his faithful old mate, his roadie, his spare wheel, and tell him of the terrible dream he had been having here in the heart of his dominion, in solitude, in great solitude, in the desert chill of the evening.

What happened in your dream, Mr Bear?

I'll tell you, Mr Roadie. It was the monkeys. It was what they did, or rather what they did not do, as I bore them safely within me through the world.

And what was that, Mr Bear?

They did not fast, Mr Roadie.

Of the wives, Elspeth alone remained at his side.

"I had a nap," he growled. It was the evening of their days. His eyes filmed over. He spoke gently so she would not take fright and hobble off for good. He spoke more in sorrow. He said, "I have decided about the cottage. It will be demolished."

Down there on the grass, she and her children wore their tortoise looks.

"It's your property," said Elspeth.

Sydney stood suddenly behind her. The therapist stood behind Sydney.

"Phone's out of order," she said. "I'll send a message into town. Where's the key so I can turn off the fence?"

"Swallowed it," said Puffy Bear.

Backing away, the therapist fell over the owner's foot. Blood spurted from a new seam. But life continued. Puffy Bear's eyes finally sealed shut again. The summer night passed. No, he thought in anguish as the dawn began to burn, no no no. The sun cast lances of phosphorescent flame through the sunken boughs of the Lebanon cedar and he closed his blemished eyes again. He awoke into the caldera of noon. Sahara slipped like a shadow past his left flank, on her way once again to the pond. Don't leave, he tried to say, but could not part his lips. There was a sound of flea-shrieks, the children were playing hide-and-seek with the seven gnomes. Elspeth and Sydney bathed the lower parts of his body in water, but his body steamed with blood. Something seemed to split down the middle. He grew.

By the pond, suddenly, there was a cloud of smoke.

Third-wife ran around his head with her therapist in the direction of the boathouse, which seemed to be smouldering.

Puffy Bear attempted to raise his great right arm to fend off the sun. The skin on his arm had splintered into a chessboard of tiny rafts. They were leaving him, Alexandria burning.

"Percival!" Sydney shouted, "Percival!"

She was holding her son, who was only slightly burned.

He had discovered fire.

Then Sydney said "What?" and she said "Show me. Show me."

Then they crouched down by the weeping willow, and gazed into the water, and Sydney cried out very loudly:

"Sahara!"

The dwarf therapist zigzagged back past Puffy Bear.

"What?" mouthed the director, his lips cracking open like a knot splitting in the fireplace.

Almost quicker than the eye could catch, Elspeth mooched past him toward the pond. Her head doddered. He was splitting open. He had been abandoned. He was breached.

Finally his mouth worked well enough for sounds.

"Sahara?" bellowed Puffy Bear in a voice that rattled the wives and children like jumping beans in verminous Mexico. He had become oblivious to the intensity of his pain, he rolled over onto his side to see more clearly. The wives and children were doing the *cucaracha*. They were buzzing.

His elbow ploughed into the turf, rocking the cedar.

The therapist skipped past his arm with a hoe, and began to poke the water. There was something under the water.

Clutching the bole of the Lebanon cedar, Puffy Bear hoisted himself to his knees. Blood and water streamed down his flanks. Within, bones began to pop. Straining himself to the uttermost, he clambered finally upright, embracing the cedar like an orang-utan flensing a shrub, for by now he was taller than the cottage. His shadow fell over the wives and children, as in the old days.

A child danced batlike by the edge of the waters of his kingdom. Its mouth was open. Through the rippling surface of the pond, something was visible that had the texture of a Plantar's wart.

They all seemed to be trying to free it.

They stumbled and whinnied.

A skateboard shot to the surface, articles of clothing scummed the waters. Draped in the remnants of Sahara's clothing, the Narcissus broke the surface of the water with a plop.

Puffy Bear gasped.

Sahara, he tried to say, but his mouth had dried out. His heart dropped like a stone through the relics of the chassis of the man, and broke. His eyes sealed shut, and he was blind for good. He began to fall back into his element, and the wives and children scuttled, to and fro, like spiders, dodging the fall.

"It was only a joke," whispered Bjorn.

Puffy Bear fell onto the Earth, shaking it, and into the pond, hurling apart the waters and half-drowning Sahara, who had paddled almost all the way to the bridge. From high in the air, it might have seemed like the death of a giant carved in chalk. For some time, like a shell abandoned by its tortoise, one eye remained visible.

The children were scattered to the ends of the Earth.

MARY GENTLE

BLACK MOTLEY

ILLUSTRATED BY CHARLES VESS

A HAND RAPPED the rickety dressing-room door.

"Ashar! *Two minutes!*"

In no apparent haste, Ashar-hakku-ezrian leaned forward to the mirror and applied greasepaint. The flyspotted silver reflected his dusty yellow hair, guileless blue eyes, and a baby-fat face marked with kohl-lines that it wouldn't acquire in reality for ten years or more. He preened a wispy almost-beard.

"*Ashar!*"

He straightened, easing the sash around the middle of his black robe to conceal his plump waist, and twisted himself to check right profile, left profile . . . His thin tail coiled about his ankles. Its plush fur dappled brown and a darker blond than his hair. As he pulled on his gloves, he flicked dust from his hem with the whisk-end of it.

"I'm here."

He pushed past the tumbling act, trotting through the dark and cluttered backstage area, and halted in the wings as the compère's voice rang out:

"And now, ladies and gentlemen! All the way from the world's end, and brought here at great expense – for your delectation and delight: the Katayan with the marvellous mind, the master of prose and genius of rhyme – *Ashar-hakku-ezrian!*"

Saturday night, all the week for a reputation to build . . . In the dazzling space beyond the naphtha footlights, applause roared.

"Good introduction," the small female engineer-conjuror remarked, waiting in the wings beside him.

"It ought to be. I composed it." Ashar flashed her a grin, tightened his sash, and walked out onto the music-hall stage. Applause hollowed the high spaces of the auditorium; the stalls crammed full of workers in worn doublets and patched knee-breeches.

"Ladies and gentlemen, you see me *honoured* to appear before you!" He swept a deep bow. Beyond the row of naphtha footlights, bottles and pewter cutlery shone. Smoke-

haloed and dazzled, easily five hundred men and women stared up at him; those there from earlier in the week banging their fists enthusiastically on the scarred tables.

"This evening my poor talents are at your disposal, entirely at *your* command – "

Close to the front of the stage, one woman wiped her mouth with her doublet-sleeve; a man bent across to whisper to a friend. Beaming, Ashar advanced downstage.

" – I will rhyme for you, I will compose for you; each monologue of mine is, as you know, *completely* extempore – no one like another, no night like the last!"

He swung his gaze up from the smoke-filled stalls to the circle. Merchant families slumming in factory-new finery; frockcoats and periwigs; one man laughing loud enough to drown him out. He fetched voice-projection from the pit of his belly:

"And to prove it, sir, to *prove* what I say, you may give me any subject and I'll begin – *any* subject that you please! Yes, you, sir! And *you*. Anyone!"

He backpedalled, hand ostentatiously to his ear. Raucous voices prompted from the stalls. Ashar crossed upstage, light glittering from the silver braid on his black robe, pointing randomly and encouragingly into the auditorium: waiting for his previously-rehearsed subjects to arise. He backed far enough to get the boxes into his line of sight – unprofitable, most evenings; and sure enough, either side of the stage, both empty.

No. One box occupied.

"Do us a monologue about the Queen!"

"Naw, make it Lord William. The bastard!"

" – one on pretty girls!"

"As you command! Wait, now." He held up both hands until silence fell, then stood straight under the spotlight. Piano accompaniment rose from the orchestra pit:

"Lord *William* treats her Majesty

Like a meeting in Hyde Park:

Harangues and preaches, talks and teaches,

Not a word of cheeks like peaches,
Shining eyes or love's bright spark.
Lord *Benjamin* with trembling lip
Speaks soft and low of legislation:
Handsomely sighs, bats his eyes,
Compliments, flatters – I can't say, lies –
And governs the whole nation!"

Under cover of the loud applause, Ashar slid a swift glance left into the Garrick Box. Naphtha flares dazzled his sight. Jewelled sword-hilts glinted in the interior of the box.

"Want one on *love*!"

"What about the pawnshop?"

"What about my missus here!"

A tall black Rat leaned up against the carved pillar at the back of the box. Some five foot ten or eleven inches tall, with a lean-muzzled face, black fur scarred with old sword-cuts; and a plume jutting from his silver headband and curving back over translucent, scarred ears. The Rat wore the plain harness of a swordfighter.

Devilment spurred him. Ashar clapped his hands together. "Lord Benjamin *again* did I hear? Yes! Yes, *and* – ?"

Other Rats crowded into the box. Not unusual to see a drunken Rat Lord sprawled there some evenings, slumming, but this . . . They wore the sleeveless blue jackets that are the livery of the Queen's Guard.

Ashar hooked his tail up over his arm, bowed to the stalls, and held up both hands for quiet.

The music-hall auditorium hushed.

"In honour of our esteemed visitors." His hand swept out grandly to indicate the box. The black Rats faded back into further shadows. He grinned. "I give you a completely new monologue, concerning our noble Lord Benjamin, minister to our Queen – "

"Gawd bless 'er!"

Ashar bowed expansively to the stalls at the interruption.

" – Lord Benjamin, together with that most delicate of sweetmeats, that most rare *candy* – "

217

"Ashar-hakku-ezrian!"

A female Rat's voice cut him off. He drew himself up, mouth opening for his usual response to hecklers; then shaded his eyes as he stared down into the stalls.

A Rat pushed between the dining-tables, her sword already drawn and in her long-fingered hand. Her white fur gleamed in the reflected footlights. Leather sword-harness crossed her silver-furred breast, and she wore a sleeveless, belted black jacket. She stood lightly on clawed hind feet, scaled tail out for balance, staring up at Ashar challengingly.

He glared back, uncharacteristically bad-tempered.

"Damn you, Varagnac, I warned you! That's what you'll get for *interrupting* me."

"I'll give you a subject for a monologue," she shouted. "A renegade King's Memory! *Take him!*"

Long-clawed feet scrabbled as the Guards leaped the low wall from the box to the stage. Steel grated from scabbard. Ashar swung round, open-handed, weaponless. A brown Rat blocked the nearest wing, sword drawn; others blocked the far side. He turned. Varagnac shoved two tables aside and grabbed for the edge of the stage.

A black Rat Guard walked tentatively out onto the exposed boards towards Ashar, one slender-fingered hand up to keep the light from his eyes.

"You're under arrest!" Varagnac shouted over the growing noise. A bottle crashed past from behind her and shattered on the stage. Feet stamped. Men and women hung over the edge of the circle, screeching abuse. Those in the stalls backed away, unwilling to confront Rat Lords. A child shrieked.

Ashar halted, dead centre-stage.

"I—"

He put his fists on his hips, sucking in his plump belly, and glared at the chaotic auditorium. Noise defeated his attempt to speak. He scowled, and stamped his left heel twice on the boards.

The stage trapdoor fell open.

He plummeted through, robes flying, arms and tail

upraised; knees already bent for the mattress-landing below.

"Stop him!"

Varagnac heaved herself up onto the stage and leaped forward. One of the Rat Guard threw himself down into the gap. She stopped on the very edge and stared down into darkness.

"Have you got him?"

A chop-bone from the auditorium clipped her shoulder, smearing grease on her white fur. She straightened, speaking to the other Rats. "Keep this lot quiet. Clear the building if you have to. You down there! *Well?*"

From the open darkness of the trapdoor, the black Rat's voice drifted up.

"Nothing, ma'am. There's nobody down here."

The woman sprawled back in her chair at the crate serving for a desk, one booted heel up on the heaped cash-books; her fingers steepled. Dawn air nipped her chin and nose. Through the open warehouse doors the river-air gusted in, loud with the shouts of dockworkers unloading clipper ships.

She tucked her hands up into the armpits of the black redingote, slightly too large, that swathed her.

"Have you found him yet, master Athanasius?"

Her husky voice sounded over the efforts of men wheeling trollies, women shifting crates; shouts and grunts; all the bustle of the warehouse being stacked full. Athanasius Godwin spared a glance at the high brick interior, the stacked wooden shelves, and bit back his resentment at being summoned.

"I regret to say – not yet. Madam."

"I've heard *not yet* until I'm very tired of it. For the best part of ten days."

Jocelyn de Flores sat up. Grey streaked her shining black hair, that curled to her collar; and she looked up with a confident and capable smile.

"Now walk with me, sir, and I'll explain something to you, and *you* can explain it to the Academy of Memory."

Athanasius Godwin pulled his cloak more tightly around his thin shoulders. The damp morning spiked rheumatic pains in his hip. Leaning on his silver-headed cane, he followed the woman through the crowded warehouse – she calling directions to left and right, not pausing in her stride – and came up with her out on the quayside. She stepped back against the warehouse wall, out of the way of a carter and his team. A Percheron huffed warm, equine breath.

"Madam, I also was a King's Memory, before I retired to teach. I remember what you said at our last meeting. *'There is a contract at stake here, master Athanasius. The way that the world is going, you may wake up one fine morning, and find yourselves more* Merchant's *Memories than King's Memories. Remember it. Though I mean no disrespect to our Queen, God rest them.'* The Academy of Memory is not unaware of that."

She nodded at his word-for-word recollection.

"Perfect as ever, master Athanasius. I believe you don't have to tell me you're good. We wouldn't use the Academy of Memory if it failed us, too much – " Her bare hand swept out, taking in the dock, the forests of sail-hung masts, and the tarpaulin-shrouded cargoes. "Too much depends on it."

"You have no choice about using us. We are all there is."

"I would to God I was allowed to write down words, as I'm licensed to set down figures in my account-books! But the world isn't made as I like it."

"Written words have too much power."

The early sun brought out crow's-feet around her eyes. Light gilded her sallow skin. Her shadow, and the masts' shadows, fell all toward the west. She thumbed a silver watch from her waistcoat pocket, flicked it open with a fingernail.

"I can't spare you much time. I'll be square with you. You King's Memories set yourselves up to be the records of the country. You set yourselves up as trained and perfect memories, to hear all agreements and contracts and recall them at demand. Now, when one of your people goes renegade, and runs off, and takes with him the only proof of *my* contract – "

A call interrupted: "Madam de Flores!"

Opalescent light shifted on the river, the east all one lemon-brilliant blaze. Athanasius Godwin narrowed his eyes and squinted. A fat black Rat strode along the quay, cloak flying. Dockworkers got out of his way without his noticing.

"Ah. The *nouveau* poor." The woman gave a slight smile, partly self-satisfaction, partly contempt. "You've met my business partner, haven't you. Master Athanasius Godwin, of the Academy of Memory. Messire Sebastien."

"I know you." The Rat nodded absently at the old man, plucking darned silk gloves from dark-fingered hands. His embroidered cloak hung from broad furred shoulders, swirling about his clawed hind feet and his scaled tail that shifted from side to side. Lace clustered at the throat and wrists of his brocade jacket. A silver headband looped over one ear, under the other; and carried in its clip a dyed-scarlet ostrich plume.

"The 'Change is busy this morning."

"Have you seen the Queen?"

Sebastien shrugged. "With what in view? The Queen is as displeased as we are."

He tucked his gloves under his sword-belt. A swept-hilted rapier dangled at his left haunch, and a matching dagger at the other. Plain, cheap weapons. The sword's velvet-covered scabbard had once had gems set into it, now the metal clasps stood levered open and empty.

"I say we should see their Majesties." De Flores folded her arms. "It's in the Queen's interest that we have this contract back in our hands immediately, before someone else finds him. Surely even you can see that!"

The Rat looked sourly at her.

"Madam partner, when they permit such as you into the audience chamber, then do you go to see the Queen. Until such time as that, permit me my own judgement as to what is wise."

He lifted a lace-wristed hand, pointing. Athanasius Godwin winced back from the accusing gesture.

"Master Athanasius, *find* this young man. Quickly. This is the height of foolishness. This Ashar-hakku-ezrian –he should never even have been acting as King's Memory to *begin* with!"

Nathaniel Marston ran up the cobbled hill from the docks. Towards the brow he stopped, breathing heavily, and leaned up against a wall, unlacing his doublet.

Indubitably, Madam de Flores, you don't know all your employees by sight, even if you claim you do!

He reversed his jacket, so that the plain hemp-coloured lining was replaced by rich blue velvet; wiped disguising dirt from his face, and rubbed a thumb over the callouses on his palm that shifting crates had given him.

But unless I miss my guess, the Academy of Memory didn't have good news for you. They haven't found Ashar-hakku-ezrian yet. And no wonder.

The sun, risen higher now, brought moisture to his fair-skinned face. He scrubbed his sleeve across his mouth. Sweat tangled stickily in his close-cropped beard.

A few men walked past, coming or going from early factory shifts; a coach with Rat Lords' heraldry on the door jolted down the hill. The city fell away in oak-and-white-plaster houses and spiked blue-tiled roofs, to the docks. Sun burned off all the spring's dawn cold. Haze clung to apple-blossom, white in gardens.

He moved off again, this time less hurriedly.

Narrow streets closed him in between barred doors and shuttered windows: a scarecrow-thin man in rich blue jacket and breeches, his hands heavy now with gold rings; and his dark red hair tangled down to his collar. Shadow slanted down. A quick turn into an alley – beyond that, he stepped from congested streets into an enclosed square.

Dust skirled across the great courtyard between sandstone walls. Thin ogee-arched windows flashed back the light. Wisteria, some eighty or ninety years old, spidered purple blossom all across the carved and decorated façade of the east wing. Students clustered on the steps leading up to the great arched entrance, talking; or ran, late for seminars.

"Nathan!"

A lead-paned window creaked open on the first floor and the Reverend Principal Cragmire leaned his elbow on the sandstone sill. The tall man beckoned. "Get yourself up here, man! I want to know what's happening."

Conscious of curious student eyes on him, Marston nodded acknowledgement, straightened his back, and strode up the steps and into the building.

This early, the corridors were full. Anglers and curbers waited to be led out for practicals in the city. A false beggar sat in a window embrasure painting on a scar. Two graduate nips and foists stood discussing the finer points of dipping pockets with a research professor.

"Excuse me." Marston eased between a doxy and a mort, answering the latter's practised smile with a pinch on her buttock; and slid thankfully through into Cragmire's room.

"Come in, Nathan, come in. You look as though you've had a busy night."

Sun gleamed on the panelled walls. He caught a wing-armed chair, pulled it up to the Principal's desk, and sank back into it with a grunt. "Damn busy. What *I'm* worried about is my teaching load. Who's taking care of that while I'm watching Ashar-hakku-ezrian?"

The tall bearded man grunted. "Sulis is taking your class in knife-fighting. Chadderton can handle the sessions on dangerous drugs and poisoning; and I've given first-level card-sharping and basic disguise to young Dermot. Ah . . . the administrative work you'll have to clear up yourself when you get back."

Nathaniel Marston grunted. "I thought as much."

"So what's happened?"

"I really *don't* know what that young man thinks he's doing. If I were Ashar-hakku-ezrian I'd stay under cover and pray to ship out of the city. *He's* making himself a career on the stage! Last night he didn't even bother to use a false name."

"He's still at the Empire?"

Marston scratched the hair at the back of his neck and chuckled.

"Not after last night! We were right – they've put Varagnac onto the boy. A misjudgement, I'd say; but then, we know Varagnac better than they do . . . "

"She found him?"

"Even she couldn't miss him. I'd have stepped in, but there wasn't any need. If Ashar-hakku-ezrian wasn't a King's Memory, I'd sign him up for us tomorrow. I'll swear he was about to spill the whole thing on-stage, Lord Benjamin and all – at any rate, Varagnac thought he was. She all but pissed herself."

Cragmire frowned. "To go renegade is one thing. I could almost understand that, with the particular contract that he's carrying in his head. But then, Nathan, wouldn't you hide, if it were you? And what does he do?"

"He goes on the stage. Under his own name." Nathan shook his head, marvelling, amused. "He's quite good. No, I do him a disservice. He's very good."

There was a pause.

"If Varagnac's people found him yesterday, then they'll find him again. Ten days ago I would have said it was to keep him alive. Now . . . Lord Benjamin may be having second thoughts."

"It may be." Marston shrugged.

"What about the commercial cartel?"

"De Flores has no idea where her missing contract is, and neither does the Academy of Memory. But they will, of course, if he goes on like this. The question is, what are we going to do about it?"

"There is the question of what the Queen . . . " Cragmire scratched at his dark beard. "I think you'd better keep a friendly eye on Ashar-hakku-ezrian. Protectively friendly. While you're doing it . . . "

He stood.

"I'll call an emergency governors' meeting of the University of Crime."

Far beneath the advancing morning, Ashar-hakku-ezrian stripped the black stage robe off over his head. His hands scraped the top of the brickwork tunnel.

"Shit!"

He disentangled himself and sucked grazed knuckles. Cobwebs trailed lace-like across his plump belly and chest. He squatted down, sorting through the heap of stolen clothing at his feet, and hooked out a pair of black knee-breeches.

Unseen outside the circle of his dim lantern, a black Rat continued to follow him softly down the disused sewer tunnel. Blue livery caught no light. She paused, translucent ears and whiskers trembling like taut wire.

One thin, strong-fingered hand went to her belt, drawing a loaded pocket-pistol. She raised it and sighted.

In the lantern-light, the Katayan knelt, ripping out part of the breeches' hind seam with a pen-knife. He sat back on bare buttocks, lifting his feet and drawing on the breeches, and reaching in to adjust himself: close-furred tail hooked out through the slit seam. The watching Rat grinned.

225

A scent bitter as ammonia stabbed her nostrils.

Copper blood in her mouth, brickwork slamming her face and body as she fell; hands that caught and made her descent soundless – all this before she could recognise the scent and taste of pain.

A man lowered the Rat's unconscious body to the tunnel floor. He tucked his lead-weighted cudgel away under his belt.

After a minute's thought, he dragged the dead-weight back into the tunnel's darkness.

Ashar-hakku-ezrian stood, belted his breeches, and shrugged into an over-large shirt. He flicked his cuffs down over his calloused fingers. The lantern cast his shadow on the wall. He turned, checking silhouettes, and combed his hair back with the whisk-end of his tail.

Whistling softly, he picked up the hurricane lamp and walked on through the disused sewer.

"Any mask put on will, after long enough, grow into the skin."

Lord Benjamin, Prime Minister and Home Secretary both, stood looking down into Whitehall. A lone carriage and pair clattered past, rattling over the cobbles. Parliament Clock struck one.

He added, "A surprisingly short time elapses before one cannot tell which is which."

The silver-furred Rat standing beside his desk grunted. Benjamin turned to face her. One of his pale hands played with the scarlet and orange cravat at his neck. His other thumb hooked into the pocket of his embroidered waistcoat, pushing back his sober black frockcoat. Where one trouser-cuff pulled up an inch, a red sock was visible.

"But this isn't to the purpose. What happened to the young man?"

Varagnac leaned one furred haunch up on the desk, reached across, and struck a match on the casing of the ornate desk-lamp. Her slender, longer-than-human fingers manipulated flame and a thin black cigar. She blew out smoke. Her scabbard scraped the side of the desk, scarring the veneer.

"You don't intimidate me. You never have." Her lean-muzzled face was sullen. "You're an outsider, and you play the fool – the Queen's fool. And you play it well. But you forget one thing. You're human. You'll always be here on sufferance."

A springy dark curl fell across Benjamin's forehead. He flicked it back. Some glance passed between himself and the female Rat, and he put his hands behind him, clasped at the back of his frock-coat, and let the smile surface.

"For now, you take my orders, Madam Varagnac."

"For now, I do, yes."

"And so – our young Katayan friend."

The Rat stubbed out her partly-smoked cigar on the polished desk. She straightened up: something close on five foot ten or eleven, all whipcord muscle: her silver fur shining.

"Do you know, he's making songs in the music-halls? If I hadn't stepped in last night, I swear he'd have put the whole contract into rhyme, and let the scum hear it!"

Impassively unimpressed, Lord Benjamin said, "And?"

The Home Secretary and the officer of the Secret Police looked at each other for a while.

"Well," Varagnac said at last, "he slipped away. We had to step in before everything was ready. My people are already paying for that one. I give it three or four days before he surfaces again. Then – "

She stopped. Benjamin schooled his features to order. In his luminous and large eyes, devilment shifted.

"Then?" he prompted, demurely.

Varagnac scowled. "Do you want him dead? It could happen, resisting arrest."

"There is the difficulty, you see, of needing to control the proof of contractual agreement, while needing *not* to have it made public . . . I think you had better take him into our private custody. I'll give you my own authorisation. But if that seems too difficult, and time is short, then it may be better if he dies."

Varagnac's lean face altered, in some way not readily decipherable. She bit at one claw nail. "If you told me the details of this contract, I could tell you if it's worth keeping him alive."

"No."

Thoughtful, the middle-aged man turned again to look down from the baroque-facaded building into Whitehall.

"Whatever I may be, madam, I'm trusted. I endeavour to continue to deserve it."

The theatre manager sorted through a cluttered desk, fidgeting among painted picture-playbills, seat-tokens, account-books, and a laddered silk stocking. Ashar-hakku-ezrian waited.

"Sixth on the bill," the plump woman offered.

"Not good enough." He stroked his wispy beard with his

thumb. "You know I'll get seats filled. I should have at least third billing."

The fairhaired woman sat back and tugged at her bodice, sweating in the afternoon heat. Her lined eyebrows dipped. "Yes, my chick, and I've heard of you from Tom Ellis down at the Empire. Half the Guard you had turning his place upside down. Oh, you'll put bums on seats all right . . . but if you do it here, you'll do it under a stage name."

Ashar, sublimely ignoring dignity, hitched up his over-large breeches. The late afternoon sun slanted in through the high garret window and into his eyes, only partly blocked by the rear of the man-high letters spelling out ALHAMBRA MUSIC HALL outside the glass.

He protested, "Who'll come to see an unknown?"

"Oh, word'll get around, my pigeon, don't you worry. I'll risk *that* for the few nights that'll make it worth it. After that, you're on your own."

Ashar-hakku-ezrian grinned. "I want more than a twentieth of the door-take. I'm *good*."

"No one's as good as you think you are, dearie."

"No one except me."

"I'll start you Thursday matineé. Don't come back here before then. In fact, if I were you, I'd keep out of sight entirely for the next three days."

At the door, her voice made him pause:

"Ambitious little bastard, aren't you?"

"Of course. What I can't understand –" Ashar-hakku-ezrian looked at the woman over his shoulder "– is why they won't all leave me alone to get *on* with it."

Athanasius Godwin walked along the colonnade, drawing his robes about him in the evening chill. The shadows of pillars fell in regular stripes across the paving. His feet scuffed the worn stone.

The feet of the man walking with him made no noise.

"He's one of you. A King's Memory. Damnation, man, what's happened to him?"

Outside the colonnade students of the Academy of Memory walked the courtyard. Most young, all with preoccupied faces and intense vision: all memorising, as Athanasius remembered doing in his youth, the *loci* of the place as a structure for meaning.

One brown-faced girl paused, placing in the palaces of her interior vision the words of a speech given by her older companion. She squinted, eyes shutting, mentally walking the memorised rooms; recalling placed images and their associated words. She repeated exactly what he had dictated.

A low mutter filled the air, other students repeating back complicated sequences of random numbers; long speeches; random snatches of conversation.

Athanasius, through shrewd and rheumy eyes, looked up at the bearded, bald man. "Master Cragmire, you have all the University at your disposal. If your sturdy beggars can't find him, being on every street-corner, nor your doxies who hear all bed-gossip, nor all your secret assassins — how am I to be expected to find one young man?"

Without detectable change of expression, Cragmire said, "I lied, he is found. Rather, we know where he is *going* to be. That may be too late. Tell me about him, master Athanasius."

"So you can predict his actions? Oh, I think not."

Irritation grated in his voice. Athanasius Godwin gripped his hands together behind him as he walked, turning his face up to what was visible above the Academy roofs of the orange western sky. Slanting sun showed up the peeling plaster on the walls; the water-stained, cracked pillar-bases. He picked words with a desperate concealed care.

"Young Ashar ... what can I say to you about him? A phenomenal memory. Very little application ... *No* application. He became Cecily Emmett's pet. Cecily — but of course, you were there when that happened. Sad."

Godwin sighed over-heavily.

"The young man was on his last warning here. His very last. Another few weeks would have seen him sent back to South Katay in disgrace. Which disgrace, to my mind, would have no effect on Ashar-hakku-ezrian whatsoever. Of all the irresponsible – *this* is characteristic, this going into hiding in the city! You wait, master Cragmire. A week or so and he'll surface, charm his way out of trouble, smile sweetly, and begin to cause trouble all over again!"

A genuine anger made him breathless. He glared at the Principal of the University of Crime.

"You sound reluctant to have him back." Cragmire shrugged. "What will happen to our young Katayan friend when you throw him out of here? Do King's Memories resign, master Athanasius?"

"We have techniques to dim the memory. Drugs."

Godwin brushed his hand against a pillar. Sunwarmed limestone was rough against the pads of his fingers.

"It is untrue, and cruel, to accuse us of turning failed students into idiots and fools. Young Ashar will lose nothing but a certain ability to concentrate."

One set of footsteps echoed back softly from the colonnade. Godwin stopped. Silence fell. He did not look at Cragmire. Above, the sky glowed blue; all the motes of the air coloured gold.

"Do you have any idea," the man's voice said, "how badly we could hurt the Academy of Memory?"

"Or vice versa?"

Aware that tears leaked from the corners of his eyes, Athanasius Godwin reached out and grabbed the man's doublet, gripping the soft leather with age-spotted fingers.

"Ashar is a stupid child. Remember that." His ability to hide desperation vanished. "Cragmire, he's not to be hurt. If you want your University of Crime to continue visible with impunity – he is a boy, he is not to be hurt in any way, he is to come back here to me where he's safe: understand that!"

Cragmire reached down and detached his grip. Athanasius Godwin stared at his own hand, flesh cramped and white; and not at the forgettable face of the other man. Breath rushed hot and hollow in his chest.

The Principal said, "If you can do anything, do it now. Your 'stupid child' is in intense danger. I think we don't even have another day."

The crowd outside the Fur & Feathers thinned now. A distant church clock struck midnight. Ashar-hakku-ezrian leaned both forearms on the bollard, and his chin on his arms, and flirted his eyebrows at the fairhaired human girl. "But *when* do you get off work? They can't keep you here all night."

She bundled her skirts back between her knees, shifting the bucket; scrubbing brush in her other hand. The wet tavern step gleamed, the slate clean now of spilled beer and vomit. "Can't they, though?"

He squatted, sliding down with his back against the metal pillar, twitching his tail out of the way of the road.

"Leave this. Come with me. I'm going to be famous." The plush-furred tail slid across the air between them, nestled gently between her caught-up hair and shabby dress, at the nape of her neck.

"Oh, Ash . . . I don't know you hardly." She rubbed the back of her wrist across her forehead. "You better get gone before the old man comes out. Get along now!"

"I'll see you back there." Ashar-hakku-ezrian nodded in the direction of the cobbled alley opposite the public house.

"Well, I don't . . ."

"Yes you do. You will. You *must*. For me." He kissed her as he stood, grinned, and loped across the road. The noise of music, and quarrelling voices quieted as he entered the alley.

A slight thud sounded.

Curious, he turned. Several other alleyways split off from the main one, none lit, all now quiet. One of his eyebrows flicked up in momentary puzzlement.

He shoved both hands in his stolen breeches pockets and walked on, tail switching from side to side; debating whether the fairhaired girl was a sure enough bet to wait for, or if the Pig & Whistle would repay a visit.

Six yards up a side alley, an unconscious brown Rat's heels

231

jolted over the pavement as Nathaniel Marston dragged him into concealment.

"Her Majesty is receiving the Katayan Ambassador," the brown Rat majordomo said. "If my Lord Benjamin would care to wait."

Benjamin inclined his head to her. "I shall always have time at Her Majesty's disposal, I hope."

He walked across the corridor to the arched window, tapping his folded gloves against his trouser leg, whistling softly under his breath. Light slanted down from above. Red, blue, gold, white: rich colours falling through a black tracery of stone.

The brown Rat appeared again, opening the antechamber's high door as a portly black Rat in lace and leather arrived. Benjamin moved smoothly forward, stepping through on the heels of the visitor with a nod to the doorkeeper, calling ahead:

"Messire Sebastien!"

The pudgy Rat turned, unlacing his cloak and dropping it for the anteroom servants to pick up. "Benjamin. I – you – that is, my duty to Her Majesty – "

Benjamin met the gaze of bead-black eyes and smiled only slightly. "How interesting to find you here, Messire Sebastien. Perhaps we arrive on the same business, hum?"

"I don't think so. I'm sure not."

"How prescient of you, messire. I don't believe that I mentioned what my own business might be . . . "

The black Rat's eyes gleamed, set deep in fat and furry cheeks. He folded his arms across his broad, velvet-doubleted chest; scaled tail sweeping the stone-flagged floor. "Now you take good notice of one thing, *boy*. When all this scheming comes out, and has to be denied by certain highly-placed people, no one of *us* is going to stand the damage of it. For that, they'll pick a man. I'll let you speculate about which man it might be."

"'Speculation' is not a word you should be using at the moment," Benjamin said.

Squat white columns held up the anteroom's groined ceiling. Two men in Court livery scuttled away with coats and cloaks. Benjamin glimpsed through the square window the finials and carved façade of the other side of the palace courtyard.

Sebastien tugged his doublet down, pulling the lace at the wrists forward over his ringless fingers. "I'll use what words I please, boy, and you'll have to show me a much better return on my investment before I stop. I don't believe you ever intended to go through with this mad scheme, it's all just to line your own pockets!"

"I think you should carefully consider what you're saying."

"We've suffered you too long, in any case; and it's the last straw to be *cheated* by – "

Benjamin raised his hand and struck the Rat a stinging blow across the face with his folded gloves.

"I will not be insulted by some down-at-heel has-been with a grudge and the brains of a mayfly! Will you complain? Do so. Do so! And the next time I see you I'll carry a horse-whip, and give you the thrashing you deserve, public scandal or not!"

The black Rat waddled back a step, long jaw dropping; made as if to speak; abruptly turned and flung out of the exit, pushing the doorkeeper aside with a furious oath.

Lord Benjamin stared, fabricated anger subsiding; sucked his skinned knuckles, and broke into a coarse laugh.

"Do you think the Prime Minister is going to fight with you in the streets like a barrow-boy! Such *stupidity*. Ah, but it has its uses. It does. I can well do without your company here today."

The further anteroom doors stood shut, great black iron hinges spiking across the oakwood. They slid at his slight touch, gliding open, and he walked through. He stood a moment while his eyes accustomed themselves to the gloom.

The great arched throne room opened up before him. Traceries of white webs snarled the walls, spindles of spider-thread curtaining off other doors and the lower, blacked-out windows. Webs dripped from the arched ceiling. One torch

233

burned low in a wall-cresset, soot staining the already black masonry.

Kneeling priests flanked the walls, each at a low mausoleum-altar. Benjamin crossed himself thoughtfully, walking past them towards the high end of the hall. The Ambassador was gone. Perpendicular windows slotted down a little light. Upon the dais at the end, where all windows had been bricked up, a great mass of stonework stood. Close up, this could be seen to be an immense baroquely-carved and decorated tomb, Latin inscriptions incised in silver below the legend SAXE-COBERG-GOTHA.

"Your Majesty!" Lord Benjamin beamed effusively. "To see you in such health is a privilege – to see your beauty, a delight given to few men in any age of the world."

Below the tomb, on the granite platform, a profusion of black silk cushions lay scattered. Small stools had been set amongst them. Nine slender black Rats lay asleep, or sat sewing, or with folded hands and melancholy eyes gazed up at the tomb. They wore black silk robes.

On a larger cushion in the centre, attended by a brown Rat page, the nine Rats' tails rested: coiled into an inextricable and fifty-years grown-together knot.

Some of the Rat-Queen looked at Lord Benjamin.

A slender Rat who sat sewing at a sampler left off, extending one long-fingered dark hand. Benjamin bowed over it, kissing the narrow silver rings.

"We welcome your presence, Lord Benjamin. We were thinking of our departed Consort, and I fear falling into a sad melancholy."

"Your Majesty might marry again. Such beauty will never lack admirers."

"We could not be unfaithful to the memory of our dear husbands, Lord Benjamin. No, we – " She bit off a thread between front incisors. A more bony and angular Rat seated at her feet raised her lean-jawed muzzle:

" – could not think of it. What news have you for us, dear Lord Benjamin?"

Benjamin pondered *Only that the world misses you who are its sunlight* and decided to leave that one for another occasion. A third Rat-Queen shifted around so that she sat facing him, this one with something of a sardonic gleam in her eyes. He bowed again, floridly.

"I should ask news of you, dear lady, you having most recently spoken to the Katayan Ambassador, or so I hear."

The third Rat-Queen frowned. "They came to protest the siting of another garrison on their north coast, even though we are only there to protect them. Really, it is – "

She reached out to the tray of tea being offered by the brown Rat page. The Rat-Queen who had resumed her sewing completed:

" – most provoking. Do not make that the subject of your visit, I pray you. Dear Lord Benjamin, we have been giving serious consideration to your suggestion for our Accession Day Festival."

"And your Majesty desires?"

"We think that we will indeed have a theatrical performance in the palace – "

235

" – by our command, this performance – "

" – because it will please the dear children," another, more bony and angular Rat-Queen, cut in. "And therefore we should have theatricals, songs, tricks, jugglers; all drawn from our great capital's theatres and places of entertainment. What – "

" – do you say to that, Lord Benjamin?"

"Admirable. Stunning! Quite the best notion I have ever heard." His large and liquid eyes shone.

"So you should say, when it was your own." The sardonic Rat-Queen smiled. "We see through you, dear Lord Benjamin. But we know – "

" – that you have our best interests at heart."

A tiny echo came back from each word, the Queen's high voices reverberating from the Gothic stonework. Further down the hall a torch guttered; and the scent of incense came from where the priests constantly prayed.

"A celebration would be much in order," he said.

"We have drawn out a list – "

" – of those performers we hear are suitable. Our noble friend the Ambassador of South Katay recommended one young person, who sounds most amusing."

He reached out to take a paper from one of the Rats laying amid the silk cushions, bowing as he did so; casting a rapid eye down the list until the name *Ashar-hakku-ezrian* leaped out at him.

"Yes, your Majesty."

He rubbed an ungloved hand across his forehead, slick with a cool sweat, and smiled.

"And something else most intriguing came from our meeting with the Ambassador." The Rat-Queen lowered her sleek muzzle over her sewing. "We hear – "

" – interesting things of this most new discovery of the lands about the East Pole. We wonder – "

This black Rat fell to grooming the fur of her arm. The bony

black Rat beside her opened onyx eyes:

" – whether we might receive ambassadors from them, as we do from South Katay. A peaceable treaty might lead to much trade, Lord Benjamin – "

" – do you not think so?" the first Rat concluded.

"Indubitably, madam. I'll be only too pleased to discover, for you, how this may be brought about." Lord Benjamin, flourishing his yellow gloves, bowed himself out of the throne room.

A horse-drawn carriage took him back to Whitehall. He sat with his chin on his breast, slumped down in the seat, no expression at all on his face. Not until he stood again in the office overlooking Whitehall did he break silence.

He picked the telephone-mouthpiece off its stand, dialling a confidential and automatically-connected number.

A click, the phone picked up and answered: "Varagnac."

He nodded once to himself, silently, said, "Kill the contract. Immediately," and put the telephone back on its rest.

"I tell you, Benjamin will sell us out!"

The fat black Rat slammed his fist down on the makeshift-crate accounts desk, his voice cutting through the noise of work in the warehouse.

"Every penny I have is tied up in this, and as for every penny I *don't* have – I'll be ruined."

Jocelyn de Flores sank her chin lower in her greatcoat collar. Slumped in the chair, so low as to be almost horizontal, she moved only her eyes to look up at Sebastien. "So?"

"So we ought to destroy all trace of our ever having been involved in this scheme. Especially the contract. Gods, woman, even a sniff of the *candy* trade and we'll end up in Newgate!"

The Rat moved from clawed hind foot to foot, rolls of fur-covered flesh shifting. He pulled out a darned lace kerchief to dab at his mouth.

"I trust our friend Benjamin as you do." Jocelyn remained still. "That's to say, not at all. Messire Sebastien, do try not to be stupid – please, listen. I think we ought to have that contract safe. Very safe. Remember, it isn't only we two that it implicates."

The black Rat began shakily to smile.

"Benjamin."

Jocelyn de Flores came to her feet in one movement, coat swirling, striding out towards the quay.

Ashar-hakku-ezrian passed the clockshop's window, paused, stepped back, and stared into the dark glass. After a moment's thought he brushed his blond hair further back behind his ears, preened his beard, and tried a left and then a right profile, gleaming his eyes at himself in the reflection with a grin.

"You could lose a little weight but you'll do."

The glass reflected plane trees behind him, planted in a triangle of earth at the junction of two streets, their leaves rustling in a spring gust. He turned away, towards the main road further down, seeing noon and horse-drawn carriages and the corner of the Alhambra, and a man shifted out of the next doorway.

The man gnawed absently at a knuckle, among gold-ringed fingers. His greasy dark-red hair and beard straggled down over the collar of his royal-blue coat.

Ashar smiled very pleasantly, side-stepping. "Good afternoon, sir."

"A word with you, master. I've got a message from your sister."

Coldness stabbed him just in the pit of the belly. Ashar shrugged.

"Which one? My father has ten wives, that gives me a number of sisters to choose from—"

"Not half-sisters, Master Ashar. Full sister. Ishnanna-hakku-ezrian."

"How do you know about her?" Ashar stopped. The spring wind blew through the thin weave of his stolen shirt. He clutched his arms across his chest. "Who are you? Have you seen her? Where is she? Is she all right? What does she say?"

"Don't listen to him," a woman's voice cut in. "All Katayans look the same to him anyway. He hasn't got any message. Have you, Nathan?"

Ashar looked away from the red-haired man. A woman walked up the cobbled road from the direction of the Alhambra, her black coat open and swinging about her calves. She stopped, hooking one thumb in her waistcoat pocket, and inclined her sleek head momentarily to him.

"Nathan?" she needled the man.

"I find your presence, madam, entirely superfluous."

"On the other hand." Grey eyes shifted, caught Ashar's gaze, and he blinked at that impact. "The University of Crime has a way of finding out most information, even that the elusive Ashar-hakku-ezrian had a sister."

Ashar made a jerky bow. "Madam de Flores."

"You remember me. For a moment I was worried about your memory — not that it isn't much on my mind in any case." She smiled mordantly.

Her remark barely irritated him. He stared at the man. A

lean, pale face; not to be read easily. Words cascaded through his mind, all of them drying up before they reached his mouth. He shook his head, shivering.

The thin sun showed up grey where it shone on de Flores' hair. She thrust her hands into her greatcoat pockets. "How old are you, young man?"

Ashar swallowed. "Sixteen. Ishnanna's – she was twelve."

"You're old enough to make judgements. I want you. I want what you have in your head, and I want it safe." Jocelyn de Flores shrugged. "I can't say the same about Marston here. He's been hanging around my warehouse for the past fortnight. One of Cragmire's men – that ought to give you some idea. Come with me now."

The man shook his head. "He goes with me."

"*Do* you know anything about Ishnanna?" Ashar shuddered. "I don't think so. I really don't want anything to do with this contract. It's boring. I don't know what you're all making a fuss about."

Uncharacteristically abrupt, he shouldered between the two of them and walked on down the street, feet knocking clumsily against the cobbles and making him stagger. The wind smelled of dust and horse-droppings. He sensed rather than heard them stride after him.

He wanted – momentarily wanted so hard that he could not breathe – the dusty rehearsal rooms of the Alhambra: the piano with one key missing, the dancer's discarded stockings, sunlight through the brick-arched windows; sweat, effort, repetition.

The two called his name behind him. He broke into a run, swinging towards the corner stage-door; dodging between two passers-by, jigging a yard left to avoid the matinée coaches pulling up at the kerb.

Movement and mass in the corner of his eye made him stumble, shy away.

Neatly, hands went under his armpits from behind.

"*Hey–!*"

Two thick-set brown Rats in blue livery bundled him

239

towards the nearest carriage's open door, his heels skidding across the cobbles, head ringing from an unfelt blow. Steps, seat, and floor scraped his hands as he thudded across the carriage's interior. Cloth muffled his head. A horsewhip cracked. The carriage jolted into immediate motion.

A red-headed man and a woman in a black coat walked moderately rapidly in opposite directions, heads bent concealingly against the cold spring wind.

The theatre manager stared down from her office window at the carriage pulling away and resignedly tore up the sticker to be stripped across that night's billboard:

SPECIAL ATTRACTION!!! WORLD-FAMOUS KATAYAN MONOLOGIST – ONE NIGHT ONLY!!!

"You're dead."

The copper taste of blood soured his mouth. Ashar rolled over, the shackles that hobbled his feet to an eighteen-inch stride clinking. Metal cut his bare ankles.

"Should I feel unwell, do you think?" he said lazily, pressing up against her haunch.

Varagnac, leaning against the bed's headboard, reached out with one sinewy arm and slid it under his, gripping his body, pulling him up closer. Ashar kneaded his hand in the sleek fur of her shoulder, feeling her muscles bunch and shift.

"Dead as far as anyone else is concerned. You're mine now."

Ashar-hakku-ezrian smiled. It cracked his split lip open again, and a thin thread of blood seeped down his chin. He wriggled his hips deeper into the tumbled bedsheets. Outside the inn window, a vixen shrieked.

"Well, boy?"

Candlelight gleamed golden on the timbers and beams of the room, on the bare floor and the bed. Shadows danced in cobwebs in the corners of the blackened ceiling. A cold draft shivered his bare spine. He pressed closer in to her warm pelt.

"Damn you, say something!"

"Rubbish. And you know it."

Livery coat, swordbelt, and featherplume lay strewn across the floor, discarded. Ashar-hakku-ezrian eased the silver-furred Rat a little over onto her side and began to manipulate and knead the tense muscles of her back. She grunted deep in her throat.

"You know something about my sister." He read the giveaway message of stress through his fingertips. "You do! I always thought so. From the very first time I came asking!"

Her arm pushed him flat. Long grey-skinned fingers traced a line down his chest, claws leaving the thinnest trail of reddened skin. It patterned across other scored lines, raised and swollen. Her bead-black eyes shone, reflecting candlelight.

"You won't keep me," he said softly. "Even now you're thinking: it was a moment's mistake, how can I get back to the city without being stopped, how can I put it right?"

He smiled. It had no malice in it. His fingers plunged into the softness of her fur: throat, chest, belly. He curled up and lay his head across her chest.

"Which is not impossible. If it finishes all this, and it means I can get on with doing what *I* want to do, then yes! I'll tell you what to do to get out of it." His breath pearled on her fur. He sensed her lean forward: sharp incisors just dinted his bare, scarred shoulder.

Ashar knotted fists in soft fur. "What just happened was fun; but why did you think you had to go to all *this* trouble?"

Varagnac sat back and laughed.

Her chest vibrated. Ashar straightened up into a sitting position, shackles chinking. The Rat, head thrown back, wheezed for breath between paroxysms of laughter; at last reaching out and putting her hands on his two shoulders and shaking him, a half-dozen times, hard.

"Damn you! Well, and what do *you* suggest, if you know so much?"

"Ishnanna-hakku-ezrian."

"Yes, I know what happened to her."

241

Toneless, no hint in the voice; no clue in the language of her lean body. Ashar sat back on his heels, his tail coiling about hers.

"Tell me that and I'll tell you . . . what the contract was." He grinned. "You were there. Well, almost there. Present, shall we say; even if you didn't know what went on – "

Her claw-nailed finger touched his lips, silencing him momentarily.

"Fast talker."

The long-fingered hand straightened, patting his cheek hard enough to redden his skin. Her lean, long body shone in the yellow light; shadows lining jaw, eye, and translucent ears.

"At least I had you." Varagnac chuckled in her throat. "For a short enough time. It may be just as well. You bid fair to be unbearable."

Ashar grinned. "And then I'll tell you how we go back."

The wind guttered the candle. Below, horses stamped in the stables. The silver-furred Rat grunted, rolled over, and retrieved her livery jacket from the floor, diving into the pocket for a thin, black cigar. She tilted the candle to light it.

"So."

"So . . . it was hot." Ashar rubbed his bare arms. "You may not remember. I, obviously, do. Two weeks ago, at the official opening of the Royal Botanical Gardens . . . "

. . . The ribbon being cut, the assembled dignitaries wandered now between tall lines of palms and ferns in the main body of the Palm House, none climbing the spiral iron staircases to the higher balconies.

Ashar stared at the thermometer in a pained manner. Spring sunlight through several thousand panes of glass added to the under-floor heating: the silver mercury line topped out at 95° Fahrenheit. Humidity quickened his breathing, put black sparkles across his vision.

"Ashar!"

He flicked his tail down to push aside a palm-frond. Wetness sprinkled his shoulders. Five or six people walked on this high railed balcony. The elderly King's Memory Cecily Emmett, at the rear of the group, beckoned furiously:

"Come here!"

He smiled as he approached. "I'm listening. You don't really need me for this, you know. I could just slip away and not be bored—"

Cecily Emmett stepped back and grabbed his arm. Her weight startled Ashar momentarily. He braced himself as the large woman's support.

"I'll be bored, then."

"You'll pay attention!"

A short, slender man in a black frock coat stood with one hand on the balcony rail, the other gesturing. Curling black hair fell across his sallow forehead. His cravat was wide, striped candy-pink and white; and his top hat sat rakishly cocked to one side. Ashar, fascinated, caught the man's eye across the intervening yards.

"Two King's Memories?" the man queried.

"Ashar-hakku-ezrian, your Lordship. My apprentice."

The man signalled acceptance with a hand in which he held sweat-stained yellow gloves. "I understand. Very well."

"That . . . " A slight wheeze hissed in Cecily's undertone. ". . . is Lord Benjamin himself. Sebastien you know. De Flores you know."

Lord Benjamin's light, penetrating voice cut through the humid air. "Forgive me if I took advantage of this official opening for us to meet. It seems secure, and opportune."

Ashar saw, over Lord Benjamin's shoulder, the hard jawline of a familiar face. Jocelyn de Flores. The fat black Rat Sebastien stood beside de Flores, talking across the trader to one well-dressed black, and two brown, Rats. Ashar leaned his elbows on the balcony.

Below, out of earshot, stood a silver-furred Rat in plain leather harness and the indefinable air of covert authority that argued security police.

The Rat lifted her head. Varagnac.

Varagnac and he stared at each other. Cecily's voice hissed in his ear:

"Listen to me, boy. You're on parole already. I want this meeting repeated back word-perfect from you; as perfect as my official record, *is that clear?*"

He beamed. Varagnac turned away.

"Of course."

A brass band played on the lawns outside the Palm House. Music came muffled through the arching glass walls. Here, the fronds of giant ferns swept down to shield the balcony from sight. Isolated by height and occasion, the group halted.

"Master Cragmire." Cecily introduced a tall, bearded man; balding, in a plain frockcoat, whose image would not stay in the memory for more than seconds. "From the University of Crime. And not an ornament to any of these discussions, Ashar, at least as far as we're concerned."

The dark-bearded man laughed. 'I'm not prolix. A little verbose, perhaps. Veritably, that's the worse criminal infringement you can accuse me of, Cecily."

"Will you *listen* to him." Amused, the fat woman shook her head.

Ashar stared between his booted feet, through the open ironwork floor of the balcony, looking directly down on water and the wide leaves of water-lilies. He lifted his head. White-painted iron chairs and tables stood on this wider part of the balcony, and Lord Benjamin already sat at one table, pouring out tea from a silver service.

"Gentlemen. Ladies."

The trader, de Flores, fell into the chair beside Lord Benjamin, pulling at her high collar to loosen it. Sweat pearled on her face, and her grey-streaked hair plastered to her forehead.

"*Damn* stupid place for a meeting, my Lord."

"It has its advantages. Messire Sebastien?" The Prime Minister passed a fragile china cup up to the black Rat. Messire Sebastien shook lace ruffles back and took the cup in fat, ringless fingers.

Cragmire drew out a chair for Cecily Emmett to sit; then seated himself beside her. The three Rat Lords took chairs. Ashar hitched himself up to sit on the balcony rail.

Lord Benjamin lifted an eyebrow, then sipped cautiously at the hot tea. "Well, now . . . "

Prompted, Cecily Emmett looked up from arranging her long skirts and surreptitiously loosening her bodice. She blinked against the refracted sunlight. "I speak now, officially, as the Academy of Memory directs. *You are heard.* What is said now, will be remembered. What is recalled by King's Memories is valid in law, in custom, and in the eyes of God. You are so warned."

"I believe that is what we are met for. If someone would like to outline the proposition . . . ?" Benjamin set his cup down on the white-painted iron table, and leaned back with his arms resting along the spiral chair-arms. His large eyes moved from the King's Memory to the larger group.

Ashar hooked one ankle about the balcony-strut he sat on and, balanced, leaned back into open space. Sword-bladed palms shone dully green around him, trunks rooting a dozen yards below.

245

Jocelyn de Flores said, "For my part, it's simple. I want to open up trade with the newly-discovered East Pole. Since one of my skippers came back from there last autumn, I've realised that it isn't as simple as sending a clipper-ship and a cargo."

"Your ship?" Cragmire queried.

"The *Pangolin.* The master is a man I trust."

A Rat in a red jacket, with gold epaulettes bowed, frigidly, to Jocelyn de Flores. "You have described this new territory to us. Savages, ruled by theocrats."

Inattention; a sudden quarter-inch shift – every muscle from ankle to thigh locked. Heart hammering, Ashar leaned forward and slid back down onto the balcony floor. His tail coiled about one strut. Across the group, he locked eyes with Cecily Emmett as the elderly woman wiped her sweating face with a handkerchief. Paleness blotched her skin.

"And the Queen?" Another Rat asked. "Lord Benjamin, it is common knowledge that you – make yourself agreeable – to her Majesty . . . "

The sallow-skinned man smiled. He waved one hand expansively. "Messire, I flatter the Queen, and I lay it on with a trowel. The Queen is not fool enough to believe me."

"So why do it?" Ashar asked. Cecily Emmett glared at his daring to open his mouth.

"The Queen's pride is to see through me. I am quite transparent about it, you see. A rogue may get away with much, when making no pretence to be anything else." Lord Benjamin turned to the brown Rat. "Have no fear of their Majesty. The Queen is always interested in new territory."

"The lands that lie about the East Pole are *rich.*"

A raw edge scraped in Sebastien's voice. The sun through the glass shone on his plump-jawed muzzle, glinting from his bead-black eyes. The light showed scuff-marks on his sword belt and scabbard inexpertly concealed with polish.

"Rich," Sebastien repeated. He tugged at the faded lace at his throat. "Benjamin, you know all this: we can import enough in herbs, spices, and exotics from the East Pole to make all our fortunes ten times over. We'll never do it. Not while their Order of the White Rose is in power. The Autarch wants nothing to do with foreign lands: *he* says, they need nothing from us, and will give us nothing."

"And bribery?" Lord Benjamin looked to Jocelyn de Flores.

"Tried and failed, my Lord. Their peasants have done nothing for centuries but toil and worship; and the Order nothing but rule and *be* worshipped. Money doesn't mean anything to either."

Here she shifted down in her chair, the collar of her shirt rucked up around her neck with the movement.

"Let me hear your suggestion again," Benjamin asked mildly. "For the record."

"The question is, what do we have that they don't. And the answer's simple, if not obvious. We have this."

Jocelyn de Flores took her hand out of her breeches pocket

and stood a small phial upright on the table. Her black eyes gleamed, looking around the circle.

"I see you gentlemen don't frequent the docklands. This is called *kgandara*. More commonly, *candy*. I always have trouble with my deckhands using it. It comes from Candover," the woman said thoughtfully, "and it really is an extremely addictive drug."

Lord Benjamin stretched out an ungloved hand and took it back without touching the phial of yellow powder.

"What does it do?" one of the nameless Rat Lords asked.

"To your people, my Lord? I don't know. It gives us dreams." Again, that smile. Ashar blinked. Jocelyn said, "Dreams are always better. I don't use *candy* myself. I have known men kill for half a gram of it. Once introduced into the new territories, we have a demand that will *always* exist. After that, I think trade might move very briskly, and we might set our own prices for what we please to have."

Cragmire sat forward, his heavy hands dangling between his knees. "Part of the price being that the White Rose, also, sell *candy* as middlemen."

"Oh, yes."

The bearded man sat back. One of the anonymous Rat Lords asked, "Are you serious?"

Lord Benjamin shrugged. "It is no worse, I dare say, than introducing muskets into Candover; which as I recall my predecessor undertook to do. With some success. Cragmire, you can supply what is necessary?"

"Indubitably, my Lord. The University has connections with the *candy* trade."

Ashar reached across Cecily Emmett's fat shoulder and helped himself to a cup of tea, now pleasantly cold. Sweat trickled down between his shoulder-blades, and he scratched at it with the tip of his tail. The several unnamed Rat Lords bent their heads together in conversation; de Flores whispering to Sebastien.

Ashar squatted briefly beside the elder King's Memory. "What a bitch of an idea."

Cecily Emmett coughed. "It's your business to remember. Not judge."

"Not even admire?"

"More trade means more employment, of course." Lord Benjamin nodded approvingly to de Flores. "Now, as to my own part – "

Cecily Emmett's elbow slammed across Ashar's hands.

The china cup flew, splintered on the iron balcony floor. He put a foot back, tail hooked out on the air for balance; and caught her arm as she slumped across him. Her chair tilted and fell. The fat woman's body fell, pressing him against sharp angles of chair, table and balcony as the group sprang to their feet.

"Madam Cecily!"

Ashar got his shoulder under her back.

The weight lifted suddenly as Jocelyn de Flores and Cragmire cradled the King's Memory and eased her down against them.

"Fetch a doctor!" De Flores thumbed up Cecily Emmett's half-closed eyelids, and rested a hand against her throat. "Quickly. My Lord, if you call – "

Cragmire said tersely, "A stroke."

Lord Benjamin stepped back from the balcony. Beneath, the clatter of running footsteps already sounded; Varagnac's voice yelling orders. He held up one hand.

"Messires, my people will see the woman to hospital, and notify the Academy of Memory." His wide-nailed hand shifted to point at Ashar. "This meeting should not be interrupted, being so hard to bring about. Messire Ashar-hakku-ezrian, you will act as sole King's Memory now. I'm sorry you have to end your apprenticeship in this way."

"I – yes."

He stepped back, not remembering standing up; watching in horrified interest as men and women from Lord Benjamin's staff stripped off frockcoats and, in their shirtsleeves, began to lift and manoeuvre the woman down the spiral iron staircase to the exit.

"King's Memory!"

Ashar-hakku-ezrian turned, hands thrust deep in his breeches pockets. "I'm listening."

"My last words?"

He met Lord Benjamin's gaze. "'More trade means more employment, of course. Now, as to my own part – "'

"Excellent." The flamboyantly-dressed man took a last look over the balcony, and reseated himself beside Jocelyn de Flores. "You need have no fear of Her Majesty's disapproval. Let them wink and say they saw nothing. When 'Empress of the East Pole' is added to the Queen's other titles, I think you'll find yourself rewarded well enough."

He steepled his fingers. "My notion is to float a somewhat larger company than you at present can, Madam de Flores; invite investment, and then further investment when the market proves itself open. More initial capital will come from these gentlemen here – "

He nodded at the Rat Lords. One sniffed, adjusting an epaulette.

249

" – and the returns will be, I imagine, quite magnificent. It wouldn't do for their Majesty's approval of the scheme to become widely known; therefore, I think, we make secrecy one of our prime concerns."

"It'll take cash to finance the introduction of *candy*." Jocelyn de Flores glanced at Cragmire. "I won't inquire into the University's methods, but you'll want funds."

"Among other things."

"Government resources." De Flores looked back at Lord Benjamin, who spread his hands.

"As you say, dear lady, government resources. Which you will have. The House will approve it as part of the confidential budget, my colleagues here assure me."

Jocelyn de Flores looked at the shabby black Rat, and Sebastien inclined his plump head. "Well then. The University of Crime will undertake to supply *kgandara* for a substantial share in the East Pole Trading Company. We'll handle transportation and trade. Lord Benjamin will – "

" – as I have said, expedite matters," the flamboyant man cut in. "King's Memory, do you hear?"

Outside, the brass band shifted into a martial tune played in three-quarter time. Under a blue sky, the sun blazed down on crimson and blue flowers in ranked beds. Ashar-hakku-ezrian slitted his eyes against green interior light. Sun shattered in through glass and ironwork. A fragile fern brushed damp against the skin of his sweaty upper arm.

"I hear."

"I set my word to this as a binding contract: Benjamin."

The black-haired woman licked the corners of her mouth. "I also set my word to this as a binding contract: Jocelyn de Flores."

"And I, Sebastien."

"My word is given for the University: Cragmire. This binds me."

Ashar cocked his head, gazing at the Rat Lords.

"Seznec: this binds me."

"Ammarion: this binds me."

"De L'Isle: this binds me."

The Lord Benjamin nodded once, sharply. "So. It is remembered."

" . . . and that's all." The Katayan leaned his elbows back on the thwarts.

Varagnac shipped oars and held up long fingers for silence. The stolen wherry grated on shingle. She stared up at the underside of the bridge. The tide being out, they beached some thirty feet from the bank.

"You did it. We're home." She heard admiration a little too ungrudged in her own voice, and chuckled throatily. "I don't have to ask if you remember what I told you, for if we're separated?"

He leaned over the edge of the boat.

"I'm going to get my feet wet. You couldn't get this thing further inland?"

"No!" Varagnac swore. She vaulted over the side, landing

lightly on mud-slick shingle. "Move."

The wind, bitter cold from the river, blew in her face. Her ears twitched. She loped across the shingle to the shelter of a pillar, tail out for balance. Her swordbelt bounced against her haunch.

"Now."

Only pale hands and face visible, the black-clothed young man slid out of the boat and ran towards the bank. A soft noise triggered her reflexes in the same second as Ashar-hakku-ezrian swore and sat down heavily in the mud.

"*Damnation –!*"

A scream sounded over his whisper. Varagnac sucked her fingers, where the tip of her throwing-knife had caught on leaving her hand, and widened her eyes. Night sight showed her a slumped body at the foot of the embankment. She caught the Katayan's wrist and threw him into the shelter of the pillar behind her.

A voice rang out above:

"*Ashar-hakku-ezrian!*"

"Nearly home," Varagnac amended.

The voice came again:

"Ashar! I want to talk. We *must* talk."

The young man shrugged easily. "I can talk to him. Why not?"

Varagnac drew her oiled blade soundlessly from its sheath. She pressed up against the wet masonry, every knob of her spine grating on the stone, back protected. A glance showed her Ashar-hakku-ezrian on the river side of the pillar, watching the other direction.

From the bridge above, the male voice sounded:

"You know she'll kill you, don't you? She has her orders."

Tidal water lapped the shingle. The stolen wherry lifted, rocked, settled. Moonlight strengthened as clouds dissolved. She met Ashar's gaze.

"Ask her!" The voice rang out above, some yards differently positioned. "Benjamin ordered it. Yesterday. At five-and-twenty to six."

Varagnac's mouth quirked. "So the University of Crime are tapping departmental telephone lines."

A blink: his lashes covered dark, glowing eyes. "That's a man called Nathaniel Marston. De Flores calls him that, anyway."

Varagnac reached out a hand to the Katayan, steered him running, miraculously sure-footed in the river slime, to the shelter of the next bank-ward pillar. Another voice came from further down the bridge:

"Ashar! You know we don't mean you any harm. We want the contract preserved. We've got every reason to keep you safe."

"Cragmire," the Katayan muttered. "I told you he was at that meeting."

"He's a liar, too."

Moonlight shattered on the river. A bitter wind ruffled her fur.

"If I go with them, will they let you alone?"

It was said with a serious, pragmatic curiosity. Varagnac didn't smile. "You're the proof – the real proof – that they're involved in the *candy* trade."

"I don't care about *kgandara!*" His careless pronunciation was flawless.

"Your conscience does you credit," she remarked acerbically.

"Those people are a long way away, and my friends are here and now. Mistress Varagnac, I'm going with Cragmire. If you wait until we're gone –"

"Listen. You're proof. Unless you can lose your memory." She grinned toothily. "And people have ways of testing that! Failing that, you *stay* a very condemning proof. Now, you do as I damn well tell you."

Varagnac stepped out from under the bridge support, left hand going up to her shoulder-sheath and forward in one movement. A high shriek echoed across the city, ripping at the bitter cold air, ringing from warehouse walls.

She caught Ashar's hand and ran five yards, pulling him

towards the steps rising up through one arch to the road.

"Because . . . "

At road-level she pushed him down beside her where she knelt, in a wall's shelter, peering out. Every sense alert for sound or movement, she murmured:

"Because I can tell you about Ishnanna."

"Tell me!"

"You must go *now*. When I say."

"Varagnac . . . "

Varagnac ruffled his brown-blond hair. It stuck to the drying blood on her hand. She winced, laughing.

"You know how to get there?"

"Yes."

"Go in the way I told you and you'll miss the security systems. Once you're in, ask for that name."

He reached up one hand from where he crouched at her side, running his fingers down the long line of her jaw. She pushed him: he stumbled into a run, fleeing towards the warehouses, bare feet soundless on the cobbles.

She stood up from the stair's concealment. The full moon flattened itself against a blue and silver sky, drowning stars, chilling the air, spidering the pavement with shadows. The lean Rat turned, silver fur shiningly visible. She hitched up sword-belt and wiped mud from her doublet. There was no sound.

Varagnac bent down, scraped a match along the pavement, lit a cigar that made a minute red ember in the night, and let them come to her.

Morning blew cold off the river.

"A command *performance*?" Jocelyn de Flores sat up at her warehouse desk, incredulous.

Sebastien nodded, halfway between satisfaction and hysteria. "Ashar-hakku-ezrian performing monologues in front of Her Majesty themselves. Madam, you think I'm a fool. Well, even this fool can guess what we'll hear from that stage!"

253

He had the satisfaction of seeing her quiet for a second.

"This is certain? He's alive?"

"The young man was found this morning by Lord William, in the grounds of the palace. He's keeping him as Her Majesty's guest until tonight. One place in the dominion where none of us can reach him!"

Sebastien slumped down on the desk, tail shoving account books onto the warehouse floor. He pulled his headband off and scratched at his sweaty fur, looked at the broken plume, and threw it down vehemently.

"I'm ruined. I'll get nothing back from that bastard Benjamin. When this blows, we all go bankrupt, if not to prison!"

"You must shift for yourself," the woman said coolly.

"*We're* ruined!"

He hardly noticed the woman leaving until she was a dozen yards away. He looked up, opened his mouth to call, and, too dispirited, made no sound.

Outside the river lapped at the dock. He wondered to what distant port the *Pangolin* might be sailing next.

Staring across the crowded palace anteroom, Jocelyn spotted very few human faces among the assembled Rat Lords.

She pushed her way through towards a young man in a half-unlaced black leather doublet, leaning casually with one arm across a sofa-back, the other hand moving in rapid gestures. Several Rats leaned up against the back of the sofa – a sharp brown Rat in linen and leather, fidgeting with the point of her dagger; a slender black Rat in mauve satin; two of her sisters in black sword-harness – debating across his head, fiercely, on subjects of his devising.

"What do you think?" He and a buxom black Rat had their heads together over sheets of paper that, Jocelyn saw, bore line-sketches.

"Well, I don't know, Master Kit; I think it comes perilously close to the forbidden art of writing."

"Oh, no. No. Not at all. It's graphic art. Wordless graphic art – silent comics." He riffled through the pages. "I don't know about this, though . . . I had the artist do my signature-portrait three-quarter profile, but it makes my nose look big. Do I really look like that?"

Leaning over the drawing, comparing it with the original, the buxom Rat traced a jawline and nose with a slender claw; then raised her hand to touch the young man's face, presented for her inspection with a certain complacent vanity.

"Kit!"

He excused himself politely and turned, with a ready sweet smile. "Yes, sweetheart?"

Jocelyn de Flores folded her arms, hands in the sleeves of her overcoat. "Who's got the ear of the Queen right now? Who are they listening to?"

The young man reached up and took off darkened spectacles, blinking thoughtfully. His smile flashed. "Well, let's see. Yes. There's the very person. Imogen!"

A striking and statuesque woman in black leather stood in the centre of another group, one finger raised, halfway through the conclusion of a reported conversation:

" . . . completely evocative. I mean, total madeleine-city – but I said to him, a battle of wits, yes; but why should I fight an unarmed man?" She halted, turning to the young man and speaking in a slightly breathless, husky voice: "Yes, Kit?"

"Imogen, this is Jocelyn de Flores; she runs the East Pole Trading Company; Jocelyn, this is Imogen, wit, truly wonderful person, and . . . well." Kit smiled and put his darkened-glass spectacles back on. "What can I tell you? She'll know what you want to know."

"I need," Jocelyn said with a degree of determination, "to see the Queen. Today."

"Now let me see, who would do . . . " Imogen lifted her chin, lively eyes searching the assembly. Poised, questing, she mentally sorted through faces and names. "They won't be giving an audience, as such: I was just saying to Vexin and Quesnoy."

Jocelyn looked blank.

"Oh, you don't *know* them." Rapidly, apologetic, breathless. "Vexin is the woman who's owned by Seznec."

"Seznec?"

"Seznec left Barbier for Chaptal."

Jocelyn gave it up. She glanced back at the young man.

"Look, I have to go." His gaze moved to the group of Rats at the sofa, the dynamics of which had shifted towards dissolution without him. "Imogen will look after you. Call me if you need me; I'll be right there."

Imogen, who had looked enthusiastically ready to continue the conversation, spotted a face across the audience chamber.

"*Ah.*"

She turned and swept off, Jocelyn stepping rapidly to keep up, and bore down on a small red-headed woman dressed in black. The woman stood talking to a brown Rat:

" . . . Kit gave me the line: *Why, this is the Invisible College, nor am I out of it* . . . Hello, Imogen."

"Æmilia, you can do this for me, can't you? Jocelyn needs to see Her Majesty. Sorry, I *must* rush. Hope it goes well for you, Jocelyn." Smiling, breathless, a little hurried; she moved with utter confidence into the crowd.

Æmilia lifted a dark eyebrow. She wore black breeches, boots, and a shirt embroidered in baroque death's-heads. For a second she stood with her weight back on one heel, surveying the far end of the hall. The glass of red wine in her hand wavered slightly. "Right . . . See that door there? In about three minutes you'll see the guard leave it. Go through. Got that?"

"He'll leave?"

The woman grinned. "You watch. Have a little trust. Honestly, the things I *do* for people . . . "

Jocelyn stared after her, losing her among the crowd of tall black and brown Rats. The background noise rose. She sniffed, smelling sweat and fur and scent, not the spices and tar of the docks; and stared the Rat Lords up and down with some contempt.

The Rat guard turned his head as the door behind him opened a fraction. He nodded and strode away, business-like, towards the entrance. Jocelyn walked without any hesitation up to and through the door.

The heights of the Feasting Hall opened around her.

Brown stone arched up into Gothic vaults, by way of carved niches full of figures of saints, statesmen, monarchs, and Rat Lords of antiquity. Blue velvet drapes curtained some draught from the hall doors. A spiky-branched candelabra hung down from the peak of the ceiling, candles as yet unlit.

The Rat-Queen in their close group stood, some directing servants in their cleaning operations, some supervising the erection of the makeshift stage, one reading in a prompt-book. Brown Rat servants made rows of chairs, and two velvet-lined stage boxes: a theatre set up in miniature.

Jocelyn swept a bow that left her greatcoat brushing dust from the hall floor. Some of the Rat-Queen turned. A sleek-faced one gestured to the page nursing their knotted tails; he set down the velvet cushion.

"Ah. One of our merchant-venturers, we believe. We hear that you wish to see us, Madam de Flores."

"Mercy!"

Jocelyn de Flores, with a mental and ironic acknowledgement to Lord Benjamin, theatrically fell on one knee.

Another sleek black head turned, wearing an expression of bemusement. "Whatever for, Madam de Flores?"

"I know something that I must tell to your Majesty," Jocelyn said. "A crime. Of which I myself am not entirely innocent."

Ashar-hakku-ezrian looked down with an expression somewhere between embarrassment and searing relief. The girl's arms locked about his waist, her face buried in his chest: only the top of her head and buttercup-yellow hair visible.

"Varagnac told me where you were." He tentatively stroked her back. Her plush-furred tail looped up and coiled snake-tight about his forearm. "But I'd have got round to looking here pretty soon."

He brought his free hand round and shifted her embrace, getting fingers to her pointed chin and forcing it up. The twelve-year-old leaned back slightly and fixed him with impossibly large eyes.

"*Sure* you would."

A head-and-a-half shorter than her brother; with cropped blonde hair, brown skin dotted with a hundred thousand pale and minute freckles, a body whipcord-thin: Ishnanna-hakku-ezrian.

Malice flicked her inflected speech: the dialect of South Katay.

"Oh, and if you think that, you tell me what I'm *doing* here."

The midday sun shone with a new warmth on the formal gardens of the palace. Topiary yews cast shade over grass walks, and, where they stood at the edge of the grand canal, the water reflected hedges, the palace's Gothic heights, and the blue sky of spring becoming early summer.

Ashar-hakku-ezrian ruffled her cropped hair. "So what did you run away to be, shorty?"

The Katayan girl stepped back and held up her hands. Black gum smeared her fingers, palms, wrists, and one elbow. Ashar began tetchily to examine his shirt where she had hugged him. "What the hell is that?"

"Cartography." Ishnanna's white-blonde tail whisked dew from the flagstones, dipped into the canal, and brought up water for her to dabble on her ink-stained hands. Her big eyes gleamed. "I'm nearly trained, Ash. The Queen's mapmaker has five apprentices, but *I'm* the one he's going to send on the *Hawthorne* when it sails to look for the West Pole. Oh, can't you just think of it!"

"Miles of empty ocean, ship's biscuits, storms, uneducated shipmasters, no destination, *seasickness* – yes, I can think of it."

"Ash . . . "

"Did I *say* I wouldn't come with you?"

The girl smiled, short upper lip pulling back from white teeth. She squinted up at him, against the sun. "Well . . . it's not for a year or more yet. Ash, what are you doing here? Did you just come looking for me? How's mother? Did she say anything about me? Why didn't you get here sooner? Why did Lord William bring you in this morning? Are you in trouble?"

"Who, me?"

Ashar-hakku-ezrian grinned and looked up past her, at the sprawling bulk of the palace that squatted black and spiked and perpendicular in the sunlight.

"We are *most* displeased."

The Rat-Queen's tones were icy. Benjamin bowed deeply. "Your Majesty."

"An attempt to undermine the ruler of these East Pole lands – why, the man is a monarch! As we are. How dare you even contemplate such action?"

Lord Benjamin put his hands behind his back, gripping his folded yellow gloves. Just to his right, the stout and sober figure of Lord William waited.

"I had thought to make your Majesty's dominions wealthy with trade."

Nine pairs of eyes fixed on him. Some of the Rat-Queen folded their hands in their laps. Lean-jawed faces stiffened, stern.

"And what example will you give the mob, Benjamin, if you begin by bringing down a monarch from his god-given station in life? How will the rabble out there think of *us*? Would you have us condescend to explain – "

" – our actions for their good, that they, being the common herd, cannot understand?"

High voices reverberated from the white-cobwebbed walls.

"Or excuse ourselves – "

" – when our responsibility is solely to ourselves and the god that gave us this land to rule?"

"You may not do this thing! We are angry with you, Lord Benjamin. We think it best – "

" – that you conclude this sorry affair now. End it. Never more speak of it."

259

One of the Rat-Queen laid a gloved hand on the edge of the baroque marble tomb, her face thoughtful.

"Lord William is to be our first minister in your place. We are sorry you should bring such disgrace on yourself, my Lord. Be thankful the punishment is no worse."

Lord Benjamin swept a bow, turned, and, as he passed Lord William on his way out, murmured to those impassive, craggy features, "Make the most of your turn in favour, my Lord. While you have it."

Two thousand candles illuminated the Feasting Hall. The naphtha jets stood unlit. A heavy scent of wax and warm flame filled the air.

Varagnac eased the sling cradling her fractured arm, buttoned into her livery jacket; one sleeve hanging empty. She undid another button. Analgesic drugs buzzed in her head. She grinned lopsidedly, standing at the head of the steps and surveying the crowd.

Stage and royal box faced each other across thirty feet of hall space, the wooden frameworks bright with purple velvet coverings and the royal crest. Stage-curtains hung closed as yet. Some fifty plush chairs occupied the intermediate space, and between them Rat Lords in evening dress and satins stood drinking green wine and talking. Varagnac eye-checked the positions of her plain-clothes Guard.

"Madam Varagnac."

"Sir." She walked down to join Lord William at the foot of the steps. Stout and stolid, he gazed across the hall.

Beyond the rows of seats, in front of the stage, Ashar-hakku-ezrian stood talking with Athanasius Godwin. The old man frowned. Ashar spoke, tail cocked, head to one side; and Godwin chuckled. Ears shifting, Varagnac caught a fragment of their conversation:

". . . accept hospitality. . . Academy . . . "

The Katayan took the offered glass from Godwin, drained it, and wiped his wispy beard. Varagnac saw him grin, and vault up onto the stage and peer through the closed curtains.

She gazed up at Ashar-hakku-ezrian on the platform. In black evening dress, and with a silver sash slightly disguising his plump waist, the young man raised arched blond brows at Varagnac, and tipped her a twitch of his groomed tail.

"Isn't he something?" She shook her head and looked down at the stout man beside her. "Sir."

"Undoubtedly." Lord William's tone was dry. "However, he still carries dangerous knowledge. He knows more about certain people's business than is entirely wise for any of us."

Varagnac rubbed lightly at her splinted arm. Through the crowd she glimpsed a red-bearded man leaning up against the empty royal box. His blue doublet had been abandoned in favour of formal dress; he moved stiffly.

"So Marston survives? Hrrmm."

"Exactly. Watch the young man. I believe that that is all we can do. And I fear it will hardly be enough."

Lord William bowed formally and continued to plough through the assembled dignitaries, towards the doors by which the Queen would enter. Varagnac circulated, checking more guard-points. She impressed in her mind the positions of Athanasius Godwin, and a small troop from the Academy of Memory; and Jocelyn de Flores and two other ship owners. She searched keenly for signs of the visible Nathaniel Marston's invisible associates.

A voice some yards away said:

"I'm surprised that you're still here. After the fall of your patron."

"Sebastien . . ." She gave it a toothy emphasis.

"That's Messire Sebastien to you." Fat and sweating in leather and lace, the black Rat narrowed his eyes in her direction. Varagnac chuckled.

"The security services are always here . . . If you're looking for Madam de Flores, she's over with Lord Oudin. Or do you think that even a human won't welcome your company now?"

"Don't be insolent!"

"Don't be ridiculous." She dropped humour and spoke concisely. "My department has sufficient proof of your involvement. I know how deep in debt this puts you. If you're thinking of repairing your fortunes, go overseas to do it. You won't take a step here that I don't know about."

A brown Rat brushed her elbow as she strode off, sending pain up her arm and shoulder. She swore. Wax dripped down from the spiky chandelier, spotting the silver fur of her haunches. Her tail whipped back and forth a few irritated inches either way.

"Fool!"

She clapped her hand to her sword-hilt, avoiding spearing two black Rats in identical cerise silk, and took a few paces closer to the stage. Ashar-hakku-ezrian slid in between the closed curtains. She halted.

"Good god." She failed to keep the amazement out of her voice. "Lord Benjamin?"

Benjamin acknowledged her with a wave of his free hand. Resplendent in evening dress with a pink tie and cummerbund, curly hair shining with oil, he walked with a very young woman on his arm. Varagnac blinked.

"Varagnac, I don't believe you know my acquaintance of this evening. This is Mistress Ishnanna-hakku-ezrian. Queen's mapmaker."

Enormous dark eyes looked up from a level somewhat below Varagnac's collarbone. Freckled, darker, and with dandelion-fluff hair: the girl stood with all her older brother's aplomb.

"Apprentice Queen's mapmaker." Her tiny voice was husky, accented. "You're the one Ash tells me about? *Mmm . . .*"

Hackles ruffled up Varagnac's spine. "One of your family patronising me is quite enough. Benjamin, are you mad? You shouldn't be here. She certainly shouldn't."

"And for his own safety, nor should the lady's brother. I hold him no ill-will; what's happened has happened —" The ex-minister broke off. "Speak to me after this. Ishnanna, look, there: Her Majesty."

"Oh, I've met Her Majesty; they like me."

A fanfare of silver trumpets interrupted, slicing the air like ripped silk; notes dropping a silence over the fifty or so Rat Lords and humans.

Heels clicked across the tiled floors: the uniformed trumpeters retired. The great doors swung open. A line of three Rat priests padded in. Varagnac automatically crossed herself. Censers spilled perfumes. With a rustle of cloth, the crowd sank formally down on their knees.

"*God save the Queen!*"

Slender, pacing slowly in a close group, the Rat-Queen entered. Open-fronted black silk robes rustled. Diamonds flashed back the candlelight from rings, pectoral plates, and headbands bearing slender black ostrich plumes. Onyx mourning jewellery weighed down their slim bodies.

They spoke no words, only looking with black bright eyes at each other, and sometimes smiling as if in response. Some of the Rat-Queen walked arm-in-arm, some with hands demurely folded before them. The royal pages carried the knot of their intertwined tails on a purple silk cushion.

"*Regina!*"

Varagnac narrowed her eyes. Nathaniel Marston knelt with only his dark-red hair showing, head bent. Two of her officers flanked him, with another cater-wise two yards away. Lord Benjamin, kneeling next to Lord William, was muttering in the sober man's ear; Ishnanna-hakku-ezrian, peering everywhere but at the royal entrance, waved to someone –

Ashar, looking out from backstage.

Guards unobtrusively shadowed the Rat-Queen down the hall and up into the royal box. Individuals approached to be presented by the majordomo.

Varagnac sighed with relief, surprised at the strength of her feelings. She got up, dusting the fur of her knees, and slipped between the crowd as they took their seats. She ducked around the curtained edge of the stage and into the backstage area.

A tall Rat faced her: blue livery half-unbuttoned, sword slung for left-hand draw; silver fur spiky with exhaustion.

Lean, lithe; clawed hind feet braced widely apart, tail out for balance . . .

Varagnac moved around the conjuror's mirror.

Rails of costumes, trestle tables, standing mirrors, and a confusion of people crowded this blocked-off corridor. Varagnac stepped back as musicians piled past her, a furious argument in progress that stopped instantly as they emerged onstage.

"Ashar."

"I'm here." He drew the edge of a finger along his eyebrows, darkening them, and met her eyes in the make-up mirror. He grinned. "House full?"

"Full of people who are dangerous." She ticked off points on long, claw-nailed fingers. "I don't count de Flores, she's only lost one opportunity. Sebastien may hate the person responsible for his ruin, but *Sebastien* . . . Benjamin will merely wait his turn out until he's in again. But you're a witness against the University, and I see Marston out there; and no doubt there are more of them here that I don't know."

The Katayan stood and put his hands in his evening dress pockets.

Varagnac's left hand strayed absently to her splinted arm. "Lord William's spoken to the Katayan Ambassador. You're going back next week."

Music and song resonated through from the Feasting Hall. In a sphere of silence, she watched him.

"There are things even *you* can't do anything about, Ashar-hakku-ezrian. In a year or two it won't matter – some other company will have contracted to supply *candy* to the natives, and her Majesty will have been persuaded into turning a blind eye. For now, you're a serious embarrassment, and a high risk."

He stepped closer to her, raising his chin so that he could look her in the eye. Varagnac stroked the side of his face. Cosmetic dust adhered to her long grey fingers.

"Rough night." Without quite touching, his hand sketched the shape of her bandaged arm.

"Don't you hear what I'm saying!"

Head cocked to one side, he flirted eyelashes at her in a deliberate parody; she laughed; and he, soberly and easily, said, "I've got it under control. Don't worry. Trust me."

With the air of a respectable grandfather, he bent over her hand and kissed it. His fingers caressed the sensitive short fur under her wrist.

Varagnac remained staring after him until minutes after the young man had walked through onto the stage. She moved back through the side exit into the hall and positioned herself unobtrusively. Decorous requests for monologues were already being called out to Ashar-hakku-ezrian, poised on stage in the full light of two thousand candles.

He shone.

"Master Katayan." The Rat-Queen's silvery voice cut across the theatre. "Oblige us, please—"

Ashar-hakku-ezrian flourished a deep bow, tail cocked behind him. His eyes were brightly expectant. The candlelight dazzled on his black clothes and blond hair. Varagnac watched him spread his hands a little.

"I am entirely at your Majesty's disposal: command me!"

Two of the Rat-Queen looked at each other, relaxed, laughing; with the unconscious condescension of royal enjoyment. A slim Rat-Queen spoke:

"We know your skills are in spontaneous verse—"

"—but we find a great desire to hear a poem of yours which is somewhat famous."

Ashar-hakku-ezrian bowed again.

"We would hear your rhyme of—"

One of the Rat-Queen unfolded a fan and hid her face. A bolder one continued:

"—of the flea."

Ashar snapped his fingers at the instrumentalists without even looking at them. He put his hands behind his back.

Varagnac's gaze shifted across the assembled company. Ammarion, Seznec, and L'Isle: Commander-General, Speaker of the House, and first Lord of the Treasury. A cluster of judges, one with her pectoral badge showing four capital verdicts handed down. And merchants, businessmen, one theatre-owner; and Jocelyn de Flores with the literary mafia: Kit, Imogen, Æmilia.

For this second, all their eyes were on Ashar-hakku-ezrian. Obsessively she checked that her security officers were in their places ... Athanasiús Godwin of the Academy of Memory had Nathaniel Marston seated next to him. She scowled, moving in their direction.

The drum beat: Ashar's voice filled the hall.

"Young Frederick, a famous flea,
Ambitions had to climb, you see,
Be bettered in the social scale,
And buy a better-class female.
He found a King whose mighty itch
Was for a —"

A silence fell. Varagnac glanced up at the stage.

Ashar smoothed back his hair with both hands. He glanced down at the leader of the musicians, nodded, and began again:

"A king whose mighty itch— "

He hesitated, stopped.

One of the Rat-Queen frowned, ready to pardon satire wittily expressed, but not ineptitude.

Varagnac's hand went to her sword, her eyes fixed on Marston. The red-bearded man's mouth opened in a momentary, amazed O, only aware of the stage. Ashar-hakku-ezrian stood, red under his cosmetics, one hand still outstretched as if he could summon up the words: a royal fool became a plain fool, evening dress become motley.

" – and so to scratch – " He wiped the back of his hand across his wet forehead. A shiver constricted Varagnac's spine. She dropped her gaze, not able for sympathy to look at him.

"I ... " Ashar's voice faltered. His eyes narrowed, dazzled by candles. He stared into the fallen silence. "I don't . . . don't remember it."

From a mutter, the buzz of voices grew louder, masking his;

one unidentified woman laughed, loud and coarsely.

"—nothing but a child with stage-fright!"

Varagnac's hand clenched. A movement in the row of seats beside her caught her attention.

Athanasius Godwin put his hand into his lap and then took it away. A cut-glass phial rested on the brown velvet folds of his robe. A tiny glass: empty.

Nathaniel Marston threw back his head and added to the laughter. Varagnac moved soundlessly to stand behind his chair, and overheard:

"Your Academy believes in precautions, doesn't it? Just as well, Master Godwin. Trying to hold him as a threat over us would have been dangerously stupid."

The red-bearded man pushed his chair back and, under cover of the noise of people talking, changing seats, calling for drinks, and flocking around the royal box, walked past Varagnac towards the exit.

The heat of a myriad candles and gnawing pain from her arm dizzied her. She smiled, the expression turning sour. Weariness hit every muscle. Left-handed, Varagnac buttoned one more jacket button and straightened up.

Ashar-hakku-ezrian stood in front of the purple silk curtains. Sweat plastered his brown-blond hair to his face. He ignored a persistent hiss from the wings to come off, hardly seeming to notice.

"How can they!" Ishnanna's tiny gruff voice sounded beside her. Varagnac looked down. The pallor of anger showed up the girl's thick robin's-egg freckles. Tears stood in her eyes. Varagnac rested a sinewy furred arm across Ishnanna's shoulders.

"It's for the best—"

And then she saw it.

A split-second exchange. Ashar's head lifted slightly, his face red and sweating, and his gaze searched out and found Athanasius Godwin. The old man sat serenely. And the slightest movement curved Ashar-hakku-ezrian's mouth into a momentary smile. He gave an almost imperceptible nod of recognition and thanks.

"Damn me." Varagnac re-checked, glimpsing between Godwin's age-spotted fingers the glass stained with an unmistakable residue. *And people have ways of testing that.* She looked up again with something approaching respect.

Ashar-hakku-ezrian very quietly walked off-stage.

" – trust me," Varagnac finished.

BIOGRAPHIES

TERRY PRATCHETT took the heroic fantasy, shook it, shoved a custard pie in its face, and made it adult entertainment again. His Discworld novels — *The Light Fantastic, Equal Rites, Mort* and *Wyrd Sisters* among them — are some of the best comic fantasies ever written.

GILBERT SHELTON is a cartoonist and writer whose most famous creations are *The Fabulous Furry Freak Brothers* and *Fat Freddy's Cat*, two underground comic strips which have achieved mainstream popularity around the world.

RACHEL POLLACK won the Arthur C. Clarke award for her third novel, *Unquenchable Fire*, and is generally recognised as an expert on tarot and other esoteric areas of knowledge.

JAMIE REID is one of Britain's best-known artists. His graphics (for Suburban Press, the Sex Pistols and the Anti-Poll Tax campaign among others) and his paintings of the last three decades have been widely published and exhibited around the world. Reid is a member of the art and design group Assorted Images.

JOHN SLADEK is one of SF's premier wits and parodists, whose novels and collections include *The Muller-Fokker Effect, The Steam-Driven Boy* and *Roderick*. He is also known as an enthusiastic debunker of cults and pseudo-sciences in books like *The New Apocrypha*.

JAMIE HEWLETT's most famous creation is his avant-garde heroine, *Tank Girl*, in *Deadline* magazine. His work has also appeared in *Atomtan, A1, i-D, 2000 AD* and will be appearing in *Revolver*.

COLIN GREENLAND, a former editor of *Interzone* and a well known SF critic, is the author of several novels, among them *Daybreak on a Distant Mountain* and *Take Back Plenty*.

MICHAEL KALUTA was a member of 'The Studio' in the early '70s, producing *The Shadow* and establishing his impressive reputation as a comics artist and illustrator. He has also drawn *The Shadow* graphic novel, an illustrated version of *Metropolis* and the comic book adaptation of the movie *The Abyss*.

ANN NOCENTI is one of the most talented writers in comics today: her work on *Spiderman* and *Daredevil* has revived those books and her graphic novel *Longshot* has moments of dreamy grandeur and pathos.

ART ADAMS's own distinctive style led to his first comics work on *Longshot*. He has also illustrated *X-Men*, *New Mutants* and *Web of Spiderman*. His *Longshot* graphic novel reunites him with its author Ann Nocenti.

IAN WATSON made his name with novels like *The Embedding* and *Miracle Visitors*, which varied the formulae of SF with material from new sciences, linguistics and cult beliefs; he is also a Labour councillor.

OSCAR ZARATE illustrated *Geoffrey The Tube Train and The Fat Comedian* with Alexei Sayle and is working on a project with Alan Moore, entitled *A Small Killing*. His work regularly appears in *Crisis*.

MICK FARREN, originally known as a rock commentator and lead singer with the Deviants, has acquired a second career as a writer of hard-boiled SF thrillers like *Exit Funtopia* and the *DNA Cowboys* series.

SAVAGE PENCIL has illustrated numerous record covers for bands such as Sonic Youth and Big Black, and most recently for the independent labels Sympathy For The Record Industry and Shock. He is currently working on his own comics project *Corpsemeat*.

JAMIE DELANO is best known as the writer of *Hellblazer*, DC's comic about John Constantine, a psychic shamus. He has also written *Captain Britain* and *Dr Who* comics as well as a six-part series *World Without End*.

JOHN HICKLENTON is 'somewhat of a ladies man'. His startling artwork first appeared in the comic *2000 AD* in 1986, for whom he went on to illustrate *Nemesis the Warlock* books 7 and 9. He has since worked on *Third World War* for *Crisis* and is currently drawing *Judge Dredd*.

BOBBIE LAMMING won the David Higham prize for her first novel, *The Notebook of Gismondo Cavaletti*, a historical novel which makes Renaissance Florence one of the nastiest places to live in fiction. She has published SF and fantasy in *F&SF* and *Other Edens*.

DUNCAN FEGREDO has illustrated *Third World War* in the comic *Crisis* as well as book and magazine covers. He is currently working on the project *Kid Eternity* with Grant Morrison.

NEIL GAIMAN burst into prominence as a comics writer in the late 80s with graphic novels like *Violent Cases* and *Signal to Noise*, and with (marginally) more conventional comics like *Black Orchid* and *Sandman*. His first novel *Good Omens*, a collaboration with Terry Pratchett, has just appeared.

SIMON BISLEY won instant acclaim with his first professional artwork *The ABC Warriors* with Pat Mills for *2000 AD*. He followed this with *Slaine: The Horned God*, also with Mills, and is currently drawing the *Lobo* mini-series for DC with Alan Grant.

STORM CONSTANTINE is the author of the three Wraethu books, *The Enchantments of Flesh and Spirit*, *The Bewitchments of Love and Hate* and *The Fulfilments of Fate and Desire* and the recent *The Monstrous Regiment*.

STEVE YEOWELL studied three-dimensional design before moving into comics. He is best known as the artist on *Zenith*, relating the exploits of a superhuman pop star, and *The New Adventures of Hitler*, both written by Grant Morrison.

LARRY NIVEN made his reputation in the 60s with the *Known Space* future history — *Neutron Star*, *Ringworld* and so on. His high-tech, politically conservative collaborations with Jerry Pournelle — *The Mote in God's Eye*, *The Foot* and so on — are classics of their kind.

DON LAWRENCE has been drawing comic strips since 1954. For over a decade he drew the science fiction epic *The Rise and Fall of the Trigan*

Empire and developed the richly detailed illustrative style that is his trademark. Since 1976 he has drawn the world famous strip *Storm*.

DAVID LANGFORD is the doyen of British fanwriters, and the author of the SF novel *The Space Eater*, the comic novel *The Leaky Establishment* and such non-fiction works as *War in 2080* and *The Third Millennium*.

RIAN HUGHES is a designer and illustrator who has designed numerous record sleeves and book and magazine covers. He has drawn a comic strip — *The Science Service* — and is currently working on a revisionist *Dan Dare* for *Revolver* magazine.

JOHN CLUTE has, ever since *New Worlds*, been one of the most stimulating critics in the SF field; *Strokes* collects many of his best essays. He is the author of one novel *The Disinheriting Party* and various short fictions and is the co-editor of *The Science Fiction Encyclopedia*.

DAVE McKEAN is the acclaimed illustrator of the graphic novels *Violent Cases, Batman: Arkham Asylum* and *Black Orchid* as well as the cover artist for *Hellblazer, Sandman* and numerous other books and magazines.

MARY GENTLE is the author of *Golden Witchbreed* and *Ancient Lights; Black Motley* is set in the world of her new novel *Rats and Gargoyles*, which sets agendas for the genre-breaking fantastic fiction of the 90s.

CHARLES VESS is best known for the graphic novel *Raven's Banner*, the comics mini-series *The Warriors* and has also produced many book and poster illustrations. He recently completed a *Spiderman* graphic novel.

MOEBIUS's first published work was the celebrated western *Lieutenant Blueberry*. He adopted the pseudonym Moebius in 1975 to identify his breakthrough science fiction and fantasy stories, including *Arzach* and *The Incal*. As well as illustrating many book, record and magazine covers, he has acted as a visual conceptualist on many films, including *Tron, Alien* and *The Abyss*.

ROZ KAVENEY was educated in London, in Leeds and at Oxford. She made her reputation as a SF critic with work for *Vector, Foundation* and *Books*, and is a regular contributor on SF, comics and a variety of other matters literary and political to the *Times Literary Supplement, City Limits* and *The Evening Standard*. She earns her living as a publisher's reader and is one of the co-editors of the forthcoming *Midnight Rose* series of anthologies. She has a marginally less exotic private life than she used to, but her cats are still variously obnoxious.